D1377729

SEP   '   2020

THE

BLACK

SKY

THE
BLACK
SKY

BY TIMOTHY D. MINNECI

Reverbose | Columbus, Ohio | 2020

Book design by Timothy D. Minneci
Layout by Jason Dziak
Cover images by Mike Winkelmann

Library of Congress Control Number: 1734521309
ISBN: 978-1-7345213-0-6

This is a work of fiction. Names, characters, places, and incidents either are the product of the author's imagination or are used fictitiously. Any resemblance to actual persons, living or dead, events, or locales is entirely coincidental.

Manufactured in the United States of America.

10 9 8 7 6 5 4 3 2 1

First Edition

Subjects:

LCSH: Apocalyptic - Fiction. | Thriller - Fiction. | Dystopian - Fiction. | Military - Fiction. | BISAC: FICTION / Science Fiction / Hard Science Fiction | FICTION / Science Fiction / Apocalyptic & Post-Apocalyptic | FICTION / Science Fiction / Military | FICTION / Science Fiction / Action & Adventure | FICTION / Thrillers / Military | GSAFD: Science fiction. | Suspense fiction. | Adventure fiction. | Dystopias. | War stories. |

For Nina & Katie

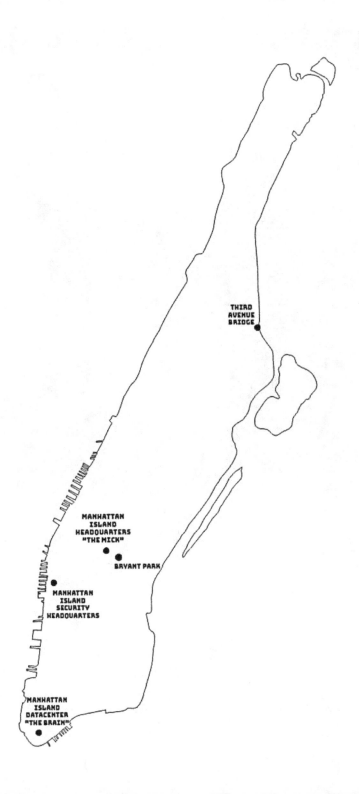

THIRD
AVENUE
BRIDGE

MANHATTAN
ISLAND
HEADQUARTERS
"THE MICK"

BRYANT PARK

MANHATTAN
ISLAND
SECURITY
HEADQUARTERS

MANHATTAN
ISLAND
DATACENTER
"THE BRAIN"

CHAPTER 1

Bishop, at the door of his superior, steadies his breath after the walk-sprint from Drone Operations Center through the dim concrete corridor. Endless permutations concerning what is about to unfold land on two very different conclusions. Either he is about to be promoted, or he is about to be fired.

Superiors don't make small talk.

Bishop spoke to them upon his hire a year and a half ago - a perfunctory welcome and nothing since. He blinks at the door plaque.

Commander Robert Fenton, Manhattan Island Security.

⁂

Until the last thirty minutes of his recently completed shift, Section Eighteen of the Manhattan Island perimeter had registered zero incursions for fifteen consecutive days. Bishop had stared contently upon the assigned bank of unchanging monitors. Since no outside paraphernalia or distractions are allowed, Bishop drew from hazy memory some of his favorite albums and replayed them in his mind to pass the grind. It was the only way he could avoid sinking into shamed thoughts about his wife off-island, from whom he had been separated from over a year, thanks to his current position.

Other operators made small talk. A few were loudmouth gadflies, including the milquetoast Operator Burns, who would announce with faked astonishment, "look at this Asshole" or "I got another Asshole in Section Twelve."

Asshole was his go-to descriptor for any person who attempted to cross the Hudson River to Manhattan. It was a source of irritation two-fold for Bishop. Number one: it was repetitive and bland. There was a veritable bounty of diverse derogatory language to draw from to describe those who attempted to jump the line at the various borough intake centers and gain safe entry onto Manhattan Island. He was like a bad comedian who drove home a tired punchline, growing more desperately demonstrative each time. Second: Burns monitored a section along the Hudson, which comparatively speaking, almost no one attempted to cross. The Harlem and East Rivers are where the action occurs daily.

Bishop knows it.

All the other Operators know it.

But nothing slows Burns' tedious mouth.

Section Eighteen, covering the bottom tip of the island just before spilling into the Atlantic, witnessed below average incursion attempts compared to the others. With thirty minutes remaining in his shift, the Early Warning Surveillance System detected surface dislocation, of which Bishop took note. On occasion, debris dumped into the river set-off the E.W.S. as it drifted out to sea.

This was not one of those occasions.

Through the thick muck constituting the atmosphere, a never-ending dreary overcast paired with a thin chemical fog, he could discern the silhouette of an object on approach - a rowboat. Once positively identified and relayed to the room Shift Lead, he launched his perimeter security drone.

Shift change ticking closer; Bishop felt his regular hunger pangs. The laser-guided mini-Python missile incinerated the boat, and whomever the junk dealers had conned into another foolhardy journey. Not a single person had ever managed to climb the high sea wall encircling Manhattan Island, but they were happy to push the lie and add to their sellable wares in exchange.

Hand over your good pair of boots, a compass, canteen, or some other useful scrounged item. In return, your ticket to out of the death and despair of the lawless wasteland known as the Free Zone, which constituted every inch of what used to be North America except for the fifteen walled-off corporate-controlled cities.

No soul ever returned from these excursions.

They either succeeded or died trying, right?

To imply his indifference would be untrue, annoyance would be more accurate. He had waited in a borough camp queue for almost a year for this seat. It wasn't like there was a long line of skilled drone pilot operators standing in his way. His opened thanks to a promotion. Some higher-up dropped dead, and the previous pilot got the bump. It's how things worked. This wasn't like before; there was no on the job training. When the call came, you either stepped in and did the job, or you were gone. Island management did not take kindly to people who padded their resume with exaggerated experience or know-how.

He would never say he was happy, the separation from Tessa extinguished the consideration, but he was safe, he was housed, he was fed, and he was doing a job he had trained for years ago.

Like everyone else in the room, he had a military background. His was at Creech Air Force Base in Nevada, flying drones over Syria, Iraq, and parts of Africa. Those were the big birds that maneuvered like a plane. The version Bishop and his fellow virtual pilots, both along the wall and within the city now operated, were closer to the multi-directional, over the counter version you could have bought at your local electronics store or off the internet. These were military upgraded, necessarily mobile for close contact "urban pacification." As in, hunting down individual targets on city streets without taking out the block and creating an ugly collateral damage situation.

With the section cleared, he guided the drone back to its charging dock atop the wall. The end of the intense eight-hour shift completed when the Lead radioed privately to Bishop, via the in-ear monitor all operators wore, that he was to report to Commander Fenton's office immediately. No explanation.

He nervously eyed his replacement enter the room and waited for them to be within visual distance of the monitor to stand up. A nod between the two was it, no idle chit-chat, as Bishop hurried out of the room, sweat already beading on his forehead.

♟ ♟ ♟

Upon entering Fenton's office, Bishop makes quick work

assessing the room. Straight ahead sits Fenton behind a nondescript desk scrolling through a handheld computer tablet. To his left, a wall-mounted television screen. To his right, a well-worn couch. What catches his eye is the shelving unit behind Fenton. It houses a variety of communication devices: an old C.B. radio, a large satellite phone and docking station, a ham radio, a pair of UHF military walkie talkies, old school rotary and push-button telephones, and a dozen or so different makes and models of cell phones. *An odd collection to keep in an office*, he thinks.

"Shut the door," says Fenton, eyes on the tablet, an imposing broad-shouldered frame even when seated. Bishop depresses a button on the wall, and the door slides closed, emitting a low whine as the gears turn before it locks tight again. "Take a seat." Fenton's deep voice concurrently calms and unnerves Bishop.

"Operator Bishop Dawes, good to see you. You have a stellar performance record in your time here. I'm going to get to the point. I have an off-the-books operation suited for someone with your background. I know your service history, and I know you survived a long time before getting your spot here. I can't give you specifics up front due to the sensitive nature of the op. I can tell you the compensation is generous."

"How generous, sir. If I may ask?"

"You can. Any remaining citizenship debt you have will be cleared. And, your wife will be granted entry, no debt. You can start over together." It is all Bishop needs to hear.

"That's pretty generous, sir." Bishop knows the debt is a scam to keep people indentured, but the lure is too good. Once a spot opens, citizens pay for the privilege of entering Manhattan Island with a down payment of half a million credits. Paid daily at shift end, most of his meager salary allocates to food and shelter. What little he has leftover pays down the debt, so he signed up for the second income lottery and scored the envious job of trash collector, riding shotgun in a garbage truck. The extra credits help make a quicker dent, though eight hours in the truck and eight hours on drone patrol leave him exhausted daily. At the current rate, he'll be debt-free in two years instead of ten, but it would still be another two years without Tessa.

"So, that brings us back to yes or-"

Bishop does not let him finish.

"I'm in. I'm in, sir. Whatever you need me to do."

Fenton barely cracks a smile as he types on the tablet. On the wall-mounted screen, a woman appears in blue-gray business attire. The background behind her is an exterior window looking over the city, what would be a beautiful view if one still existed.

Bishop recognizes her immediately from whenever he watches the island's televised corporate news feed: Sandra Nolan, Deputy C.E.O. and Senior Vice President of Manhattan Island Security, second in command to Manhattan Island C.E.O. and de facto leader Elton Vinick, and Fenton's immediate boss.

If getting called to Fenton's office was alarming, speaking to an executive like Nolan face to face meant something is catastrophically fubar'd.

"I'm glad you've accepted the offer, Lieutenant Colonel Bishop. I'm Sandra Nolan."

"Yes, ma'am." He found it funny she referred to him by his actual Air Force rank, which no one did anymore. She had obviously just glanced at his file moments ago. "I've seen you on the news a few times." Nolan blows past the acknowledgment. "I assume you've heard the rumors regarding Elton Vinick and his health."

"Yes, ma'am. I have." Street-level whispers, nothing more. The news feed is 24/7 company propaganda, useless for anything other than air quality reports and lottery numbers. The Vinick news had been inadvertently confirmed when instead of his face showing up for the recent year-end "state of the island" infomercial just a few weeks prior, Sandra Nolan appeared in his place.

"What I am about to disclose cannot be repeated or shared with anyone, not even your wife."

"I understand."

"No doubt you've heard the rumors that Elton Vinick is ill. Information regarding his health is closely guarded. Two weeks ago, a surgeon who was to operate on him passed away unexpectedly. Unfortunately, he was the only one on the island qualified to perform the procedure. We have information a similarly capable doctor is stationed at a large encampment in Bangor, Maine. You are to travel to Bangor and retrieve Doctor Marion Wolcott. When you return with Doctor Wolcott, you will be debt-free, and you will be reunited with your wife, whose entry fee will be waived and will be matched with a suitable job."

"What's the deadline, and what if he resists?"

"The deadline is forty-eight hours. We do not anticipate Doctor Wolcott will come willingly. We know his skillset is a limited commodity, so he's protected in the makeshift community that exists in Bangor. Commander Fenton will provide you with a full briefing and the tools necessary to extract him."

Bishop promptly assesses, "what if I get back with the doctor before forty-eight hours are up, but Vinick has passed away?"

"We will uphold our end of the deal, just worry about getting

Wolcott back to us."

"Yes, ma'am."

Nolan's image on the monitor flickers off. Gears turn in Bishop's brain. *How do they know about Wolcott? What is wrong with Vinick? How am I suited for a kidnapping mission? How am I supposed to get to Bangor?* He looks over to Fenton.

"Any questions?" asks Fenton, staring intently at Bishop.

"No, sir."

▲ ▲ ▲

Tessa brushes the whetstone with a mineral oil rag, making sure to evenly distribute across the rough surface to ensure a uniform sharpening of the knife's blade. She runs her thumb along the edge of the stone, about the size of a chalkboard eraser, and feels the accumulated burrs. Picking up the next in a pile of dull knives, Tessa places the blade atop the stone opposite her. With the confidence one gains from a thousand repetitions, she slides the edge towards her, over and over.

In the hierarchy of Free Zone weaponry, she long ago learned to respect the knife more than the guns utilized by most survivors. Guns had their place, and from time to time, she had required one to escape a jam, but guns couldn't skin rodents for food or quietly dispatch an unwanted guest when silence was paramount.

Raised by her hard-drinking, hard-living survivalist father in the desolate outskirts of Palm Desert in California's Coachella Valley, she had plenty of teenage free time to spend on basketball, cheap booze, and assorted mischief. It was the kind of adolescent misbehavior that would have made the helicopter parents in nearby Orange County apoplectic. She didn't just run with the boys; she usually ran them over.

Worn down by the same sleeplessness, malnourishment, and drudgery for daily survival all Free Zoners face, her once peak physical athletic conditioning is shrunken to its hard-carved sinewy base. Her skills on the college basketball court long since made irrelevant; she now trades in reconditioned knives for shelter, food, and any other needed amenities. Though the bullet trade is far more profitable, the gangs have it on lockdown wherever something resembling a functioning economy exists. Her specialty mostly hides under the radar, allowing her to operate as an independent in a world where gangs and tribal law rule outside the walled corporate cities.

Eventually, in whatever town they had found temporary refuge in, some desperate or overconfident (sometimes the same) Free Zoner would attempt to separate Tessa from her stash and tools. Most met their demise thanks to a pair of rare knives from her father's collection, the Australian Jagdkommando.

Three edges, twisted to a single point, made from one solid piece of twelve-inch stainless steel. Tessa housed a pair in leather sheaths tied around her wrists, easily accessible and exceptionally lethal. When the time had come, and a few interlopers made clumsy attempts to jump her, they found themselves disemboweled, the curved blade simultaneously penetrating and extracting thanks to a series of intentional imperfections that grabbed and clawed during retraction. She had earned a reputation as someone not to mess with, but one cannot survive on reputation alone.

Each day, she exits her Walton Avenue second-floor apartment she rents from a pair of juiced-up Italian brothers, conveniently known as "The Italian Brothers," who have muscled ownership of the entire block of six-story complexes. She heads to the barter market residing in the old Yankee Stadium less than half a mile away. Though Manhattan Island is a free market free-for-all where all types of once illegal drugs, prostitution, and any other vice is readily available for purchase, the Stadium takes it to another level, adding a diverse roster of weaponry and slave trade. You name it, someone will make a deal for it.

Except for the Jagdkommandos, all her knives are traded, most for food, some for clothing she can't stitch together herself, like replacement boots, which she is in desperate need of. Though it perplexes her, gold and silver have returned as a commodity. If she couldn't eat, wear it, or use it to defend herself, she has little use for it.

But others did not share her minimalist approach, including the Italian Brothers. Some of her reconditioned knives are sold for these precious metals, which she then uses to purchase bullets from various gangs, and then turn around the bullets to the Italian Brothers. They had not taken over several city blocks of housing on charm. They love and hoard every gun and bullet they can get their hands on. Entire apartments in their complexes house massive collections of ammunition even well-stocked forward operating military bases would envy.

Sure, they can buy the bullets themselves from the gangs, but interactions are avoided at all costs. Smartly, the Italian Brothers rarely leave their tightly controlled and well-fortified complex. Anyone who rents an apartment from the Italian Brothers pays in either guns or bullets. Their blocks are known as the most secure in what remains of the Bronx.

Tessa has watched the temporary security of neighboring boroughs slowly crumble, the way their previous short-lived residencies in Trenton, Harrisburg, and Rochester had all crumbled before. She knows the Italian Brothers have earned the begrudging respect of the bullet gangs, but eventually, a turf war will break out. And she doesn't want to be around when it all goes to hell again. Like it always does.

She needs a way into Manhattan, and waiting on Bishop to earn her way in will mean moving again, maybe twice. He is putting every credit he makes towards paying his own debt before he can buy her ticket in, but at the current rate, it will still be years. She doesn't know if she has another two years on this side of the wall left in her.

Tessa flips the whetstone to the refined side and applies the mineral oil, then slides the knife back and forth, over and over, an occasional glance at the gray mist through the window outside, her trance shaken by a ring from the videophone monitor.

⚔ ⚔ ⚔

Bishop stares at the video screen in Fenton's office as Tessa's face materializes. Thanks to a few buried and mostly operational landlines, conversing with someone off-island in the Free Zone is still possible. Only a few off-island buildings in the surrounding boroughs have service, which of course, drives up the price of the housing.

"Bish, what's going on?" She knows he should be at work, her happiness tinged with concern. Their conversations are routine, once a week after his shift end, for thirty seconds. All Bishop can squeeze out of his budget for the street level phone booth. It means skipping one meal during the week, but it's worth the hunger pains.

"I got a job offer, a mission. When I get back, you're coming inside with me."

"Get back? Where are you going? Are you leaving the island?"

"I can't go into details, but I will come to you when it's complete. Stay close to home, I will come to you."

She knows he's holding back, but doesn't push, even with the alarm bells going off in her head.

"I love you, be safe. I'll be here."

"I love you, too."

Bishop kisses his right index and middle fingers and holds them up, and Tessa does the same. Fenton points the remote control at the screen, and the image dissolves to black, then picks up a small computer tablet and hands it to Bishop. "This is everything, all the intel on Wolcott. Follow me, I'll bring you up to speed, but we need to get you on the road."

He follows Fenton, exiting the office and into the concrete-walled hallway –

"We have had seven missions before yours, each providing us with useful intel. We know Wolcott has round the clock private security. They are with him at home, when he travels, everywhere…"

-past a series of unmarked doors, the drone operations room –

"He has no wife or children we know of. The city is isolated, most of it is intact."

-arriving at a windowless and handle-less door marked AUTHORIZED PERSONNEL ONLY – CLEARANCE LEVEL 2 lit by a red light above the frame –

Fenton places his index finger on a black wall-mounted box, and the light above the door changes from red to green. They step into the elevator and descend further than Bishop had ever traveled, unaware of the city beneath the city. As he slides his index finger across the tablet, he activates a cluster of boxes: Bio. Maps. Blueprints. Video. Photos. Audio. Drone.

"Don't mistake civility for weakness," cautions Fenton. "There is barely a central authority, everyone is well-armed, and if they've survived this long, they are more than capable."

"Is that how the seven before me-"

Fenton interrupts before he can finish. "As far as we can tell, only two ever made it to the city."

Bishop registers the information while flipping through photos. Quick swipes reveal an average looking male in his forties or fifties, salt and pepper hair more likely salt than pepper these days.

Out of the elevator, they step into a blackened room. A cascade of motion sensing overhead lights ripple on and illuminate a cavernous garage filled with an assortment of military vehicles - tanks, personnel carriers, jeeps, light armored trucks, mobile anti-aircraft systems and more. Prior to his time at Creech, Bishop had spent time becoming intimately familiar with a variety of fleet vehicles, but seeing such a wide array in one locale is unexpected.

"Jesus...," mutters Bishop as they pass several experimental combat and tactical vehicles he had only heard about. Fenton smirks.

"When the Pentagon is having a going out of business sale, you buy everything you can get your hands on. We don't even have time to get to the good stuff."

Going out of business is a curious way to describe the collapse of a government, but it wasn't inaccurate, thinks Bishop. There were three years between the discovery of a chunk of rock roughly the size of Hawaii, formerly connected to the minor planet circling the sun known as 975 Perseverantia, and it impacting the forests of the Republic of Tuva in Eastern Siberia. Over time, three different plans were conceived, designed, implemented, and executed with varying degrees of failure. And they all cost money.

Despite the threat of all life on earth in danger of being obliterated in either a fiery hell-storm or the post-apocalyptic atmosphere choking aftermath, contractors and corporations still wanted to get paid. That became a tricky proposition when tax collection ended, economies ground to a halt, and currency lost all value. Instead of war profiteering, the next gold rush market was apocalypse profiteering. Military assets were the first to go. Eventually, entire cities became acquirable in exchange for services. It is how Solear, a multinational bioengineering, commercial aircraft, real estate, mining, drilling, media production, and most importantly, aerospace conglomerate, came into receivership of the island of Manhattan.

They cross the garage and enter a room marked "Armory" filled with rows of black metal lockers, gun racks, and well-stocked shelving. After a moment to take it all in, Bishop eyes the tablet again and scratches his chin.

"Do you have a shopping list?" asked Fenton.

"Yeah, one of everything." Bishop places a semi-automatic CheyTac M200 sniper rifle on the table and positions himself behind the scope as Fenton grabs the appropriate magazines and boxes of rounds like he has for the seven soldiers who proceeded this mission.

"A popular item, I'd also recommend these." Fenton opens a black cabinet and pulls out a metal box the size of a briefcase, pops open the latches and swings it around to Bishop. Inside, tucked into foam, a dozen dart syringes, glass vials, and needles along with a smaller deconstructed rifle, barrel, and detached scope.

"We need him alive. Those are for taking down elephants, so, you know, don't overdo it."

After snatching a pair of pistols, holsters, sheathed knives, a bandolier of grenades, night vision goggles, and binoculars, he strips out of his civilian clothing into head-to-toe black waterproof fatigues paired with a bulletproof vest and pieces of light armor on his arms and legs. With his gear zipped into a hefty duffle bag, he stops at a full-length mirror to examine his ensemble.

"Are you checking yourself out?" snaps Fenton.

"Just making sure I've dotted all the I's and crossed all the..." Bishop trails off in thought. "Wait a minute, the tablet has a drone program."

Fenton smiles and leads Bishop to yet another room, lined with shelves filled with dozens of drones like the one he operates daily in defense of the seawall. Fenton grabs two off the shelf before keying open a vault the size of a dorm refrigerator.

"These will run off your tablet, same capabilities, but I've got an upgrade for you." He pulls out the small box with the skull and crossbones, which would have made the hair on Bishop's arms stand at attention if it were not suppressed under the cotton/synthetic hybrid material and strips of flexible Kevlar.

"To go with your standard mini-Pythons, I've also got these." In the box lay a dozen twelve-inch rounds marked with the ominous label, and beneath it lettered S-A-R-I-N. Bishop is more than willing to do the job, but this was some of the nastiest chemical warfare ever developed, and he looks to Fenton as if to say, *really?*

"Trust me, we haven't even talked about Boston yet."

So, more rumors are true.

First Vinick, now Boston.

The only incorporated city in the United States to fall to the gangs, who now controlled every inch inside interstate ninety-five, from the South towns of Quincy out West to Newton and North through Reading to Peabody. To restrain all traffic in and out of New England, over the last year or so, they had systematically demolished every interstate, highway, bridge, and tunnel west of the city to Syracuse, funneling any desperate and unsuspecting traffic straight to them for pillaging. This is what stands between Bishop and Bangor.

They pack up and return to the garage. Bishop immediately surveys and crosses each vehicle off his mental list for various reasons - too slow, too small, not enough armor, not enough battery range. He realizes therein lies his biggest problem.

The early twenty-first century saw the development of a variety of combustion-free electric vehicles. Still, the ranges were paltry, with the first to market Tesla models barely able to hit three hundred miles. Advancements increased this to a maximum range of about five hundred miles, the distance just to get to Bangor in a straight line. It's not like there would be a charging station waiting for him while he grabbed a latte at the nearest local coffee shop, which made the return trip something of a non-starter.

Fenton makes his way to the end of the garage opposite their entrance point. Bishop hurries after him hauling, the rifle and overstuffed duffle bag, catching up just as a metal garage door lumbers open. Light and sounds escape beneath.

Inside is a garage filled with more than a dozen personnel in gray one-piece jumpsuits tending to a variety of civilian vehicles Bishop has never seen on the streets. He thought this odd considering his half-hour-long walk between the Drone Operations Center inside security headquarters and his one-room apartment gave him plenty of time to observe the daily life of Manhattan Island.

"All corporate personnel have their vehicles serviced here," explains Fenton as they walk past several service bays. "The old subway tunnels were repurposed for the executive fleet to move V.I.P.s around town." Bishop is stunned at the world he never knew existing beneath his feet.

"But this one is yours," Fenton says, stopping at a black four-door vehicle, commonly known as a Humvee or Hummer.

"You're joking, sir. Right?" From the annoyed look on Fenton's face, Bishop understands he is not. The fact this is already a gas sucking hog immediately bewilders Bishop, but the extra armor plating he's spotted drive the minuscule mile per gallon near zero.

"Silva," yells Fenton. From under the hood of a nearby sedan, a pony-tailed twenty-something rears up. He wipes his hands on a rag and hustles over.

"You explain it better than I do, Silva. Tell him how it works."

"So," Silva starts as he opens the rear tailgate. "We got three batteries on a chain. They all start fully charged, max distance about two hundred fifty miles each thanks to the weight. Now I know what you're gonna say, 'cause this is what everyone says at this point. You're gonna say, 'but that doesn't get me back.' Trust me, I know. I did the math, too."

Bishop smirks at the confidence, curious about what he is looking at because it was unlike anything he has ever seen in the back of a military Hummer.

"Here's what we did. We replaced the standard single cooling fan up front with eight smaller turbine fans, which will simultaneously cool the engine and, get this, recharge a portion of the depleted batteries."

"What percentage?" inquires Bishop.

"You get about half of each battery back the first time, on a second-round recharge, maybe twenty-five percent. Max, an extra five hundred miles, give or take. Then it has to be dock recharged."

"That is…"

"Amazing? Brilliant? I know, thanks."

Fenton rolls his eyes, "Just show him what he needs to know, and quickly. I need to get him on the road." Silva leads them to the driver's side, opens the door and points to a mounted tablet wired into the dash.

"Those are battery readings. The first battery depletes, the engine automatically switches over to number two, then three. Once you burn down one and switch to two, number one will be slowly charging, etcetera, got it?"

"Yeah, I got it."

"Also, you've got other goodies. On the dash, buttons N1 and N2 - those are your nitrous boosts. Double your horsepower, but don't double up. One at a time, or you'll tear the damn tread off your tires. You've also got some countermeasures, all of them are marked." Silva motions to a line of toggle switches - oil, smoke, flares, chaff, and others.

"This is like the ugliest James Bond vehicle ever made," quips Bishop.

"Ugly," scoffs Silva. "Whatever. Last thing, it's got a self-destruct. Use your ignition key, under the dash, there's a second lock. Turn it, the countdown is five minutes, no kill switch. It's packed with enough Semtex to take out a city block."

"I'm driving a massive bomb is what you're saying."

"Pretty cool, huh?" Silva says with odd enthusiasm.

"Enough, it's time to get on the road," barks Fenton, clearly disinterested in the banter.

Bishop loads his gear and climbs in with instructions preloaded into the dash tablet on navigating the tunnels to the Third Avenue Bridge. A secondary garage door marked "EXIT TO TUNNELS" creeps open, and Bishop follows the turn-by-turn instructions through the dimly lit passage.

Being on the southeastern side of the island, congested surface traffic might have taken him an hour to cross to reach the bridge, but thanks to the tunnels, it would be a quick ten minutes. It is enough time for him to mentally revisit what has just happened and what he is about to do.

A half-hour ago, he was ending his daily shift. Now he is about to navigate a Hummer full of Semtex into the Free Zone *on purpose* with the intention of driving through gang-controlled Boston - not once, but twice - kidnapping someone seven previous attempts have failed to do, and get back in forty-eight hours.

After he reaches the surface street at Lexington Avenue and crosses several heavily armed checkpoints to East 129th, followed by the entrance of the Third Avenue Bridge, he waits for the raised steel traffic bollards to descend so he can cross. On the tablet, he changes the navigation to Wolcott's last known address, which gives him an estimated travel time over the hundreds of miles it will take to reach Bangor.

He watches the bollards lower, accelerates onto the bridge, and let loose a string of expletives so vulgar and creative, Operator Burns' head would have promptly burst in horror.

2

Fenton shuts the door upon the return to his office, snaps up the remote from his desk, and aims it at the wall-mounted video monitor. A digital menu appears. He swiftly navigates the list of options and lands on "Remote Tracker." As he settles in at his desk, a digital map appears onscreen, and a small red dot creeps up Highway 87 parallel to the Harlem River.

Across the screen, a block of text flashes: "Incoming Call - Sandra Nolan." Fenton uses the remote to minimize the tracker and accept the call.

"I'd like an update," says Nolan, not looking at the camera while typing off-screen.

"He departed ten minutes ago. I'll send updates as they come in."

"Hourly," Nolan interrupts. "Text them to my secure mobile. I don't want to wait until something happens anymore. Has the next contingency been identified?"

"There are additional options available if needed, but that

number is declining."

"Do you think we'll be needing them?"

"Lack of intel is a continuing issue, but I believe we've addressed some of our previous failings and provided improved support this time."

Nolan stops typing and looks to the camera lens.

"I hope so. Updates. Hourly."

She looks off-screen to click a button, her image flickers off Fenton's screen as the tracker reappears. He retrieves a tablet computer like the one he previously provided to Bishop, swiping to activate.

Using a stylus, he selects a folder titled "Bangor," and it cascades open, revealing all the previous folders present on Bishop's with one additional document titled "Candidates," which he taps with the tip of the stylus. A spreadsheet opens, the first column filled with names, followed by additional data in the columns to the right: military background, current position, identification number, and more, with the last titled "personal information." In the column by Bishop's name, the field contains the following info: Wife (off-island).

Seven names appear in the rows above Bishop, all colored red. Fenton selects Bishop's row and changes the color to green. Below Bishop, over two dozen names appear.

He clicks the first row and highlights:

Regina Sanders
Navy First Class Petty Officer
City Patrol
ID # 189-773-630-519
Child (16)

He gets up from his desk and approaches the wall-mounted monitor, tablet in hand.

From the digital menu, he chooses the "City Surveillance" option. A box appears on screen with the text: "Enter ID Number." Fenton swipes from the bottom up, which causes a digital keyboard to appear on the screen. He selects the identification number on the tablet.

Instantaneously, several video monitor screens appear with multiple views of the same city street. All public space on Manhattan Island is covered by multiple cameras, and every citizen is required to wear digital tracking identification. Along the sidewalk, in front of a row of glass doors and windows, bundled pedestrians walk in both directions. Floating above each of them, their identification numbers appear like apparitions, all grayed out except one. 189-773-630-519 is lit up in red above a police officer.

Fenton settles back into his chair, accesses the tablet menu, and selects the Video option. From a list of Recent Contacts, he chooses "Garage" with the stylus. An image of the garage appears, and Silva steps into frame.

"Is the next vehicle prepped?" asks Fenton.

"Yeah. We lose him already?" responds Silva sarcastically. "Because I bet the over on Boston on this one."

"No," says Fenton without any acknowledgment of the gallows humor. "But we can expect an accelerated timetable if it does."

"You got it, boss," says Silva as Fenton selects the End Call option on his tablet, terminates the transmission, and turns his attention back to the wall-mounted video monitor.

He picks up the remote and uses the menu to split the screen - the left half shows Bishop's red dot move north on Highway 87, the right half is a live video feed following Regina Sanders.

Fenton wearily rubs his eyes with his thumb and forefinger. He's already sent seven assets before Bishop, seven good soldiers in his estimation, on what he considers to be a suicide mission. The fact any of them made it past Boston is a not so minor miracle.

Only two even made it to Bangor, and their tracking beacons went down soon after, no doubt taken out by Wolcott's security detail. Without satellite surveillance, disconnected and unable to penetrate the sludge permeating the atmosphere, his intel has been reduced to a red dot on a screen, a simple beacon.

Like the seven times before, he sits and steels himself for the inevitable eighth disappearance of the red dot.

♙ ♙ ♙

On the day Robert Michael Fenton of Fairfax, Virginia, turned eighteen, he enlisted in the United States Marine Corps.

The Fenton family extended back enough generations to claim distance relation to family members who fought in the Civil War. However, no immediate member of Fenton's family tree had served with any branch of the armed forces since then. Avoiding through circumstance, academia, deferments, and such.

There was no indication in his teenage years a decision this dramatic was on the horizon. His above average but not spectacular high school grades and affable personality with an analytical bent pointed towards a reasonably priced

state college education in a catch-all major like business administration. Robert Fenton was destined for middle management, which is why his decision and transformation confounded nearly everyone who knew him.

Something snapped as if he had been in a soothing, comfortable coma until doused with a bucket of freezing water. Perhaps it was a sense of helplessness from a childhood of nightly news broadcasting a parade of terrorist attacks, both domestic and abroad, a deteriorating economy, school shootings, or increasingly polarized politics. Or maybe it was none of those things. Maybe he just wanted to put boot to skull.

His rise in the Marine Corps was nothing short of meteoric. Held back at each rung by service and grade time, or excessive numbers ahead of him, he consistently scored highest at each rank, impressing superiors, and earning begrudging respect of his fellow enlisted.

By the time the United States military had become permanently entrenched in the Middle East protecting petrol dollars, he had already reached Corporal, and continued advancement supporting operations in Afghanistan and the Horn of Africa. Ten years later, he had ascended to Gunnery Sergeant and before age forty, Sergeant Major, the second-highest level for an enlisted.

His accession to the top rank for an enlisted, Sergeant Major of the Marine Corps, seemed a foregone conclusion. It would take ten years for the conclusion to become a reality, combining the dual admiration of the men he served under for this razor-sharp analytical mind and near exhaustive attention to detail, as well as vigilant advocacy for every Marine in his charge down to the rawest Private.

Preceding his fifty-first birthday, the Commandant of the Marine Corps announced Robert Michael Fenton as the twenty-first Sergeant Major of the Marine Corps as of the coming July. A few months later, the world would learn of the asteroid, and he would be the last Sergeant Major of the Marine Corps.

Like so many qualified military personnel, he found gainful employment post-asteroid impact in the security of a corporation run city. Given full command of operations, he took great pride in securing Manhattan Island, creating an impenetrable fortress that had not allowed a single successful incursion during his command.

It was only natural Fenton's pride experienced the greatest insult when Sandra Nolan informed him of mission parameters several weeks ago, seemingly so absurd they bordered on lunacy. He knew he would be sending good men to their death, something he had been forced to by previous superiors during anti-terrorism operations in the Middle East, parts of Asia and Africa. Still, this order came with no explicit explanation of an end game. Nolan had made it clear the circumstances surrounding Elton Vinick would not be fully revealed, and his suspicion was the rationale for acquiring Wolcott did not match the reality of the situation.

⁂

Sandra Nolan types at her desk on the fifty-fourth floor inside the rechristened Bank of America Tower, now known as the Manhattan Island Corporate Headquarters, referred to colloquially as "the Mick." As a member of the Manhattan Island corporate hierarchy, along with her staff and personal security team, they occupy the entire floor, with residences, offices, meeting room, workout facility, kitchen, and more at their disposal. As C.E.O., Elton Vinick occupies the top floor, one above Nolan, rarely departing except for the quarterly shareholder meetings held by Nolan.

In a building retrofit to combine corporate and personal space, each tenant on the top floors rarely makes excursions downward. Foot traffic funnels upward, slowly being reduced as privilege and access become more restrictive. Outside of his staff, Vinick might be visited solely by Nolan for weeks at a time. Like the previous attempts to recover Wolcott, she would make a personal visit to Vinick to brief him on their current status.

She knows she has approximately five hours until her first briefing with Vinick, the time it would take Bishop to successfully reach and pass the city. With Boston in the rearview mirror, another four hours would place him in the outskirts of Bangor by predawn.

In the corner of her eye, Nolan sees Zach McCall, her top assistant, approach with familiar energetic urgency.

"I know, I know," Nolan sighs.

"They're already through the first course," responds McCall.

"Of course they are," says Nolan as she locks her computer with a keystroke, grabs her mobile phone off the desk, slips it in her pocket, and rises to face her young but nervous number two. "None of them have a decent chef."

She whips past McCall, who follows closely behind, out of her office and down a well-lit but sterile windowless hallway. Their shoes click in unison on the marble tile floor. They navigate a corner to a glass-walled conference room, and Nolan strides through the open center entrance double doors. Eight men of varying middle age and casual business dress sit in well-worn leather chairs around a heavy wood veneer conference table. The men immediately end their random conversations and focus their attention on Nolan. While Vinick may be the figurehead leader, in their minds, and reality, Sandra Nolan runs Manhattan Island.

She walks across the room to the buffet against the far-left wall and fills a clear glass with water from a pitcher.

"The new asset was deployed about twenty minutes ago," she says as she pours.

"We need to talk about the real contingency plan," says Chief Information Officer Nathan Lamb, seated furthest from Nolan across the room. The most vocal of all board members, as well as the youngest with nary a gray hair, has positioned himself as the dissenting mouthpiece on the board, a consistent thorn in Nolan's side.

Several members of the service staff enter with covered plates and distribute them around the table, removing the domes and refilling water glasses as Nolan takes her place at the head of the group.

"I appreciate the position of the board, but we're still several weeks away from a discussion, Nathan."

"With all due respect, Sandra, you've been keeping us in the dark. No one besides you has seen Elton in over two months."

Nolan eyes the service staff as they exit the room and close the door behind them, then turns her attention back to Lamb.

"We have three weeks until the scheduled shareholder meeting for the new fiscal year. It gives us plenty of time in the event we need to send additional assets."

Lamb spins his fork in the bowl of spaghetti, spooling a few noodles into an oval before dropping the utensil with an overdramatic flair Sandra chuckles at from the across the table.

"He needs surgery for who knows what, there has to be

recovery time, correct? I've said it before, and I'll say it again, if he is incapacitated at the time of the meeting, we will have no choice but to name a replacement."

"Sandra, Nathan is being practical," interjects Chief Financial Officer Lloyd Rust, the senior member of the group, a lanky fair-skinned man with thinning white hair. "We are operating in a vacuum. I've known Elton the longest of anyone here, and this behavior is unprecedented, even for a recluse like him."

She scans everyone in the room. *Nathan is making such a blatant power play*, she thinks.

Who is with him that he feels this confident?

"I'm not going to second guess the man who kept this city together."

Lloyd Rust wouldn't; they go back too far.

"A man who had the foresight to see the collapse before it happened."

Pete Birkman is a Lloyd Rust sycophant; he'll side with him.

"Who laid the groundwork every other secure city would emulate."

Dan Jensen and Ravi Zafar will back Lamb.

"If it wasn't for the man you are so quick to discard," Sandra snaps, "how long do you think you would have lasted out there, Lloyd?"

Tony Verma, Bob Waugh, and Al Lu are the wildcards.

"I am not dismissing what Elton has done," retorts Rust, who stares at Nathan instead of Sandra. Nathan shifts in his seat, annoyed by the attention.

"Nobody is cutting the man down," Lamb interjects. "If not for now, then at some point in the future, a contingency is going to be needed. While we all have personal feelings and loyalties to deal with, I want us to focus on the realities and facts, and not let emotion cloud our decision making."

Nolan focuses on her three wildcards, Verma, Waugh, and Lu. Body language, facial tics – clues to their leanings. From the way they avoid eye contact with her, she has the unfortunate answer.

"Put something in writing," she says. "We can shape it up as we go."

"I'll work with Nathan on a first draft," says Rust, nodding to Nolan.

"Sounds like a plan," responds Lamb, digging back into his spaghetti.

Nolan smiles without smiling, pulls the mobile phone out of her pocket.

No new messages.

♟ ♟ ♟

The black Hummer speeds along Highway 87 past the barren Hillview Reservoir towards the Central Park Avenue off-ramp connecting to the Hutchinson River Parkway. Thanks to accurate projections of where the asteroid would make its final impact, there was no mass exodus in the United States from major cities, leaving the highways and interstates mostly uncluttered. No place would be left untouched, so there was no need to seek a safe haven.

Aside from the random abandoned vehicle, his primary concern are the assorted bridges, overpasses, and toll booths, providing ample cover for ambushes by desperate Free Zoners. The smart raiders will simply let him pass, aware a military vehicle of his type is shielded and well-armed, not worth the hassle. While some will take on the challenge, the better bet is a civilian target.

Still, he must remain vigilant, keeping his thoughts focused on the road, locating and assessing every possible threat in real-time. On occasion, without provocation, something as simple as a color or outline of a far-off building triggers a momentary mental drift. He snaps from the lapse to refocus on the deserted highway. At this moment, his mind drifts not to memories of Tessa, but his loudly complaining stomach. Bishop grabs for the latch on the center console compartment, realizing he missed his meal after guard duty several hours ago and flips open the lid. *Thank you, Silva.*

Inside are half a dozen water bottles and a dozen vacuum-sealed bags of various sizes all marked M.R.E. (Meal, Ready to Eat!) in large lettering. Chili with beans. Beef stew. Pork Rib. Sloppy Joe. Nothing ideal while driving. He digs his hand deeper, rummaging around until he feels the brick-like density of a military issue energy bar. He pulls one out, rips open an end with his teeth, and bites down. Dairy-based, calcium-enriched blandness never tasted so good.

The mass of black steel glides along the barren highway with no regard for the nearly faded lanes. Bishop will likely not encounter another soul until he reaches the edge of Boston. While this has been a mild Northeastern winter, with some freezing rain and little snow, none which had stuck, previous winters had ranged from brutal to inhumane.

Outside the fourteen corporation-controlled cities and their surrounding boroughs, neighborhoods, and adjacent suburbs, much of the rest of the country was simply abandoned, especially in the northern states where subzero winters had driven the remaining Free Zone population south. Canada seems wholly forsaken, and Alaska's coastal cities had been wiped out by tsunamis. Bishop was surprised to learn Bangor even had residents, let alone some sort of loosely organized society.

As he gnaws on the hardened energy bar, his mind focuses on Boston.

He will arrive in the nighttime void in just over three hours. He figures he will need to penetrate multiple checkpoints along Interstate 95 as he moves north, checkpoints which had most likely already been assaulted in recent days, perhaps repeatedly. He has no idea of their success rates, if any.

Have those checkpoints been worn down and reinforced?

Are they still operable?

Have they doubled-up on their security measures?

With no satellite imagery or long-distance communication, he figures Fenton is blind, save for a simple tracking device no doubt implanted in his Hummer.

Bishop considers the best he can hope for is the detonation of the self-destruct in previous attempts had significantly damaged a checkpoint or two, a sobering prospect he wishes not to encounter himself.

CHAPTER

2

Tessa examines the current selection of refurbished weaponry strewn across the bedroom floor on top of a frayed nylon tarp.

-A pair of steel double-edged fixed blades with aluminum wrap-around grips.

-Three stainless steel switchblades of varying lengths.

-A seven-inch meat cleaver with a pearl handle.

-Two black stainless-steel boot knives with leather sheaths.

-A set of three five-inch throwing knives and a nylon sheath.

-One thirty-two-inch Messer long sword with scabbard.

She has been finishing the current crop for the past week in anticipation of visiting the Yankee Stadium trading market in the coming days. Her schedule is now accelerated, thanks to the call from Bishop.

When they were together, before Manhattan and out in the Free Zone, they had developed a non-verbal communication system, mangling basic sign language into a private correspondence to be employed when necessary. Each finger, in combination with a facial feature, meant something different. When he touched his index and middle fingers to his lips, what looked like a kiss goodbye was a message. One Bishop did not want Fenton or Nolan to overhear - two days. Whatever was happening, Tessa would not hear from him for roughly forty-eight hours. When she did, she would need to move hard without hesitation.

Not a problem, as her backpack fits all her possessions. Always ready to go – a few days' worth of clothing, a medical kit, essential tools and utensils, a canteen and water purifier, respirator mask and clean cartridges, tent, sleeping bag, poncho, winter gear, two weeks' worth of dried meats and canned fruits, and assorted items she has collected like flint steel, a signaling mirror, flares, and other useful odds and ends.

As she carefully rolls the nylon tarp in preparation to depart for the market, she contemplates the message from Bishop.

He's on some sort of recon mission, something with a forty-eight-hour turnaround. Either we're running, or he's buying my ticket in. She didn't want to, but still briefly entertained the worst-case scenario. *If I don't hear from him in forty-eight hours...*

She wipes it from her mind as frenzied as it enters, but already knows what she will do. She cannot endure another northeastern winter. Despite the Italian Brothers' fortifications, the gangs grow more brazen and desperate in their nearby power grabs. If the safety and security of Manhattan are removed as an option, she would rather live out her days in the abandoned wasteland of the southwestern United States. She will head home.

Anxiety-fractured thoughts race through her head, half-realized. What she desperately wants is for Bishop to make contact in the forty-eight hours he silently promised.

Before they reach the deadline, she needs to head to the market with her collection to barter. Her pair of steel-toed, waterproof boots have long passed their use-by date, and the exceptionally wet winter has only accelerated their decline. Reinforcement with discarded (and easily torn) plastic bags, a plentiful supply in the makeshift landfill across the street, is a short-term solution. She also needs to eat, and her foodstuffs are over-rationed as is - time to make some deals.

Tessa stuffs the rolled tarp into a black duffle bag and zips it shut. She sits down on the only chair in the apartment, a wobbly wooden kitchen piece with a missing spindle, and slips a pair of plastic bags over each foot. They are currently warmed by a pair of thick but aged camping socks, and finally the worn boots, for the last time she hopes, pulling the cuffs of her army surplus digital camo pants over the tops of the footwear.

She traverses the small bedroom to the crooked three-drawer dresser, upon which her Jagdkommando knives rest. She slips the first leather and nylon wrist support over her right hand, then the left. On her palm side, she guides the Jagdkommando into the long leather sheath sewn to the backing, buttoning each end to secure the knife in place, then repeats on her other hand. With a hidden flick of her middle finger, she can release the knives into her hands in an instant.

Previously, this roughly five hundred square foot apartment would have fetched a quarter million on the market in the early 2000s. Now it rents for a bucket of bullets. She leaves the bedroom and moves into the combination dining and living space, and then to the hallway, which splits right to a bathroom and closet, left to the front door. While spacious only by New York apartment standards, the high ceilings fool the eye into thinking the rooms are much bigger than they appear. For example, the hallway into the apartment is only four feet wide. Thanks to the perception of height, the narrow entrance, lit by a large ornate chandelier, isn't as claustrophobic as expected. Real estate agents relied on the impression of value when the same space would not muster a quarter the monthly cost per square foot a few miles away in Jersey City.

From the hook on the hallway wall, Tessa grabs and slips on the black polyester winter coat, zips up, and draws the hood over her head. She pulls the fingerless knit gloves from each pocket and slides them on each hand, snaps up the duffle bag from the floor, and inhales a deep breath. The same deep breath she has taken in a hundred times before. Nothing can be taken for granted on the outside, there are no rules, and there is no law. *Remain focused*. Keep her edge, her daily mantra. One last breath, she opens the door and steps into the hallway.

Tessa shuts the door, locking it with the lone key in her possession and moves with purpose past the three doors remaining in the second-floor hall to the stairwell, speedily descending the flight of rusting metal steps to the ground level. She enters the first-floor hallway and proceeds briskly to the first-floor lobby entrance, the only ground-level access point in the building, fire codes be damned.

What was once a welcoming lobby reception desk is now outfitted with a makeshift guard station operated by a pair of well-armed, steroid-enhanced sentries employed by the Italian Brothers, complete with a tripod-mounted M-60 machine gun. Never one for unnecessary conversation, Tessa nods to the sentries on her way towards the front pair of bulletproofed glass doors, receiving a disinterested silent approval from both. This is the regular extent of her interactions with them.

The late afternoon cold slaps her cheek as she steps out onto the sidewalk, scanning in a one-hundred- and eighty-degree view of the street and her surroundings. She spots an older man fifty yards in the opposite direction she'll be headed bundled in a mishmash of clothing and blankets push a shopping cart filled with metal scraps on the opposite side of the street. She turns right and starts for the stadium, a six-minute and thirty-second walk she has timed down to the footstep.

Although the market has no opening or closing time, most traders close before nightfall. This gives Tessa ample time to barter and get back to the apartment. She does not want to get caught outside at night. No sane person does. The gang's rule, but as the song goes, the freaks come out at night. Some are out just to destroy and cause mayhem because they can, liberated from the constraints of a judgmental and lawful society.

On a typical day, Tessa would arrive early to the market, layout her tarp, and let customers come to her. It tries her patience, but she is usually able to move all her supplies in a day or two, stocking up on several weeks' worth of food and bullets for the Italian Brothers. It was one of the two trips outside Tessa would make regularly, the other to scavenge for new knives to recondition. If she happened upon a book while out, occasionally, she would pick one up. She made a habit of never keeping more than one book at a time, she had learned long ago not to save more than she could carry. Stay lean, stay agile.

Her quick stride puts her at one hundred fifty steps per minute, but she never runs. Anyone who runs looks desperate and weak. Those who keep their heads down look fearful and timid. *Confident movements, head up.*

Oddly enough, it was her college basketball coach who had imprinted the phrase in her head regarding her ball-handling skills. Like most everything post-asteroid impact, it had been repurposed.

She makes good time down Walton Avenue crossing East 157th Street and 158th up to East 161st, a personal best time by her estimation. This is always the quiet stretch. As she makes the left onto 161st, she spots people walking to and from Yankee Stadium on the street and sidewalks. There are no friendly faces, no smiles or nods of recognition. Dressed in frayed oversized clothing, gaunt eyes focus forward on nothing while simultaneously watching everything.

A tenth of a mile goes by briskly and as she marches towards Gate 6 of the stadium. What was once a monument to the most famous and popular sports franchise in the United States now serves as an overcrowded flea market of equal parts desperation and vice. Folding tables and makeshift displays are filled with anything and everything. She knows most of the faces, few of the names. The endgame is a small old man named Charlie, who is, for lack of a better description, a cobbler. Everyone wants pretty much the same thing, insulated waterproof steel-toed boots. Since no new boots have been manufactured since shortly before the asteroid strike, Charlie has carved out a decent niche for himself repairing old boots and upgrading other less desirable footwear.

Like everyone in the market, he avoids trouble with the local gangs by cutting them in on the action, in his case, by merely keeping them outfitted with proper footwear. In turn, any discovery of useful boots or shoes found in the Free Zone gets funneled to Charlie. The trouble Tessa has is Charlie has no interest in her knives, so a straight-up trade isn't possible. She will have to swing a few deals to acquire materials Charlie will want to secure a new pair. She anticipates the shopping list. He already has all the tools he needs, but he has a consistent number of consumables to replenish, including beeswax, hemp, and leather. None of these are cheap, nor are they easy to come by.

Tessa has the added burden of initiating the barter rather than letting people come to her, immediately putting her in a position of weakness in negotiations. These are not all traders she has dealt with previously, so there is plenty of legwork ahead. She must talk to each, and best-case scenario, make a straight-up swap for goods. More likely, she will deal with a third party, exchange for gold, food, bullets, or some other useful commodity. None of this is going to be fast, she still has tomorrow, but these bartering sessions tend to drag on, and the forty-eight-hour countdown is present in her head.

As she ambles through the curving concrete tunnel past the various stalls, she spots the middle-aged couple at her first destination a few hundred feet away by Gate 5. Rick and Rita, along with their seemingly endless number of teenage and adult children, operate the secondhand clothing shop, one of the few permanent fixtures at the market for as long as Tessa has been coming here. More importantly, Rita and several of her daughters had become the go-to seamstresses in the area, fixing just about any garment thrown their way. Having a useful skill is about on-par with being an accurate shot to staying alive, though it's good to be both.

With her eyes laser-focused on weaving through the modest crowd of buyers and sellers, Tessa doesn't notice the footsteps flank each side of her. A black-gloved hand slides expertly over her nose and mouth, a wet rag doused with the synthetic opioid Kolokol-1 knocks her out instantly. The two figures slip her briskly through the "Employees Only" door on the right, disappearing her down a long, dark hallway.

♟ ♟ ♟

Bishop stands below the rusted overhead highway sign - Pawtucket RI Exit 2A - in the pitch-black night. As he urinates in the median, he scans the highway up and down through the infrared night vision goggles strapped to his head. The batteries help reduce the volume of the Hummer engine significantly, but a pair of headlights negate the advantage. As uncomfortable as they were squeezing his head, night vision goggles would be his eyes to the world for the time being.

With no moonlight able to penetrate the caustic cesspool above him masquerading as an atmosphere, even the 8x attachment on his goggles isn't doing much good without a light or heat source nearby. In the desert outside Las Vegas, on a clear night with a full moon and starfield, he had worked with sniper teams on practice shots of over two thousand yards. Now he could barely squeeze two hundred yards of vision out of the lingering opaque murk. This was an ever-present concern considering the evening ahead.

Several hours alone in the Hummer provided plenty of time to sketch out a plan for Boston. The maps in the tablet gave the rough location of sentry posts along I-95, but only an estimation, as there are no notes or important details. He assumed this had been where previous attempts had ended, and Fenton was simply making the best guess. He only knew where these guys hit the end of the line, with no idea what took them out.

The first would be where I-95 meets I-93. I-95 north travels over I-93 then loops around two-hundred and seventy degrees heading northwest toward Boston. He suspects a sentry post has been built-up right in the middle of the loop since all traffic is being funneled to Boston via I-95 but will need to send in a drone to scout and confirm. There are four additional sentry posts marked intersecting Route 109 Interstate 90, Route 4, and Route 129, where the sharp turn north will take him directly to Bangor. Though he suspects there are more, yet presumably, none as heavily fortified as the north/south entry and exit points on I-95.

If the gang controlling Boston are ex-military, which everyone suspects, they will have roving patrols on either side of I-95 running between each sentry station on a regular rotation, as well as an array of anti-personnel mines and various other deterrents. The half loop around Boston should, at a top speed of 70 mph, takes one hour. He can trim ten or fifteen minutes by going the presumed suicide route and bisecting the city via I-93 and Route 1, a move made either from desperation or madness. He would reserve this option for a last resort.

As Bishop zips up the fly on his pants, he makes one last visual check of the surrounding area. Nothing. There was a time when the absence of sound and movement unsettled him, to know abandoned cities and neighborhoods he and Tessa had encountered during the first few years struggling to survive were once filled with life, with families, with futures. Nature fills the void now, opening cracks in unattended concrete surfaces, rusting metal collapsing to dust.

He climbs in the Hummer and starts the engine, removing the goggles for a brief respite and tablet prep session. Assaulting and evading the sentry posts will not be a one-vehicle operation, so he brings up the guidance controls for the drones and examines the dashboard. His plan is simple in concept - utilize the drones to scout and neutralize each sentry post. Between the two of them, there is enough lethal armament to do the job. The key will be cutting off communication so the other posts cannot be alerted.

Bishop doubts the presence of a sophisticated communication system. No cell towers or satellite dishes to deal with, most likely just handheld walkie-talkies to cover the miles between and stay in touch with the vehicles on the ground. Those vehicles would present a different challenge. He suspected something simple, two-man teams in Jeeps or pick-ups, maybe even civilian S.U.V.s or automobiles. The Hummer's capabilities, as explained by Silva, are entirely defensive, so he'll have to operate one of the drones to neutralize vehicles while driving the Hummer, not an ideal situation. He understands the shortage of capable personnel, but this was the prime application for a co-pilot.

Enough thinking.

Time for Boston.

CHAPTER

Bishop slows the Hummer to a crawl and parks beneath the Neoponset Street overpass above I-95. With ten minutes remaining before reaching the first sentry station, this is the last cover he'll have before the assault. Time for a weapons check.

He reaches behind him into the back seat and opens a box, pulling out the Python missile-armed drone, and carefully places it on the front seat beside him. He does the same for the Sarin drone, unlocking each missile rack, inspecting projectiles, paying close attention not to bump or jostle.

Nasty, nasty stuff he thinks to himself, closing the racks and returning the drone to the seat.

Next, he reviews the panel of up/down toggle switches in the middle of the dash where a radio would be in a civilian version of the vehicle. He glides his hand over the descriptions he briefly examined in the garage - oil slick, smoke screen, surface flares, aerial chaff - all useful at the right time. Below the toggle switches, he notices two buttons he did not spot at first glance.

Two small round black buttons marked "Pain" and "Mask."

Pain and mask, he considers. *What the hell are those?*

The only things coming to mind are science fiction as far as he is concerned, experimental military projects never implemented, left on the chalkboard. Best guess, he figures "Mask" is some sort of advanced camouflage, and "Pain" is, well, it could be anything.

I guess it'll be a surprise if I end up using it. Thanks a lot, Silva.

♟ ♟ ♟

The Hummer cruises along I-95 in the pitch-black night at a steady forty miles per hour, drones hovering side by side thirty feet above the vehicle, matching the speed. Bishop feels his pulse tick up as he multitasks. He shifts his night vision assisted eyes from the road ahead to the overgrown foliage of either side of the highway to the tablet crudely mounted on the dash displaying a split-screen of each drone camera, set on low light so not to blind him. No heat signatures appear with what Bishop estimates is less than six minutes before they reach the first sentry post at the I-95 exit.

Using the voice command, he instructs the drones to increase speed to eighty miles an hour, scout, and engage all armed targets for the next three miles along the interstate. In unison, the drones speed up and rapidly put distance between themselves and the Hummer. At the current speed, the drones will arrive three minutes ahead of Bishop, hopefully having cleared the area of any sentries so he can make the tricky two hundred and seventy degree turn northeast towards Boston without interference.

He watches the tablet monitors as the drone's glide above I-95 toward the interchange, each side of the screen displaying a small distance counter in the bottom right - 2.5 miles, 2.4, 2.3, etc. as they approach the interchange. Small heat signatures appear in the bushes along the highway - rodents, squirrels, nothing big enough to be a threat, but attracted to the smells and sounds of nearby humans, or what's left of them.

His heart rate accelerates as the counters drop below two miles, visual contact with the interchange imminent.

1.5 miles - he lets up on the gas pedal, slows the Hummer from forty to thirty-five, then to thirty miles an hour. *Calm down*, he thinks to himself, *let them do their job.*

1.2 miles - no movements on the screens. *Wouldn't they have an earlier warning outpost or patrol? If these guys are ex-military, something is off.*

.9 miles - still nothing on the screens, he slows the Hummer to twenty miles an hour, two miles out from the interchange.

.5 miles - the contour of the two hundred seventy-degree interchange curve is now visible on each screen. The inactivity means one of two things to Bishop, either these guys have some elaborate camouflage techniques, or…

.1 miles - the drones circle the interchange, the images on screen stun Bishop. Faint heat signatures glow inside the unfilled off-ramp. What was once a sentry station now lies in smoking ruin.

"Go to sentry mode," Bishop barks, and the drones rotate into a defensive stance, slowly circling the position, weapons out and hot.

▲ ▲ ▲

Bishop opens the door of the Hummer and carefully steps out. The smell hits him immediately, the mixture of burnt chemicals and flesh. Metal shipping containers had been laid in a circular pattern mimicking the curve of the off-ramp with a single rear entry and exit point for vehicles. Containers melted down thanks to what looks like a thermal weapon strike, along with several vehicles and two dozen or so corpses.

Since this outpost is the tip of the spear, so to speak, it makes sense repeated assaults had finally worn it down. Best guess places the last encounter at less than twenty-four hours ago, which means Fenton spoke with him shortly after the previous mission failed somewhere between here and Bangor, probably at one of the other posts along I-95.

This gives him peculiar hope - reinforcing this post is not a priority as there are other fires to put out. Maybe the gang controlling Boston is not as prepared as first thought.

He treads through the site, searching for anything of use. He notices a few of the dead bodies with melted walkie-talkies on their belts. If just one walkie survived, he'd be tapped into the gang security communication lines, but alas, the previous assaults had obliterated everything: nothing but scorched and melted plastic runoff.

Upon returning to the Hummer, he verbally switches the drones from sentry mode back to a thirty feet hover above the vehicle. He accelerates around the remaining off ramp-up to forty miles an hour onto I-95 North. *Next sentry post will be in ten minutes at Route 109 based on Fenton's notes.*

Both drone screens light up, and an ear-piercing sound fills the Hummer.

PROXIMITY ALERT – MULTIPLE CONTACTS DETECTED

Vehicle heat signatures appear on the screens, on approach less than a mile ahead. In the front, a pair of small four-wheeled trucks, Jeeps, or pick-ups with a driver and passenger. Behind them, a pair of semis pull double tractor-trailers, no doubt replacements for the melted graveyard he just left.

These are the reinforcements, perfect timing.

None of this causes him concern, the Python drone can take care of this group in a matter of seconds. What concerns him is their low speed, this group is only traveling twenty-five miles an hour. But why? His unwelcome answer arrives as the bright glow of two fifteen hundred horsepower turbine engines appear. He is now staring down the barrels of a pair of M1 Abrams tanks.

Stuck on I-95 north thanks to the concrete barrier on the left and the metal guardrail on the right backed by a seven-foot-tall sound deadening brick wall, with no apparent anti-tank countermeasure, it leaves him with one option – hide.

Get off the highway at Exit 13 as fast as possible, find cover, and let them pass. Promptly flooring the accelerator up to sixty miles an hour covers the few hundred yards in a flash, the drones match him as he slips the Hummer into the off-ramp lane. He slows back down as the road curves hard to the right and takes advantage of the substantial old-growth tree line to find an opening in the guard rail and slide the Hummer off-road for temporary cover.

"Drone one, throttle up seventy feet, rotate forty-five degrees."

The Python done immediately ascends skyward just above the tree line and pivots back toward I-95. Bishop nervously waits, hoping his decision to hide rather than engage doesn't put an early end to the mission. The first vehicle comes into view, then the second, followed by the two semis in unison side-by-side. Finally, the tanks rumble by, no sign he has been spotted. Either they are not outfitted with infrared night vision, or they're not looking much beyond the road immediately in front of them, as the drone hovers less than a quarter mile from the highway.

He recalls the drone back to a thirty-foot hover and slowly guides the Hummer out of the brush back onto the off-ramp towards I-95. He checks the rearview mirror - no sign of the convoy heading toward the first sentry post. He accelerates again, the Route 109 post approximately seven minutes out. The element of surprise is still on his side for the moment, but this recent experience presses him to reconsider his approach.

This lane is a death trap.

He looks across the median and realizes the southbound lane has no outer guardrail or barrier. The farther he proceeds, the taller the middle concrete wall rises, trapping him into a three-line wide chute headed straight at the next sentry post. Just then, the proximity alarms shriek on both drones hovering above.

A lone heat signature appears, one he instantly recognizes - a Humvee - the militarized version of what he is driving, something he was intimately familiar with from Las Vegas. And it is heading straight for him.

Between the tanks and this, Bishop has no doubt this gang is ex-military, probably from one of the nearby garrisons in the northeast. He tables the analysis for later, as he has about thirty seconds before the Humvee makes visual contact. Or less.

The Humvee's roof-mounted weapons system opens fire on Bishop with its fifty-caliber machine gun, guided by a thermal imaging system.

A row of cartridges explodes in the road directly in front of Bishop's Hummer, ricocheting off the hood and roof armor.

"Drone one, engage and target weapon system."

The Python drone accelerates forward up to sixty miles an hour, crosshairs on the fast-approaching Humvee. At half a mile, the Python fires a pair of missiles in tandem. The fifty-caliber gun raises upward into a defensive position and fires upon the incoming ordinance, successfully knocking out the left Python before being incinerated by the second.

The Humvee continues forward in an erratic swerve as the chain of exploding bullets spray shrapnel throughout the interior, blowing out the windows in a quick burst of flame and debris, shredding the unknown driver and passenger where they sit.

Hopefully, they couldn't radio anyone, his momentary optimism dashed as bursts of light blind him. He slams the brake and brings the Hummer to a skidding stop, ripping off the night vision goggles, rubbing his overloaded eyes.

Two-thousand-watt flood lights flicker on one-by-one in succession from atop the right containment, reflecting off the ice and road slush. Ten minutes into his hour-long trek around I-95, and his element of surprise evaporates. Every sentry station going forward is now aware of his presence, reinforcements being called-up along with anti-vehicle deterrents activated to make passage impossible.

What happens if I turn around and go back? Will they let me back in the city without Wolcott? Of course they won't, we'll be on the run again. Everything we've worked towards will be gone; we'll have to start over with nothing. Goddammit, why did I agree to this?

He accepted a mission that could only end one of two ways - success or death - whether he wants to consciously admit it or not. It was the big gamble, an all-in push, and he knew it.

I-95 is now useless to him. If he is going to make it through Boston, he can no longer go around. It leaves him the other option - the suicide route straight through the city. He will need to find temporary shelter, reload the Python drone, and map it out.

Bishop's eyes go wide with fearful acknowledgment when his ears catch the rotational hum in the distance. He scans the sky, trying to block out the glare of the floodlights when he spots it - an inbound Apache helicopter armed with what he presumes is a standard armament of air-to-surface Hellfire missiles.

His mind races, but only finds new combinations of desperate expletives. The end is coming for him in the form of five and a half tons of airborne death a few miles down the road and a hundred feet in the air. The flame and smoke plume from under the wing of the Apache means one thing - he is about to be face to face with a Hellfire.

CHAPTER 5

"Drone one, target rear rotor on incoming bogey. Drone two, target cockpit of incoming airborne!"

The Hellfire missile seconds from impact, Bishop instinctively recognizes his lone option - the aerial chaff. He hurriedly locates the launch button in the dashboard array and depresses the black dime-sized disk. In a split second, the cover where the gas cap metal flap is located above the left rear quarter panel opens and fires a series of six tubes arching into the air.

The fifteen-inch long canisters filled with small, thin strips of aluminum explode in a massive burst of smoke fifty feet in the air to the left of the Hummer. He kills the engine, and the vehicle goes limp, reducing the electronic signature of the vehicle long enough for the incoming Hellfire missile to reassess targets and shift its path a few degrees right into the distracting aluminum cloud.

Before he can cover his eyes, the Hellfire explodes upon reaching the countermeasure. The detonation rocks the Hummer hard enough to lift the left side of the vehicle off the ground, bringing it back down with a violent thud. It rocks Bishop, slamming his left shoulder into the door and shooting a temporary jolt of pain down his arm and across his back. He regains his composure and turns his attention to the tablet screen.

The Apache launches a series of air-to-air flares and harmlessly diverts the pair of Python missiles away from the rear rotor of the helicopter to a safe distance and discharge. The Sarin gas rockets, however, find their mark.

As the Apache banks right, rockets shatter the front and rear left cockpit windows, exploding their deadly and odorless clear gas cargo inches from the faces of the pilot and co-pilot. They immediately suffer the effects of the fast-acting chemical weapon as it attacks their nervous system. Breathing labors as neurotransmitters misfire and asphyxia sets in, their muscles betray and choke the life out of them.

Bishop watches the Apache bank right, harder and harder until it spirals downward out of control, disappearing behind the tree line. There is no ball of flame explosion, but a billowing plume of charcoal smoke tells him it was not a controlled landing. The crew had most likely suffocated to death before hitting the ground.

Even in this life and death situation, utilizing Sarin still brings on a pang of disgust. He had studied the effects of nerve agents like Sarin and VX. No one deserves to go through such a horrifying end, his only solace being that due to the concentrated doses, the suffering lasts seconds, not minutes.

"Drone one and two return to vehicle," he states after restarting the Hummer. As he watches them slink back towards the roof, he reviews his options, gritting his teeth as the pain in his arm and back swell.

Move forward, more the same. Go direct through the city, I backtrack right to the convoy and deal with those tanks. I need another option.

As the two drones hover and descend back into the Hummer, he switches the tablet back to the map of Boston and surveys his position. With only one exit between his current location and the expected sentry post at the Route 1 exit in a few miles, his options are limited. Taking an unknown route through surface streets could take hours.

There are no good options.

What's the best worst option?

Time to reload the drones to capacity and figure it out, and fast.

♟ ♟ ♟

After completing the armament refill on each drone, Bishop checks the dashboard clock: 2:47 AM. He reasons this gives him roughly three hours of pitch-black to operate before the dusty morning haze of dawn returns. With the multiple assaults along I-95 over the past several weeks, whatever viable security forces are currently operating will most likely be drawn to the perimeter, leaving the vast interior comparatively safe for maneuvers. It's how he cajoles himself as he plots the route through the surface streets of Boston's surrounding suburban and rural areas.

With travel speed most likely cut in half, the trip through will be closer to two hours than the one-hour jaunt via I-95 had promised. Bishop will need to do it headlights off, night vision goggles on, with numerous twists and turns instead of the straight-shot highway. He will need to reference mapping more often and accurately. He cannot risk repeatedly checking the tablet and take his eyes off the road, surmising he will need to utilize the drones to guide him through.

Bishop maps the route on the tablet the best he can ascertain from the current intel and uploads it to the drones. Sarin drone will be the eyes in the sky, leading the charge at five hundred feet in the air at a distance of a mile ahead to stay out of visual sight. It can real-time ground intel to the Python drone, which will fly at eye level directly in front of the Hummer at a cruising speed of thirty to forty miles an hour, and act as a guide for Bishop. And when necessary, a battering ram against roadblocks and unfriendly encounters.

This could work, he convinces himself, shifting the Hummer into drive as the Python drone moves into position ahead of him. In less than a minute, he spots the ascending off-ramp for Exit 14 to Easy Street. He smirks to himself, a rare moment of levity. *Easy Street. Sure, why not.*

Following the curve of the road, the Python leads Bishop down a two-lane street flanked by long-abandoned concrete office buildings and industrial parks. This far out from the city center, there is a good chance he won't see another soul for some time. The landscape shifts, corporate parks give way to small shops and open land. A decade ago, this was probably a sleepy small town, lined with century-old homes and even older trees. Now the branches remain permanently stripped, the remaining decay unmeasured. There is no movement or sound other than the low hum of the battery-powered engine pushing the Hummer through the pitch-black night.

♟ ♟ ♟

Tessa squints open her heavy-lidded eyes. She represses rising panic, immediately realizing her arms and legs are secured to the chair currently keeping her upright. Her vision slightly blurred, she scans the dimly lit room. No exterior windows, no sound she can make out, just a single door with a small roundish window allowing some unnatural light to shine in.

How long have I been out, she wonders.

They didn't cover her mouth, so whoever did this isn't worried about her screaming and being found. She wiggles her bare left foot enough to register a few taps of the floor. Concrete, best she can tell. As the mental fog lifts and her mind sharpens, she realizes her forearms are bare aside from the heavy rope securing her to the metal chair arm. Her jacket, boots, and more importantly, her Jagdkommando knives and sleeves have been removed.

She tests the give on her arms and legs but finds little. Whoever tied her up knew what they were doing. If they wanted her stockpile of knives, they would have robbed and left her, or killed her already. No sense in keeping her tied up in a locked room. If she was headed for the sex slave trade, she would be bound and gagged in the back of a truck headed for the outer Free Zones. For reasons currently unknown, she is alive.

As her senses return, an aching rises in her midsection - hunger and dehydration. She would have been back to the apartment by now, eaten one of the disgusting energy bar concoctions she picked up from the market and a few glasses of freshly boiled water. She runs her tongue around her mouth and feels the dryness when the convulsion of a cough suddenly grows from within. She attempts to suppress it, which causes her to lurch forward painfully and snort through her nasal cavity before she hacks involuntarily, the sound bouncing off the dry walls.

Recovering control of her breathing, she steadies herself and focuses on listening. In the hallway outside the door, the creaking of metal scraping concrete and footsteps - someone rises from a chair. The door porthole goes dark as a figure blocks the overhead lighting. Tessa's heart races as the figure stares in, the window too dirty to make out features. Just as quickly, the figure disappears, and the steps move away from her doorway.

Left? Right?

Which way did they go?

How many footsteps?

Concentrating is difficult as the adrenaline kicks in. No matter, the footsteps return, trailed by a second pair. After some unintelligible murmuring on the other side of the door, she hears the tumblers unlock from a key turn. The door opens, light from the hallway flows into the room, temporarily blinding her. The screech of metal dragging on concrete assaults her ears - one of the figures pulls the chair from the hallway into the room and places it more than arm's length from where she is seated.

With the light behind them, she has difficulty making out faces but sizes them up instantly. Two men. The larger still in the doorway in surplus military pants, boots, and a tee-shirt, six feet plus tall and muscular. Not juiced like one of the Italian Brothers' goons, but definitely not a Free Zoner. Most importantly, a holstered pistol in a waistband. The smaller one, now seated in front of her, also in camo pants and boots, but with long sleeves and some sort of baseball cap.

"Go ahead," says the seated man.

The man in the doorway reaches his arm midway up the wall

in the hallway. A single click and an overhead bulb dangling above Tessa switches on. She's now able to make out faces but recognizes neither. The man in front of her has stubble on his face. She places him in his forties and takes note of the dirty NY emblem on his hat. The hallway sentry appears much younger, mid-twenties maybe, clean-cut face and shaven head.

"Ok, Tessa," the man in front of her starts, pausing to consider his words. "I know you have questions. Just save them for now. To be honest, I probably can't answer them anyway. I'm going to tell you what you need to know. We good so far?"

"Yes," states Tessa with little inflection.

"Your husband is on a mission, you know that. I don't think you know the specifics, but it's not important. Right now, he is…" the man checks his watch, a bulky metal face on an elastic band "…about six hours into the trip. He indicated in approximately two days he'd make contact, correct?"

Tessa thinks for a moment, *should I answer him? How would he even be aware I have that information?*

"Yes," she states, with subtle annoyance.

The man takes off the ball cap, revealing a shaved head like the other. He rubs his hand over his head and face, puts the lid back on, and leans forward to Tessa. Elbows rest on his knees as he rubs his hands together.

"Here's the deal. Odds are, and I'm sorry to tell you this, but there's very little chance he's coming home. He's not the first to be offered this job, there have been, let me think. Six? Is that right, six?"

The man in the hallway responds. "I think seven, last I heard."

"Ok," the seated man responds, "So seven people have failed to do what your husband is trying to do. They're all dead. And

I've got nothing to do with it, outside of my control. The thing is, if for some reason, your husband does succeed, we can't let him back into the city with his cargo. And this is where you come in. See where I'm going with this?"

Tessa nods an affirmative.

"I got nothing against you or your husband, but my boss doesn't want him to do what he needs to do, so you're going to be our guests until this all gets sorted out. I'm sure you understand; other people would use this opportunity to treat you poorly. We're not going to do that. This is a job, that's all."

"Thank you," responds Tessa, holding back her sarcasm. "May I ask a question now?"

"Sure," the man says."

"What should I call you?" asks Tessa.

"You can call me Ward," he responds.

"Ward. Like, you're the warden?"

"Sure," he responds. "That's the popular opinion."

"Ward," she says with feigned appreciation, "I haven't had any water in a while."

"Yeah," says Ward with a weary smile, "we'll get you some water. You're probably hungry too. We'll take care of it. I'd like to untie you, but here's the rule. If one of us is at the door, you will move to the back of the room, place your head in the corner with your arms behind your back. The room is too big, if you make a move towards the door, we'll have it shut and locked before you're halfway across the floor. And then the kindness ends, got it?"

"I do," she says.

"As long as we need you here, we'll keep you fed and hydrated," says Ward. "Naturally, you're going to ask about bathrooms next. Unfortunately, we don't have one down here, so best we can do is give you a bucket. Try not to make a mess. Just let us know and follow the procedure so we can get rid of it so your room doesn't stink up. Got it?"

"I got it," responds Tessa. "One more question?"

"Go ahead," he responds, hoping to wrap up the discussion.

"You said seven people have been sent on this mission before, and none of them completed it. So, you've never dealt with that situation. What are you going to do if he does?" she asks.

Ward sighs, "He's going to try to contact you before he re-enters the city. To bring you in with him, correct? We will intercept and explain the situation. If he cooperates with us, then you and your husband will be able to walk away. If he doesn't, then... you won't. Do you need me to elaborate?"

"No," Tessa replies, realizing whatever chances she has of joining Bishop and making a new life in the city are rapidly diminishing.

"So, how about these," she says, nodding to the ropes around her arms and legs.

"No problem," says Ward. From his pocket, he pulls out a white handkerchief and slim plastic bottle. He removes the cap and sprays the cloth with a clear liquid.

"Wait a minute," squirms Tessa, realizing what is about to happen.

"Sorry, precautions," responds Ward as he stands up and places the cloth over her mouth and nose, she bucks violently until her body falls limp once again.

⚑ ⚑ ⚑

The Hummer idles as Bishop stares at the monitor. Forty minutes of traversing the unattended rural and suburban back roads outside Boston had worked out better than expected. The Python drone, currently charging its battery in the back seat, has efficiently guided him without incident through Dedham, West Roxbury, and Brook Farm up to Hammond Pond Parkway in nondescript Chestnut Hill Village thanks to their eye in the sky, the Sarin drone.

He has routed a not so straight course west of the city center, and so far, it's paid off. His best guess is whoever controls Boston is using interstates 90 and 93 as the primary routes between the city and I-95 loop. It was the case until a week or so ago when one of the previous attempts to run the gauntlet of I-95 turned east where it intersects at I-90. Somewhere in Newton, I-90 is now missing a large section of highway, no doubt thanks to Silva's weapon of last resort based on the radius of the blast crater.

Thanks to the detonation, I-90 is no longer passable, and Route 9, better known as Boylston Street, now serves as the southern route between the city and I-95. This according to images Bishop views of the slow-moving convoy, provided by the Sarin done, after returning from completing visual recon of I-90.

For the last five minutes, Bishop twiddled his proverbial thumbs in the Hummer. Tucked behind bushes and trees off to the right side of Hammond, obscured by a slight right curve in the road, he watches a seemingly unending convoy of tractor-trailers transporting shipping containers west. Moving at a glacial pace, he's clocked around thirty trucks pass by, and the end appears nowhere in sight.

The fortifications, he has no doubt, are due in part to Bishop's current incursion, as well as the recent previous assaults. He is losing time, and more importantly, the cover of darkness. With well over an hour to get through the city, and less than two before the sun commences its slow ascent, the window of opportunity is closing fast. Stealth is his goal, but as the trucks continue to plod along Boylston, he knows he cannot sit and wait much longer.

Bishop studies the video feed from the Sarin drone. His best guess, the trucks are moving between twenty and twenty-five miles an hour along the bridge on Boylston over Hammond. If he times it correctly, he should be able to sneak the Hummer up to the intersection and wait along the Boylston bridge entrance ramp running parallel, using the nearby tree line for cover, and slip under the bridge.

Time to go.

He shifts into drive, the Hummer creeps up Hammond and makes a right onto Heath Street, a block away from the Boylston Bridge. With no street connecting directly to the Boylston on-ramp, Bishop finds a home with no backyard fence and maneuvers the Hummer up the driveway and into the backyard, through some long-dead bushes and onto the pavement of an apartment complex parking lot exiting onto the Boylston side street.

The Hummer now sits ground level on the Boylston entrance, parallel to the slow-moving convoy of trucks on the bridge above. He watches the convoy through the gaps in the trees, one after the other. Depressing the gas pedal, he accelerates up to twenty-two miles an hour alongside the convoy as the intersection rapidly approaches. He needs to make the quick turn right and duck under the bridge just after the cab of a truck passes, matching the payload exactly, and before the next truck is close enough to see movement on the street below.

Bishop decelerates slightly to match the speed of a rear axle on one of the trailers as the distance closes, only seconds left before the turn. He takes one last look at the convoy, then turns back to the road ahead. The Hummer meets the intersection and Bishop swings the steering wheel around hard to the right, disappearing under the bridge. He slams on the brake pedal, sits, and waits. The sound of the convoy rumbles above him uninterrupted. No brakes firing, no sign he is spotted. Now comes the tough part.

Unlike where he came from, there is no tree line or cover to hastily duck behind up ahead. He will be exposed for long enough that several trucks in the convoy will pass and be able to spot him. It is time to create a distraction.

⚐ ⚐ ⚐

The Python drone rises out of the Hummer through the roof opening and makes a hard turn back down Hammond from where they came. When the Sarin drone ran a reconnaissance sweep of the area, Bishop noticed spread out among the various suburban neighborhoods just southeast of his current position a variety of strip malls, schools, and other professional buildings.

What he wants, and what the Python drone is currently in search of, is something combustible, like an old gas station or external container for home oil heating. Something explosive with a big, bright fireball to give him a few seconds of diversion.

A mile south of his position, a block left of Boylston, the drone locks in on a collapsed metal awning, the kind sheltering gas pumps at a filling station. This one, unattended for years, has a crumbled support beam and has teetered halfway over. While the gas in the below-ground tanks is completely unusable, the gummy residue it has congealed into, along with the fumes trapped in the tank over time, will put on the exact kind pyrotechnic display he hopes will do the trick.

The last thing he needs is for the drone to be spotted after the explosion, so he positions it fifty yards away from the gas station at street level. Using the tablet, he locates the crosshairs onto two of the six pumps and places it back onto the dash. He shifts the Hummer into drive and moves it into position at the edge of the bridge covering.

Best guess: he needs a minimum of ten seconds of eyes facing south so he can dart north and duck behind cover at the ninety-degree turn ahead.

With his hands tightly gripping the steering wheel, he gives the order, "Drone one, fire on targets one and two." The drone launches a pair of Python missiles. In a split second, they impact the gas pumps, exploding their decayed metal shells, sending flames through the pipes below, and into their underground storage tanks. The secondary explosion rips through the containers, bursting back upward with an impressive fireball.

Even from Bishop's position under the bridge, his rearview mirror lights up from the blast. He immediately depresses the gas pedal, and the Hummer lurches forward out from under the bridge down Hammond.

"C'mon, move!" he mutters to himself, the heavy vehicle accelerating slowly to twenty-five, thirty miles an hour. He spies the rearview mirror again and catches the plume of fire and smoke rising behind him. The trucks continue along Boylston, but he can hear hydraulic brakes firing.

A few more seconds and he guides the Hummer hard to the left behind a raised rock wall running along the road. Easing to a stop, even behind the cover of the layers of piled boulders, he can see the glow in the sky from the explosion. He removes his night vision goggles and grabs the tablet to return the Python drone and is immediately crestfallen.

The black screen projects two words blinking in unison:

SIGNAL LOST

In his ten-second dash to safety, Bishop never glanced over at the tablet screen, though it would not have provided him with the proper perspective of what happened to the Python drone.

While the secondary explosion from the below-ground gas storage tanks executed as intended, Bishop failed to take into consideration the half-collapsed awning resting at a forty-five-degree angle. Fifty yards should have been outside the blast radius of the explosion, but the initial burst hit the weighty metal covering and partially redirected it straight at the drone. Recognizing the threat, the drone attempted to retreat, but it was too late.

As the approaching fireball greedily swallowed oxygen, the drone was pulled forward into the heatwave, melting the blades first before being completely engulfed and incinerated along with the remnants of the gas station. Bishop can only sit and glare frustratedly at the screen. Working the drones in tandem surveillance duty has gotten him this far, losing one will make the rest of the journey through the outskirts of Boston even more difficult.

No time to mourn, he rapidly recalibrates his approach. He grabs the tablet and brings up the menu options for drone two. He finds the Virtual Control Panel and drills down the menu into Audio Settings, landing on a text-to-speech option. He still needs eyes in the sky scouting ahead with the night vision goggles, but without the Python drone to relay direction to, it is up to Bishop to receive them out loud.

"Audio test, one, two, three, repeat back to me."

"One, two, three," the digitized tablet voice responds without inflection. Cycling through the options, he switches from the preset digital voice to the "British - Male" option.

Using the tablet, Bishop guides the drone out of the Hummer through the roof opening five hundred feet above his position like before. The Sarin drone maps the area according to the predetermined route and accelerates forward. He watches the infrared screen as the drone cruises ahead, reaching the quarter-mile mark in a flash.

"Continue on Hammond Pond Parkway for one point five miles to Beacon Street," states the computerized British voice from the tablet. *That's not a bad accent, I need to name him. Alistair? Liam? Gerald? Yeah, Gerald.*

"Drone two, update call sign to 'Gerald,'" says Bishop with a self-satisfied smirk.

Before slipping the night vision goggles back over his head, he glances at the dashboard clock: 3:59 AM. *Gotta move, gotta move,* he urges himself, shifting the Hummer into drive and back into the predawn, the sunrise creeping closer.

♟ ♟ ♟

Fenton wearily raises his head from the spartan cloth and metal couch along the wall opposite the monitor, rubs his eyes, and scans his office. Once again, he is caught off guard by the alarm on his tablet. Ever since these missions commenced, he has taken to sleeping in his office while an asset is deployed overnight. With the hourly check-in Nolan now expects, sleep is doled out in hour increments and taking an exhausting toll.

An hour ago, he watched the blip representing Bishop move away from the I-95 loop around Boston into the outer suburbs of the city. His previous experiences told him Bishop was in trouble. Both prior excursions off I-95 onto surface streets had meant quick endings to those missions. As his eyes adjust to the invasive glare of the monitor screen, he is pleasantly surprised to see the blip still active and moving. He is even more surprised Bishop has penetrated further into the suburban terrain between I-95 and downtown Boston.

Arms stretch as he reaches to his desk without getting up, grabbing the tablet, and flipping through a few screens to land on a messaging application. Previously sent messages appear above his typing:

Fenton: on 95N, bos eta 3hrs - 11:00 PM
Nolan: no response, message read - 11:01 PM
Fenton: on 95N, bos eta 2 hrs - 12:00 AM
Nolan: no response, message read - 12:01 AM
Fenton: on 95N, bos eta 1hr - 1:01 AM
Nolan: no response, message read - 1:01 AM
Fenton: approaching bos loop in 10-15 min - 2:02 AM
Nolan: no response, message read - 2:03 AM
Fenton: on streets, approx 2 hrs to 95N - 3:04 AM

Nolan: no response, message read - 3:05 AM
Fenton: still on streets, approx 1hr to 95 N - 4:03 AM
Nolan: no response, message read - 4:03 AM

He types "close to 95N, last known sentry post in 10-15 min" and clicks send with a timestamp of 5:02 AM. He waits for the non-response response of Nolan's read receipt so he can lie back down for another fifty-five minutes of shut-eye. Her read time is absurdly consistent, sixty seconds or less, and never more. He mentally ticks off the seconds, waiting for the read timestamp in response.

Without looking at a clock, he senses the sixty-second marker tick near. He yawns and rubs his eyes again, fixing them back on the tablet screen in time for the message to switch from "delivered" to "read." Sandra Nolan never disappoints.

Fenton is about to return the tablet to the desk and return to inconsistent slumber when he notices an incoming typed response to his message.

Nolan: mtg w Vinick at 0630, board at 8, need up to min updates - 5:03 AM

His optimism long gone, even if Bishop successfully eludes the last sentry post, Bangor will be no walk in the park. Two of his best assets have been taken out not long after arrival. With no satellite surveillance and long-distance communication near impossible, details of what awaits anyone approaching the city are only speculation.

Rumors swirled from time to time of cities throughout the country free of corporate control able to maintain local governance, but most chatter ended up being hyperbole at best.

Gangs were the de facto rule of law outside corporate protection, yet Bangor reportedly remained free of both. Whether it was an isolated location or less than stellar climate, Bangor was still associated with words like "sanctuary" and "refuge." Aside from maps and encyclopedias, what Fenton knew about Bangor and Dr. Marion Wolcott was limited to a single transmission, sent by his third asset, former Navy Seal Arch Takeshi.

Upon arriving in Bangor, Takeshi broadcasted a brief audio message via ham radio on frequency 52.525. Fenton always kept his ham radio tuned to this, as it had been the calling frequency used by civilian ham radio operators. In the early years after the asteroid, this frequency lit up with activity, but over time, he heard less and less chatter until it went silent over two years ago.

With diminishing access to electricity and batteries, ham radios and repeaters, which extend the signal, were going extinct. Fenton still isn't sure how Takeshi managed to pull it off. He suspects Takeshi stumbled upon an abandoned tractor-trailer or some other vehicle with an extended antenna and hotwired the ham radio into his Hummer.

The message was brief and to the point, catching Fenton off-guard as he sat his desk anxiously watching the red tracking dot on his wall monitor make it further than the previous two incursions. He was, at the time, just over a week ago, mildly excited at the prospect of retrieving Wolcott, so when the crackle of noise and a voice emanated from his dormant ham radio, he was almost too fixated on the screen to register the sound behind him.

"This is Takeshi for Manhattan, this is Takeshi for Manhattan," started the weak transmission. "Time is fifteen-thirty. Site is three by one. Repeat three by one. Extract by eighteen hundred. Roger so far, Manhattan."

Fenton swirled his chair and grabbed for the black plastic handheld ham radio.

"Affirmative, Manhattan receiving," responded Fenton.

"Manhattan, are you receiving?" said Takeshi in the static.

"Affirmative, Manhattan is receiving, can you hear me?" says Fenton worriedly.

"Manhattan, are you..." Fenton waited as the static was replaced by silence. He looked up at the board, Takeshi's red blip flashed twice, then disappeared. Although brief, the message contained several pieces of information he added to the portfolio kept on the mission.

First, Takeshi's position indicated he was not far from the address they suspected Wolcott utilized for housing. Previously, it was a starting point, now it was the confirmed destination.

Second, Takeshi dropped a vital piece of coded intel. "Site is three by one" meant one thing to Fenton, that three guards were patrolling the site protecting Wolcott.

He hated losing a soldier, especially one who had made it so far. At the time, he reasoned the next incursion would be able to utilize this info and build on it. However, this wasn't the case with the fourth asset, who was termed along I-95.

The fifth, a member of Army Special Forces from New Orleans via Fort Bragg in North Carolina named Oliver "Ollie" Dubois, managed to not just reach Bangor but remained active for twenty-four hours before his beacon went dim.

Fenton had high hopes for Ollie, who was formerly a Delta Force operator before joining the Central Intelligence Agency secretive Special Activities Division, the most elite of the elite in counterterrorism and counterintelligence. He was the single most skilled and deadly individual Fenton had ever encountered. Unfortunately, he was also insufferable, known for long-winded, endlessly diverging operational anecdotes in which he would often refer to himself proudly in the third person.

"So we cross the border in El Paso over to Juárez, all muscled-up in armored Suburban's, 'cause the cartel down there just sent six to the morgue and two of 'em were spring breakers from Wisconsin. Wrong place, wrong time deal, caught in the crossfire. I'm riding with a bunch of fresh meat. And I hate fresh meat. Talking hard, but their eyes bugged. You know that look, right? Good old boys, but full of adrenaline. This is the crew I'm saddled with. Federales ain't doing shit, which is smart on their part. They don't want to lay a hand on these narcos. These are real deal, but we get a tip-off on the safe house. Bunch of their shooters responsible for this shit are laying low there, along with the typical stash – drugs, guns, you name it. Washington and Mexico City are doing their song and dance, but S-A-D gets good intel, source on the ground. It's one of those ask for permission before or beg for forgiveness after situations. At least we thought it was good. Half a click from the safe house, the lead Suburban gets lit up from an RPG. Just roasted. Quarter of our crew down in a shot. Of course, the newbs just lose it. One shoots himself in the foot. Swear to god. Blows off his freakin' toes. Didn't matter 'cause a roof sniper splattered his brains all over me a second later. I give these pant shitters an inspirational Ollie Dubois speech along the lines of 'fight on your feet or die in your seat,' and wouldn't you know it, we had some real shooters in our crew. In the end, we lost eight of two dozen but took out over thirty of the cartel's finest, including the safehouse. Now, of course, we did not get a trophy for our efforts. That's the job. But through a friend of a friend of a friend, a real six degrees situation, I hear that a family member of one of the Wisconsin kids is ex-special forces, and they send along a thank you, truly heartfelt. Makes you feel good. Some say that's the payment for this job. I'd like to think so."

"Also, the half mil in cash we split from the safehouse, 'cause Ollie Dubois can't live on a government salary and good vibes, you know?"

After Ollie, the skill set of available assets fell off considerably in Fenton's mind. Bishop is a fine soldier, smart and capable, but nowhere near prepared to deal with the known and unknown threats like the more accomplished Takeshi or Ollie. While he is encouraged Bishop has made it this far, primarily via the unconventional route he is currently navigating, Fenton is inclined to put his next asset into play before Bishop officially goes off the board.

As he reclines back down onto the couch to catch another brief slumber before the next update, he eyes the ham radio on the shelf behind his desk.

Still tuned to 52.525.

Still silent.

♟ ♟ ♟

Bishop suspects the reinforcements he previously watched convoy west to I-95 are part of a more extensive security enhancement operation, and the images the Sarin drone are currently broadcasting back to him confirm this guess. I-95 is now lined with dozens of shipping containers in an inconsistent weave pattern, making speeds above fifteen or twenty miles an hour a near impossibility.

To make the last sentry post even more challenging, machine gun nests now line the I-95 split off Yankee Division Highway paired with half a dozen tanks and towed howitzers. The multiple intersecting and overlapping lanes form an oval into what is now an inescapable death trap with a circling Apache helicopter thrown in for good measure. From the markings and his knowledge of homeland based military installations, the gang running Boston had acquired equipment not from the East Coast, but installations as far away as Missouri and Arkansas.

How did they end up this far east?

A question for another time.

Parked under a tree line on Salem Street, which runs parallel to the last ramp onto I-95, the Sarin drone lowers itself down through the Hummer roof and settles onto the back seat, blades slowing to a stop. While Bishop carefully swaps out the left Sarin rockets for Python missiles, he considers his attack strategy for the remaining sentry post.

He looks at the dash and its options one more time.

The aerial chaffs might come in handy again, but I'll be in too close for the surface flares to be useful. Same for the oil slick and smoke screen, everything is going to be in front unless they pursue north. I need to make sure they can't.

Bishop wants to test the mysterious buttons marked Pain and Mask to determine their capabilities but considers they may only work once or require a lengthy recharge period. Rendering them useless before he needs them or causing a delay and negating his small advantage could be disastrous. Right now, obscurity is his mask, so he is prepared to hold those options until necessary.

He reasons, or more accurately, hopes the reinforced Hummer armor will be able to handle the gun nests outfitted with fifty caliber Browning machine guns on tripods. The drone can neutralize the Apache; however, it is the tanks and howitzers providing the final headache. He can outrun the tracking movements of both, but the shipping containers will slow him down enough to erase the speed advantage. If he can take out the Apache with two Pythons, it will leave him enough Pythons and Sarin to assault the tanks and howitzers or create enough confusion for him to evade a direct hit for the one mile of open highway he has to survive.

He inserts the last Python missile, lowers the cartridge back into the drone, and moves it to the backseat.

Two miles, it's just two miles, he implores himself, like he's trying to finish one of the many long boot camp runs he often concluded with a round of violent heaving.

Two miles to the other side of this, then it's smooth sailing to Bangor.

He has done a lot of stupid things in his life, but assaulting a fixed military position protected by air support and heavy artillery with only a souped-up SUV and a drone is about as inconceivable as it gets. After a swig of water, he closes his eyes and tries to grab an image of Tessa from before. When the world had not yet contorted into the grim present.

He fixates on a moment when they were dating. They had cruised up the Pacific Coast Highway in a rented convertible for a weekend in wine country. It sounded kind of classy but was really just an excuse to stumble around small towns like Santa Barbara and Solvang, sampling wines by the glass before drunken lunches of tacos and over-salted margaritas. Like an aged Polaroid, the edges have grown blurry to the years passed. He focuses on their walk along Stearns Wharf, the feel of her hand in his, the smell of the ocean, and the glare of the sun off the rippling water. So close, the sensations slowly dissipate into a fog.

A moment of reprise is enough, giving him calm and focus. He slips back on the night vision goggles and starts the Hummer engine. Shifting to drive, he navigates through the tree line brush to the I-95 ramp and drives over a crushed portion of the metal guardrail. The lumbering vehicle slips onto the asphalt and accelerates into the madness ahead.

"Gerald, elevate to two hundred feet," states Bishop.

"Climbing to two hundred feet," responds the British-voiced drone via the tablet speaker.

The drone rises through the roof opening and takes a position above the Hummer as the onramp curves right, I-95 insight less than a quarter-mile away. He can already see the mass of shipping containers lining the highway.

Half a mile to the loop, one mile around, last half mile to the Forest Street Bridge. We can do this.

The bridge is his last piece of the escape puzzle. If he makes it around the loop and the sentries pursue, he will use the drone to take out the bridge supports and collapse it behind him. It would render the return trip more difficult, but he needs to worry about the next ten minutes, not the next ten hours.

In the starless pre-dawn night, the Hummer slips onto I-95 and into the maze of shipping containers, arranged in a haphazard zigzag. Bishop weaves the heavy vehicle through as nimbly as possible but is barely able to accelerate above fifteen miles an hour.

"Gerald, location of airborne bogey?"

"Distance to bogey one point eight miles, elevation three hundred feet and steady, direction northeast at ten miles per hour."

"Gerald, elevate to five hundred feet and close on airborne bogey at fifty miles per hour."

Bishop continues the frustrating crawl around and through the highway shipping container obstacle course, unable to get a clear visual on the first gun nest housing a fifty-caliber machine gun pointed right where he is heading.

"One mile to bogey."

An alarm sounds. High pitched digital chirps. "Bogey direction change. Bogey circling south, thirty miles per hour. Bogey will be in visual range in twenty seconds."

"Gerald, target main and rear rotors, fire on target lock," yells Bishop excitedly while he tries to keep his focus on the road.

The drone locks targets and fires a successive pair of Python missiles at the Apache. The helicopter launches aerial countermeasures, sending both missiles off to harmlessly chase flares and explode away from the flight path. Simultaneously, the Apache locks onto the drone with its 30mm chain gun and unleashes a steady burst of retaliation fire.

Utilizing its avoidance programming, the drone decelerates and immediately descends two hundred feet, the chain gun expertly trailing it. After a hard bank left, the drone fires a succession of three Pythons and three Sarin rockets. The chain gun switches from offense to defense and cuts down all six incoming ordinances while firing a half a dozen Hydra 70 rockets from its pair of nineteen count tube launchers mounted under each wing.

Closing at twenty-three hundred feet per second, the unguided missiles explode in an array around the drone. The successive concussions bounce it violently in the air before it is swallowed by the erupting flames and spirals out of control to the ground, crashing lifelessly in a burning heap.

Goddamnit Gerald.

Like earlier on I-95, floodlights flash on all along the highway, illuminating Bishop's position. He tears off his night vision goggles, now useless. With his second drone out of commission and night cover blown, he now sits defenseless, just a few shipping containers away from the first gun nest. From above, the Apache uses a blinding search spotlight to sweep the ground just north of his position, working its way towards Bishop.

With both drones eliminated and no weapons capable of taking out the Apache, tanks, or howitzers, Bishop considers these may be his final seconds. He grimly looks over the dashboard buttons - Mask and Pain.

"Well, what the hell," pressing the Mask button first.

To Bishop's immediate eyes, sitting inside the Hummer, nothing happens. The exterior, however, undergoes a swift and dramatic change. Utilizing an experimental polymer covering the exterior surfaces of the Hummer combined with digital imaging via multiple strategically placed three-millimeter camera lenses, the program instantly recognizes the surrounding surfaces, creating a digital rendering of the surrounding terrain to adapt.

From above, the vehicle disappears into the asphalt highway.

From the side, it matches the rippling metal walls of the shipping container.

The polymer manipulates the spectral wavebands currently being utilized by the Apache to hunt for Bishop via night vision and thermal sensors. Standing still, Bishop and the Hummer are virtually invisible.

Through the bulletproof glass of the front windshield, Bishop can see the hood of the Hummer. It melts seamlessly into the highway in front of him. He closes the roof opening, adrenaline pumping as the realization hits him - *I have the advantage on approach, but they'll see the camouflage adapt as I move. Think, think, what is Pain? An EMP wouldn't be painful, just a pain in the ass. It's gotta be physical, but there is nothing in here, no weapons, no extra tech, what the hell is it?*

Bishop pauses and turns, looking back at the Hummer's array of linked batteries currently occupying the rear of the vehicle, searching for anything that might be out of place and clue him into his last option.

"I know what it is," he says to himself, quietly at first, again with more confidence. "I know what it is!"

He steps on the gas. The Hummer creeps out from behind the cover of the last few shipping containers, continuing along I-95 toward the first machine gun nest. Awaiting him is a fifty-caliber tripod-mounted gun aimed in his direction crewed by a pair of sentries in head-to-toe cold weather camouflage gear.

In the closing fifty yards, neither guard notices the ghostly apparition approaching from the south, like a phantom displacing reality. As the Hummer nears, their ears slowly perk to the subtle hum of the vehicle's electric engine as the adaptive masking compensates to keep the Hummer invisible.

A little bit closer, Bishop tells himself, *just a little bit closer.* Realizing something is off, both guards fixate on the sound and odd movements they cannot quite register just twenty-five yards from their position.

Bishop places his finger on the button marked Pain as he guides the Hummer within ten yards of the machine gun nest.

Alright, here goes nothing.

He presses the button. The Hummer grinds to a halt as the engine and batteries shut down, turning off the adaptive camouflage, leaving Bishop completely exposed and immobile.

Bishop stares out the window at the guard racking up the fifty-caliber machine gun aimed directly at his position and strings together an impressive new combination of expletives.

CHAPTER 3

"Don't shoot it, you hear me, do not shoot that thing!" yells the sentry standing with his arm out, waving off the gunner behind the fifty-caliber machine gun.

"What the hell, man?" the gunner yells back, muffled through his ski mask. "That's the truck from earlier on the other side of 95, we have shoot on sight orders!"

"Did you see what that thing just did?" responds the first sentry. "It's got some sort of... I dunno, cloaking system. That's advanced tech, we are not going to blow that up."

"Fine," the second sentry stands and removes a 9mm Glock pistol from his waist holster. "Let's do this."

The first sentry also unholsters his pistol and they both cautiously approach the Hummer, guns raised and aimed at the driver door. The sound of hydraulic pistons firing draws their attention.

On the roof of the Hummer, four panels slowly raise, one to front, one to the rear, one to each side, until positioned at a ninety-degree angle with the vehicle, refracting light from the overhead floodlights placed along the highway.

"The hell are those things?" asks the second sentry, halting in place.

"Dunno, let's open it up and find out." The first sentry also stops, looking around confused at first, then more and more frantic. He holsters his weapon, then pats at his camouflaged winter coat and pants.

"I feel... hot. Do you feel that?" the first sentry asks with rising concern.

"Yeah, what is that?" responds the second sentry, dropping his gun to the cold asphalt highway as he unzips his insulated jacket and rubs his layered long underwear below. "I feel like...like I'm on fire!"

Both sentries drop to their knees, then sprawl to the ground, writhing and screaming in agony as their water and fat molecules respond to the radio frequencies aimed at them, boiling just beneath their skin. Pea-sized blisters form as second degree burns rapidly spread throughout their bodies.

From behind the reinforced armor of the Hummer, Bishop watches the scene unfold. In the sky, the Apache circles erratically, pilots unable to exercise control as their bodies cook from the inside. After a few seconds, it makes a hard landing behind the tree line off the right side of I-95.

Down the stretch of highway, Bishop watches as tank personnel crawl out from their vehicles while tearing off their protective winter gear. At the last moment, he realized what the Pain button was for - an Active Denial System.

Designed in the early part of the twenty-first century as a non-lethal weapon for military and local policing, it acted as a giant microwave, cooking the insides of anyone unfortunate enough to be in proximity. Over the years, the speed of deployment and effective distance increased. Based on his current visual, Bishop figures this one has a one-mile radius in all directions. A giant temporary bubble of scalding misery now surrounds him.

Unfortunately, as he has learned on the spot, the Hummer only has enough juice in the batteries to run either the engine or the weapon. Switching the weapon off and the engine back on means releasing his vice grip. It will take time for the sentries to recover, and some might try to pursue. Another thirty seconds of exposure and anyone within a mile should be incapacitated for the next twenty to thirty minutes before the swelling starts to recede and they can get back on their feet.

A quick check of the tablet map shows a relatively straight route to Bangor, continuing to I-95 for approximately the next four hours, providing him an arrival time of around ten in the morning. It occurs to Bishop most days when his overnight garbage collection route ended, he would be home and in bed by nine in the morning. As disruptive and selfish as it sounds, he knows he will need to sleep for a few hours. He doesn't want to be sloppy due to exhaustion, and the adrenaline ups and downs of the night have drained him of whatever self-produced energy bursts he will need.

He decides - shut down the weapon, restart the engine and get the hell out of town, hopefully without any pursuit. After putting enough distance between him and Boston, he will find a secure location, get a few hours of shut-eye, refuel on whatever decent MREs are available, and complete the last leg into Bangor. The other issue is the shaking in his hands.

He had noticed it a few hours back but took it as nothing more than frayed nerves or excessive adrenaline. He was slowly coming to grips with the truth - he was going through withdrawal from the diacetylmorphine spray he has been inhaling two or three times a day, a low-end cheap narcotic available at the bodega not far from his apartment. To keep him balanced, he reasoned. To steady himself in an unsteady world, to numb the mental distress of executing those trying to escape the Free Zone, to sleep without the nightmares. All the island security personnel used some sort of drug to keep themselves numbed. Unfortunately, the bottle he had purchased the previous day sat useless in the locker back at Manhattan Security headquarters.

There will be no drug store or pharmacy to shop at along the way for a refill. He is just going to have to deal with the withdrawal effects, however uncomfortable. None of this matters at this moment, as he switches off the weapon currently keeping two dozen or so sentries writhing on the ground.

Allowing the weapon to power down as the roof panels retract, he waits a moment before pressing the ignition button on the Hummer to restart the engine. It purrs to life as best an electric engine can, and Bishop wastes no time shifting into drive and accelerating past the scattered prone bodies lying next to defanged tanks and howitzers. Those not already passed out can only watch motionless as the Hummer speeds by on its way around the north bend of I-95 towards Bangor and out of sight.

Boston is finally in his rearview mirror.

⚖ ⚖ ⚖

Sandra Nolan stands in her sparse kitchen, blankly staring out the floor to ceiling window from the fifty-fourth floor onto the dimly lit city morning while she crunches a nearly flavorless energy bar. It is a city she had been observing through windows like this her entire life. The world had changed, but this was still her island.

Unlike Nolan, a large percentage of the current Manhattan residents were not a part of the immediate pre-asteroid population, having either negotiated access into the fortress or been recruited. In contrast, those existing residents without an employment purpose were pushed out, figuratively and literally. She was one of the few homegrown inhabitants, raised on the Upper West Side by her college professor father and orthopedist mother in the exclusive Central Park West neighborhood. While not an outcast per se, her considerable intellect allowed her to skip two junior high grades and complete high school at the age of sixteen to the catty remarks of her peers. She surprised her parents by forgoing higher education for medicine or law to pursue a Bachelor of Music in violin from the renowned Juilliard School, an instrument she had been obsessed with since the age of three.

She placated her parents' poncy high society ambitions as a teen but relished the opportunity to strike out on her own. Even then, she was dismayed by the careerist commercial ambitions of so many of her classmates. The violin excited her facilities for math, science, and history in ways those individual subjects left her wanting. She had only one burning desire - to become the youngest, and first female, first violin in the Juilliard String Quartet, which in the first eighty years of existence had only four people fill the role, all male. Her odds of becoming an astronaut or President of the United States were more reasonable.

At the absurd age of twenty-eight, Nolan would achieve her

dream, joining one of the most elite of classical music performing groups in the world. Like any musical performer, she would gain both a casual and more fervent fan base. Instead of pre-teens discovering pop or punk music for the first time, hers was from a stratum of society even higher from which she or her parents were familiar. She soon counted world leaders, cultural elite tastemakers, and corporate titans as devotees. It was after one of these exclusive performances that she was introduced to a quiet but intense classical music connoisseur named Elton Vinick.

The phone in her hand vibrates, shaking her from the morning mental fog after a night of too many interruptions during her restless sleep. A new text appears:

Fenton: good news, past bos onto bangor, eta 4hrs - 6:22 AM

It is the message she had hoped to pass along to Vinick in a few minutes, and the board later this morning. She finishes the energy bar and exits the kitchen to the bathroom to brush her teeth and down a quick swig of makeshift mouthwash before her trip up to the fifty-fifth floor.

"Zach," yells out Nolan. She hears the hurried footsteps on approach.

"Yes, Ms. Nolan," responds Zach advancing down the hallway.

"I need my tab-" she stops mid-sentence as he hands her the black computer bag. "Good, thanks." She rifles through, looking for something, and removing a small plastic rectangle the size of a credit card. "This might go long today; I'll text you if I'm running late for the board at eight."

"Got it," he says, stepping out of the doorway so Nolan can

exit. He follows behind as they move down the hallway to the pair of elevator doors. She presses the up button, and after a moment, they open. She enters alone, depressing the button marked "55."

"Security clearance required," announces a prerecorded voice via an overhead loudspeaker. Nolan presses the small plastic card to a black box above the elevator buttons, switching a small LED light from red to green and closing the elevator doors. She checks the time on her phone, 6:28 AM, as the elevator rises twelve feet between floors in seconds, then slows to a stop.

The doors open, and Nolan is face to face with a familiar sight - the unsmiling face of Xeno Reed, the head of Vinick's personal security detail. A short but stocky gentleman with a razor shaved head and bionic left hand and arm up to his elbow. Over each of his shoulders, the barrel of German-made MP5 9mm machine guns are leveled at her by security guards in full body armor.

"Good morning, Miss Nolan," says Xeno with matter-of-fact familiarity.

"Good morning," she responds, taking one step forward and raising her arms. Xeno glides his hand, which has a built-in metal detector in the palm, along the outline of her body, but with a perfunctory quickness.

"He's in the gym," Xeno states as he completes the check. Nolan smiles and turns right, following a similar floorplan to her own story. But while Nolan had updated various rooms with neutral tones and an occasional accent wall, Vinick had gone binary, black walls buffeted by while ceilings and floors lit by long strips of bright halogen light bulbs. Like the interior of an interstellar spaceship, it was antiseptic and sterile, words Nolan would have never associated with Elton Vinick when she met him over twenty years ago.

She rounds the familiar corners of the fifty-fifth floor, entering the gymnasium at exactly 6:30 AM. It is outfitted with the standard assortment of machines, benches, dumbbells, and weight plate racks. Across the windowless room, she sees Vinick in his usual spot atop a cushioned mat seated cross-legged in the Lotus yoga position on the floor, his feet placed atop the opposite thigh, each sole facing upward.

His eyes closed, he takes a long smooth inhale through his nose, exhaling just as deliberately through his mouth. Nolan knows to wait until Vinick is ready. It may be a minute; it may be five. He wears the same clothes she sees him in during every visit - a plain white sleeveless tee shirt and cotton white pajama pants. His thin seventy-seven-year-old frame pokes at the clothes at sharp angles. His hair has been grayed for as long as she has known him, from thick and manicured to thin and unkempt.

"Tell me something good, Sandy," says Vinick in a deep calm voice. She steps forward into the room toward him, stopping at the edge of the gym mat.

"Current active asset is through Boston en route to Bangor, a little under four hours out," responds Nolan with calm reassurance. Vinick opens his eyes, fading blue betrayed by cloudiness. His vision operates at a quarter of optimal. He stands and grabs a long metal cane leaning against a nearby workout bench. His movements slow and deliberate, a man whose body is decaying faster than his mind. He steadies himself and walks toward Nolan.

"Good morning," says Vinick with familiar warmth. His tone sharply adjusts. "This is going to take a while, isn't it?"

"Unfortunately, yes." She shares his annoyance, walking next to him as they exit the gym for an open area next to the kitchenette. Vinick opens the fridge and removes a clear plastic bottle filled with a thick dark green liquid, one of a dozen neatly lined up. He shuffles over to an upholstered medical chair flanked by an IV pole and a bank of four television monitors on a wheeled stand in front. If he was a teenage gamer, this would be the best set-up money could buy.

He places the bottle on a small table attached to the chair arm and clutches a remote, which he aims at the blank screens. They flicker on, revealing live black and white surveillance camera footage. The top left shows elevator doors where Xeno and his two guards are currently seated, to the right, the interior of the now uninhabited elevator. The bottom left is of Nolan's conference room, currently unoccupied, from the angle opposite the buffet table near where Nolan sat. The bottom right is an electronic chessboard in mid-contest, "Awaiting Player Two" flashes across the screen.

Nolan sits at the nearby kitchen table and removes the tablet from her bag along with an attachable keyboard while Vinick sips the green drink, wincing from the pungent flavor.

"I'll never get used to the taste, I don't care what's in it," muses Vinick.

"Lamb is getting bolder," says Nolan. "We'll need to be creative to keep him at bay."

"He thinks he has a play," he says, "but he's too focused on me, he's missing the big picture. The single-minded always miss the big picture." Nolan smirks knowingly. She has heard Vinick dispense pearls of homespun wisdom for decades.

"Is that why we get along?" she responds while typing. "We're big-picture people?"

"Lamb is a child," he barks back between sips of the green drink. "Lloyd was a fool to bring him in without proper vetting. It would take a good psychiatrist years to unpack the childhood issues Lamb is carrying around. Distant father, overbearing mother, some sort of self-pitying nonsense. But he's a shark, don't let his smart-alecky attitude snow job you."

"I know, I know," acknowledges Nolan. Vinick pauses after another sip from the plastic bottle.

"We get along," he finally answers, "because we know who we are. We are truthful in our actions, however difficult they may be. We recognize the world as it is and navigate as such. We are not just survivors, we are diviners." Nolan rolls her eyes just slightly, knowing Vinick is prone to bouts of verbosity.

"Don't roll your eyes at me. I've reached the age of grandiose overstatement. It would have all been in my memoirs, you know. Not that I'll have a chance to write those now."

Vinick tips the bottle up and downs the last of the green drink. As he does, a woman dressed in a white nurse's hospital uniform enters carrying a clear bag of yellow liquid marked "EV Parabiosis Batch 1741."

"This is the part you don't like," he says. Nolan focuses on the computer screen as she types while he places the bottle on the nearby table and picks up a roll of white medical tape, tearing off two pieces and adhering them on the edge of the table.

The nurse hooks it to the IV pole, then picks up a hypodermic needle attached to a long clear tube running up to the IV bag. Vinick takes a deep breath as she inserts it into a protruding vein on his left hand. With his right hand, he carefully selects each piece of tape and places it on the tube to secure it in place. The nurse grips the bag again and turns a small plastic knob at the bottom nozzle releasing a stream of liquid into the tube, along his arm, and into the needle.

"Thank you, dear," exhales Vinick. The nurse silently nods, turns, and exits the room.

"Done yet?" asks Nolan squeamishly.

"Let's get to it," says Vinick, as the fresh plasma pours into his vein. "It's time to give Mr. Lamb exactly what he wants."

⚐ ⚐ ⚐

Nolan strides into the conference room at one minute to eight, all the board members seated in the same place as the previous day. She makes her way to the head of the far end of the table without glancing at them and sits.

"Good morning, everyone," says Nolan as she removes the tablet from the bag and sets it up with the keyboard. "I've just spent the last hour and a half with Elton drafting our version of the requested succession contingency we discussed yesterday afternoon. It is a first draft, we'll have time to iron out the finer points, but it is ready for your initial review. We'll expect the same courtesy with the counter-proposal."

She types on her computer, opens the email client, and attaches the document to a new message, addresses it to everyone on the board, and clicks the send button.

"Everyone should have it now, check your inboxes," Nolan says as she gets up and steps over to the buffet behind her. She skips the various breakfast food options and instead opts for the heated synthetic caffeinated energy drink, light brown in color, and equally unremarkable in taste. After pouring herself a cup, she looks across the room as the board members review the multipage document currently occupying their inbox.

After a quick glimpse to register their reactions, her focus concentrates on Lamb. His brow furrows as he reads. *Bet you didn't see this one coming, Nathan.* She looks up at the clock on the wall and flashes a tiny smile, knowing Vinick is eagerly awaiting the coming moments via his webcam.

"What in the hell?" asks Lamb incredulously. "He can't do this. He's superseding the board's authority."

"Technically," Lloyd interrupts, suddenly understanding what is happening, "he can. The bylaws were not written with judicial or federal oversight. I'm not sure a credible legal firm even vetted them. By the time Elton and Solear purchased Manhattan Island from the state of New York and established the governance structure, it was voted on by the first board, and that was it."

"The bylaws pertaining to this are quite clear," states Nolan as she returns to her seat. "Vinick and the founders believed a time would come when the board would no longer be an effective representation of the population, this arrangement was ultimately temporary and not sustainable. A general election with, based on current housing demographics, a ward representation system would be necessary to address the needs of the city."

"So, Elton Vinick's grand plan is to bring back democracy?" remarks Lamb snidely. "I have to say; this makes me question the man's mental capabilities. The board is not going to stand for this."

"The board has no say," responds Nolan.

"Excuse me?" says Lamb with disdain. "This board can remove him anytime it pleases."

"Let me reiterate," Nolan counters. "The board has no say because Vinick and the founders built in an option in the bylaws. When fifty-one percent of the population is considered a citizen in full standing, meaning they have wiped all entrance debts from their record, board governance can be dissolved in favor of the ward system. They can then appoint a comptroller as a general representative of the wards."

"Sandra," asks Lloyd, "what is the current count of full citizens for Manhattan?"

"At the start of the new year," she answers, "it was at fifty percent with an average week to week net increase of point three. Meaning-" Lamb interrupts. "Meaning at the end of the first quarter, when we meet for first Q results, he can pull the trigger."

Nolan smiles at Lamb. *Gotcha.* She hears a vibration emanate from the computer bag, reaches in, and pulls out her phone. A new text appears:

Fenton: bangor eta 2.5hrs - 8:04 AM

"Good news, everyone," she announces. "I just received an update: our latest asset is en route to the target, only a few hours out." She eyes Lamb for any physical response, but he stares out the large floor to ceiling window, expressionless. After a moment, he rises out of his chair and walks to the window, looking out over the murky cityscape.

"The only people who can exercise this option are in this room," asserts Lamb. "And the only person who can execute it is Elton Vinick, who would rather dissolve this board than give up his power. Once the wards are in place, they would look to someone with experience to appoint as a comptroller. Maybe

Elton, maybe his second in command. I'm sure he's got a nice soft landing planned for himself as he throws this city into chaos." Lamb looks over at Nolan as he slowly starts to walk around the room.

"He is leaving us no choice," he says with rising intensity. "I am calling a vote of no confidence for Elton Vinick, and for his immediate dismissal as CEO. At which point, the board will revisit the bylaws and exorcise the ward option." Board members look at each other sheepishly in silence as Nolan shakes her head in feigned disbelief.

"You don't have the votes, Nathan." she retorts. "You need unanimous consent, and you don't have that," Nathan smirks.

Something's wrong, she thinks, *he's way too confident.*

"Then let's vote and find out."

"Wait a minute, let's not get ahead of ourselves," cautions an even-tempered Lloyd Rust to Lamb. Turning his attention to Nolan, "Sandra, would it be possible to get Elton on the intercom? I believe this serious crossroads we are at demand his participation."

"I'll do you one better, Lloyd," says Vinick, to the shock of everyone in the room, as he strides in through the doorway sans cane with a surprisingly lithe gait, flanked by his security chief Xeno Reed. His shabby t-shirt and pajama pants upgraded to sharply pressed grey slacks, a white button-down shirt, and a black cardigan sweater, finished off with a pair of glossy loafers.

"Give us some time," he says to Xeno, who retreats from the room with a steely eye on Lamb. Vinick walks to Nolan and places his hand on her seated shoulder. "If you would allow me, I'd like to say a few things before you call your vote, Nathan."

"Of course," says a red-faced and flustered Lamb.

"Thank you," responds Vinick. "Sandra has been taking the brunt of the punishment for my absence over the last several months. My physicians advised me to reduce my workload to reduce my stress as not to negatively impact my health. Only Sandra and the head of island security have been privy to the details outside my doctors."

"Why is that, Elton?" inquires Lloyd, speaking with the sincerity of an old friend. "Why the need to hide your condition from the board? To use our security to retrieve someone from outside the city?"

"Because this board talks, Lloyd," answers Vinick. "Spouses, children, neighbors, friends. Rumors would crack the foundation of authority this board currently maintains."

"But you're willing to dissolve the board," retorts Lamb.

"You're right, I am," responds Vinick. "It's a card in my hand, and whether I play it is entirely up to me. Let me ask you, Nathan. If you're are successful in ousting me today, who do you suppose will be named the successor? You? It's no secret you desire the position, but last time I checked, you didn't have the votes. Have you thought this through? How do you know that people loyal to me won't vote for my removal, only to turn around during the replacement process and install someone loyal to me, allowing me to lead by proxy? How do you know you won't get ousted yourself, overplaying your hand and exposing your weakness? That this has all been just a ruse to force you to make a move and show your cards when you didn't need to?"

Vinick pats Sandra on the shoulder with familial affection and makes his way to the door. Lamb leans back in his chair, staring squint-eyed at Vinick as he exits.

"Why are we running secret missions to Maine, Elton?" asks Lamb incredulously. "What is up there you need so bad? Plenty of doctors on this island. What aren't you telling us?" Vinick stops just before the doorway and turns to Lamb.

"There is a man there, a very special doctor, who can save my life," answers Vinick.

"With all due respect, that's crazy," Lamb spits out. "How can you know if anyone is still alive out there after all these years?"

"I know," says Vinick with a weary smile, "because until not long ago, he was a citizen of this city. And I hope... I believe we will find him. I'm afraid we did not part on the best of terms, and I would like a chance to make amends with him." Lamb's curiosity is peaked.

"Who the hell is this person?" he asks.

"He is my son," responds Vinick, who does not look back to see the stone-faced Nolan, and exits the room, Xeno stepping to his side as they disappear down the hallway.

♟ ♟ ♟

Tessa lies asleep on the cold concrete, rousing slowly at the sound of knuckles rapping the door. The dangling overhead light snaps on, and the darkness vanishes. With her hands and legs now free, she wipes the sleep from her eyes and stretches her legs.

"Breakfast," announces a voice from the hallway, "Move to the corner, arms behind your back." As instructed, she places her head in the corner, taking a step back, pressing all her weight on her neck, and puts her hands behind her back.

The metal door creaks open on the rusty hinges and in slides a makeshift tray, upon which a bowl of blueish gray mush and a glass of water reside.

"Do you want a book?" asks the voice.

"Yes, please," responds Tessa, and a paperback book is tossed in, followed by the slam and lock of the door. She pivots on her feet and cautiously approaches the tray. The mush is worriedly undefined, so she gets on her knees, bends over it, and sniffs.

"Um, what is this stuff?" she asks.

"No idea," responds the voice. She hears him settle into the chair in the hallway just outside the door. She decides to taste it and scoops a small amount into her hand, then testing it with her tongue.

It's like watered-down cream of wheat. Blech.

Regardless of the taste, or lack thereof, she lifts the bowl and drinks from it, finishing it greedily and then downs the water, finally turning her attention to the reading material. After wiping her hands on her pant thighs, she reaches for the tattered book and turns it over.

"This is a thesaurus. A thirty-year-old thesaurus. Are you serious, this is the only book you have?" she asks pleadingly.

"You're lucky you got that," responds the agitated voice from the hallway.

"Fine," she spits back. "I guess I'll just expand my vocabulary." For the first time, Tessa finally has a chance to look over every inch of the room without eyes on her. The concrete floor is smooth with only a small drainage cap in the center, no bigger than her fist. She runs her hand along the rough, unpainted cinder block walls leading up to a smooth plaster ceiling. The lone light provided by the dangling bulb a few feet above her head is threaded through a metal link chain.

Whether the chain can hold her is not much of a concern until she spots the rectangular ventilation shaft in the ceiling toward the back of the room. Unfortunately, this room appears taller than standard. She approaches the rear wall and counts the cinder blocks from the floor up. At eight inches per cinder block, she calculates the ceiling is twelve feet. With her hand outstretched, she can reach the ninth row of cinder blocks, only halfway up. She walks back to the center of the room where her chair sits and carefully picks it up, placing it directly below the hanging light.

She gently places her bare left foot on the chair to avoid noise and transfers her weight onto her left quadricep muscle to raise her entire body upward. With both feet on, she reaches and grabs the metal chain just above the bulb, which singes her wrist on contact. She gives the chain a slight tug and watches the ceiling to see if the plaster cracks. It doesn't, so she pulls harder, testing the strength of the chain links and the hook drilled into the ceiling where the wire disappears.

She decides to give it one final test, gripping the chain tightly as she gingerly lifts one, then the other foot off the chair. It holds - a way up, but not yet a way out. The room is square and not big, maybe ten feet by ten feet. *Probably used to be some sort of storage closet.* Getting to the ceiling is step one, getting the vent shaft open is step two, which will require, from what she can tell from where she is standing, a screwdriver.

Tessa carefully steps down from the chair and returns it to the original spot. "I'm done," she announces, "could I get the bathroom bucket, please?"

"Hold on," the man in the hallway announces. He rises loudly from the chair and walks away, Tessa counts. Fifty-five seconds pass before she hears footsteps again, and about a minute and twenty for him to return to the door. She places the food tray next to the door and returns to the prone position in the corner. After a quick check through the window, the guard opens the door, pulls out the tray and slides in a rolling plastic bucket, the kind paired with a mop and wringer found in every office storage closet.

"Any chance I could get a spoon with this mush next time?" asks Tessa, feigning sweetness.

"Yeah, I dunno about that," the guard mutters as he pulls shut the door and locks it. "Let me know when you're done."

She approaches the bucket, examines it from all sides. *Dammit.* The entire construction is plastic, not a single piece of metal on the whole thing. The wheels, handle, every part is molded plastic snapped together.

Well, they're not stupid.

Tessa undoes the top button of her pants and unzips the fly, squatting over the bucket to relieve herself. She looks up at the ventilation cover and studies it for a moment, then back down at the zipper on her pants. From under her shirt neckline, she pulls a thin gold band on which a small gold cross hangs, rubbing it between her fingers.

♟ ♟ ♟

As the elevator floats between floors, ascending to the fifty-fifth, Sandra checks her phone:

Fenton: on target, bangor eta 1.5hrs - 9:02 AM

It slows to a stop and the doors open, Xeno and his pair of armed guards in their familiar spot.

"Miss Nolan," says Xeno, "twice in one morning, this is unexpected." They go through the motions of the security check.

"Lots of surprises today," she responds, faking a smile.

She marches down the hallway, peering into the unused gym and then onto the kitchen and living area. No sign of Vinick. She turns and makes her way back to Xeno.

"Is he...," she points down the hallway in the other direction.

"Nope," responds Xeno, who looks and points toward the ceiling. "Said he wanted to some air. You can take the private stairs." He motions to a door off to the right of the elevator.

"Thanks," says Sandra as she pushes through the doorway and proceeds up the twisting staircase to another door, this one windowless with "Roof Access - Caution Wind" painted across in fading red. She grips the vertical metal bar and thrusts forward; a blast of cold January air immediately slaps her face.

She immediately spots Vinick, who briefly looks back at her from a dozen yards away.

"You're not dressed to be up here," says Vinick, holding a small metal oxygen canister with a clear tube running up to his nose, held in a place by an elastic strap around his head.

"Neither are you," she says, making her way to Vinick, leaning into the stiff breeze, arms wrapped around her trying to contain the abruptly escaping warmth.

"A good slap of cold to the face is invigorating," he states. "Like getting snapped with a wet towel in the locker room." She shakes her head, sidling up next to him, peering over the murk-covered city.

"Can we just get to the part where you explain yourself?" she asks indignantly. Vinick inhales deeply.

"My first wife Pasha and I were married very briefly, just after college," he says without bluster. "We had a son, divorced a few years later. Most people didn't know Carla was my second wife. I wasn't anyone until I met her. My son Marion and I had a complicated relationship. I did my best to support them, but he doesn't see it that way. Especially after his mother left..." He trails off in a manner unfamiliar to Sandra, Vinick not being a man of self-reflection.

"When did you get him into the city?" she asks, her indignity evolving to empathetic curiosity.

"About a year ago, I pulled strings," he confesses. "It's not like you can't have enough doctors, but the hospitals were fully staffed at that time. The team in charge of population control had vetoed his entry. He had been working in a community in the Carolinas that had come under attack and was looking for refuge. I exerted some influence to get him in. I thought it might help us, seeing as we were the only family left for each other. It did not. The more I tried, the worse things got between us. When he told me he was leaving for Bangor last fall, I tried to convince him to stay, but he wouldn't listen. He said he could do more good there. It was a mistake to let him go."

She eyes him, simultaneously feeling pity and frustration. She has worked by his side for so long, and yet he hid this from her. For the first time since she met Elton Vinick decades ago, when he became her patron, mentored her, guided her onto a path of professional and personal realization, what creeps into her mind was wholly unfamiliar: suspicion.

⚐ ⚐ ⚐

Bishop slowly opens his eyes and surveys his surroundings. Everything is how he left it three hours ago. The alarm on the tablet flashes "12:30 PM" in rhythm with the bell chime he programmed to give himself a brief reprieve. By a quarter after nine, his eyes had grown heavy enough he found himself nodding off once or twice while speeding down the desolate highway, snapping himself awake, but the message his body sent was clear - get some sleep.

An hour outside Bangor, he found an exit off I-95 in the long-abandoned town of Waterville. He backed the Hummer into the burnt-out husk of a strip mall coffee shop, camouflaging it from any possible prying eyes for this abbreviated slumber. As he blinks back to full consciousness, thirst and hunger are his primary concerns. He reaches into the compartment filled with bottled water, energy bars, and MRE bags, and examines his choices, settling on the vacuum-sealed sloppy joe pack.

He searches the compartment, then the glove box for a military-issue flameless ration heater to warm up the MRE pack, a luxury which had been overlooked by Silva and his team back in the garage. Time to improvise. He starts the engine and pulls the hood release from under the dash, exiting the Hummer with the MRE package. Circling to the front of the vehicle, he raises the hood and places his hand on the rectangular engine cover, feeling for heat. Finding none, he slides his hand over the engine, finally locating a warm spot to place the MRE pack, gently lowering the hood as not to attract attention with a loud noise.

He slips back into the driver's seat and checks the dash battery levels. The extra miles through Boston plus deployment of the Active Denial System weapon have drained the first battery and half the second, more than Bishop wants, but still within the comfort zone. He expects he won't be doing much driving in Bangor, so he'll be left with a somewhat full battery plus the two rounds of recharging to get him back to Manhattan.

Flipping through the menu on the tablet, he opens the map

section and slowly traces the route he will be on before reaching the outskirts of Bangor. From what he can tell, his target residence is a rural area north of the city and east of Pushaw Lake. The rear of the house off Forest Avenue butts up against a tree line, which may or may not still exist, but has no high ground for surveillance.

After a few minutes pass, it's enough to warm the MRE on the engine block. Bishop returns to the hood and extracts the package, gripping the edge gingerly to avoid a burn. Back in the Hummer, he turns off the engine and splits the MRE open along the pleat. A plume of steam emerges. The smell is nothing special, edible at best. He sadly realizes Silva forgot to include any utensils for the MRE packs, making sloppy joes a tricky proposition.

He gingerly places the steaming package on the passenger seat and exits the Hummer once again. The coffee shop is in bad shape, a fire had torn through here years ago, but he is willing to bet somewhere one spoon or fork managed to survive. He moves behind the remains of what was the counter to the left of the vehicle and pulls open drawers and cabinets covered in soot and dust. Nothing.

At the end of the counter, a single swinging door leads to what he guesses is a back-storage room. Surely whatever valuables were left have been picked clean by now, but he decides to make a go of it, stepping over a partially melted cappuccino machine to reach the door half off the hinges. As he pushes through, he spots a metal rack filled with half-burnt boxes of napkins, paper coffee cups, and lids. He looks through the boxes and, at the bottom, finally finds what he is looking for - spoons. Mostly heat disfigured and fused together, but he sorts through the box and finds one semi-respectable piece of silverware.

He makes his way out of the storage room back behind the counter and freezes in his tracks. Staring at him from outside the coffee shop stands what looks like a child, maybe twelve, thirteen years old based on the height, dressed in tattered winter clothing, hood up and a scarf covering their mouth and neck, distressed boots well past their best-by date. A twelve-gauge hunting rifle slung over their back. Standing behind the counter, ten or so feet from the Hummer, Bishop cautiously surveys the area.

Are there others?

Am I about to get jumped?

Why didn't I grab a gun?

I got complacent; the last three hours were too easy.

"Hey there," says Bishop, projecting slightly above his normal speaking voice. "You alone?" The child affirms with a nod, then raises their hands in a surrender pose and walks forward through what was once a large glass window into the coffee shop.

"You packing anything besides that rifle?" he asks, moving out from the counter closer to the Hummer, the driver side door now just a few feet away, almost within reach.

"No," says the child in a muffled voice, "Are you?" Bishop looks at the damaged spoon in his hand and smirks.

"I can do some damage with this spoon," he remarks. "What's your name?" The child stops walking, ten feet of water warped, soot-covered hardwood flooring between them. The gloved right-hand grabs the coat hood while the left grips the scarf, pulling back both. A ponytailed girl stands before Bishop.

"I'm Victoria, but Vickie is fine," she says, waiting on Bishop's response, still processing the encounter. "And you are?"

"You can call me Bishop," he says, "How old are you, Vickie?"

"Fourteen. I think. I'm pretty sure fourteen," she mulls over as she says it. "So, what brings you to my town?"

"Your town, huh?" he asks bemused. "Well, I heard you guys had the best spoon selection in the country, so I decided to come check it out. So, this is your town, huh? Are you the mayor or the sheriff?"

"I'm everything," she smiles back. "I'm the only one left. Well, my brother is here, but he's…" She trails off, Bishop stiffens his back.

"He can't travel, he was born with a lot of problems," she sighs. "Our house was built for him, so never really made sense to leave."

"Look," he responds. "I'm going to be upfront with you. I don't have a lot of time to stop and talk. Now, I was gonna sit here and eat my lunch, and then be on my way. If you want some company for a bit, I'm happy to split it with you and we can swap stories. But you're going to have to find your own utensil." She pulls out a large Swiss army knife from her jacket pocket and holds it up.

"I should get one of those."

Bishop and Vickie sit side-by-side on the coffee shop countertop, spooning Sloppy Joes out of a pair of dented aluminum mixing bowls.

"This is not good," she says.

"Jeez, beggars can't be choosers, you know," he responds defensively. "Besides, what are you surviving on, twigs and powdered milk?"

"My dad set up solar panels on our farm when they moved out here, like, twenty years ago," she responds. "They kind of still work, keep the lights on at the house. It's too cloudy to get everything running at once, but all my brother's medical equipment runs, we've got hot water, and the basement is a perfect grow house. He used to grow pot down there until, you know… Now we can grow vegetables. Not much variety. I guess people like him were kind of…"

"Hippies," interrupts Bishop.

"Yeah," she says, thinking. "He was all about being self-sufficient and living off the land. My parents were vegans. If they knew what I was eating now…"

"Oh, it's not real meat," he retorts with a chuckle. "I mean, technically, I guess it is. But it's not steak or a hamburger. There's much worse…" He catches himself, about to descend the dark path of murder gangs and cannibalism but thinks better of it. Somehow, this girl and her brother were surviving, all alone, in the middle of nowhere. "So, if you don't mind me asking when did your parents…?"

"Mom died right after it hit," she says, her voice softening. "The town flooded at first. After that, most people took off to go west. Our place is kind of on a hill, so the basement got some water, but it's still in good shape. She was on her way back from town when a wave must have hit her. Car ended up on the second floor of some house."

"Damn, sorry to hear that," says Bishop.

"My dad," she says, pushing down sadness, "he died a couple of years ago. He had cancer a couple of times, part of the reason he was growing pot. Drugs used to make him sick, the pot helped him eat, that sort of thing. He was good up to the end, like the last six months or so. He was a good dad." Her eyes well with tears, but she fights them back. She hasn't spoken aloud to someone about it other than her brother in a very long time.

Her story is familiar and temporarily twists him up. He and Tessa abandoned the West Coast for his parents' suburban home in St. Louis. They figured being away from the coasts when the asteroid struck was the safest bet. Like many who fled the seaboards for the perceived inland safety, the New Madrid

Seismic Zone had not been on their mind, unless they were frequenting conspiratorial websites that foretold impending doom on a regular basis before the asteroid.

Like it had over two hundred years prior, the earth tried to tear itself apart as middle America shook and turned upside down. Lakes disappeared as geysers of sand and dirt exploded. Crude underground fallout shelters built during the cold war were swallowed into the depths, taking the inhabitants and their survival treasures with them. Entire neighborhoods evaporated into thin air. After the first wave and the early aftershocks, the Dawes family and Tessa set out to help their neighbors whose homes had not fared as well as their own. More aftershocks, more destruction, his parents never returned. Tessa, along with Bishop's two younger sisters, spent weeks searching the area, uncovering nothing but death and horror. It was not long after that Bishop lost them as well as the blackness closed in from above, losses he still could not fully process, with his mind on survival mode every moment of every day.

"It's good that you were able to spend time with him," he says. "Lotta people who survived, their families were just gone one day. No goodbyes, nothing." He pauses to change the subject. "So, are you planning on staying here?"

"I make a trip up to Bangor every once in a while," she says, "but it's hard to trust anyone anymore, you know? Me and my brother, we're better off on our own. Just easier."

"I get it," his mind drifts to Tessa as he scoops the last bit of sloppy joe from the bowl. "So, you've been to Bangor."

"Yeah, is that where you're headed?"

"Well, this has been nice and all, but I got this thing."

"Yeah, your secret mission," she sarcastically responds. Vickie closes the Swiss army knife, slips it back into her pocket, and hops off the counter. "Well, it has been a real pleasure." She extends her hand like an adult; Bishop takes it and they shake.

"Yeah, we should definitely do this again sometime," he wants to say something reassuring but retreats to the safety of humor. "Any places I should check out in Bangor, they have a nice mall or anything?"

"Good luck, Bishop. If you come back this way, make sure to say hi," she says as she exits the coffee shop, pulling her hood back over her head. "I hope you know what you're doing." She ties the scarf back around her head, covering her nose and mouth as she trudges back into the biting January cold.

So do I, kid. So do I.

♟ ♟ ♟

Fenton strides down the stark concrete hallway to his office. The phone in his hand vibrates, he stops to read the incoming text:

Nolan: call me when private - 12:50 PM

He contemplates the message as he moves through the doorway into his office, shutting the door behind him. Back at his desk, he picks up the tablet, selecting the video conferencing option to initiate a call with Sandra Nolan from a list of contacts. The wall-mounted screen to his right flashes "Dialing Sandra Nolan" a few times before her face appears on the screen.

"I'd like an update," she says, focused on the camera.

"Asset nine was deployed ten minutes ago," responds Fenton. "Bangor arrival estimated at twenty-one hundred."

"Anything on the last one," she asks. "Is the beacon still stationary?"

"Hold on, let me bring that up," he says, typing on the tablet. The wall monitor screen splits in half, Nolan's image moving right as the map program appears on the left. The red blip appears on I-95 toward Bangor.

"Looks like he's active again," says Fenton with little inflection. "Probably stopped for a quick rest, not unusual at this point. I'd put him near the target within an hour, depending on his approach."

"Let's get the next one queued up," responds Nolan.

"If Bishop is successful, we're leaving the new asset out there high and dry," he argues. "We should stick with the plan, wait to see how Boston plays out, and then decide."

"The timetable is shrinking," fires back Nolan. "I understand your reservations, but if I had my choice, I'd be sending them out on the hour." His eyelid twitches. Under his stone-faced exterior, Fenton seethes at the implication of expendability.

"We'll wait until Bishop reaches the target, then reevaluate," he says. "Is that satisfactory?"

"Fine," responds Nolan. "Keep the hourly updates coming, please."

"Will do, talk to you-" says Fenton.

"Wait," she interrupts calmly. "There's been a development." He leans back in his chair, studying Nolan's face on the screen. She pauses to explain without explaining, choosing her words carefully.

"I can't go into specifics, but there is more to this," her voice softening. "The target may be more difficult to acquire than we first thought. Some information was withheld. There is also a secondary consideration. Internally, this isn't playing well. It could have political repercussions for all of us."

"Care to go into any greater detail?" he asks, knowing she won't.

"Let's plan to meet in person this afternoon," she says, eyes drifting back off-camera to her computer screen. "I'm not sure we're...let's just meet in person. I'll let you know the time and place soon."

Nolan terminates the call without waiting on a response. It catches Fenton off guard. He closes the video chat screen and brings up the second map on the split-screen. To the left, he watches Bishop's red dot move along I-95 approximately forty minutes outside Bangor. On the right, Regina Sanders, the new deployment, blinks a new red dot on I-95 just north of Manhattan.

Political implications? Why would she want to meet in person? he wonders. On the tablet, he returns to the "Candidates" spreadsheet and changes Sanders row from yellow to green. He highlights the next row in yellow with a stylus, then spins it between his fingers, an unconscious habit he picked up in college when studying. He could weave a pen or pencil through all his digits for hours with smooth efficiency and no attention, the physical manifestation of his churning subconscious.

Why would she want to meet in person? he wonders again. His concentration is broken by the ring of an incoming call on his tablet from Silva.

"I've got an update for you, we'll have two more Hummers prepped by the end of the day," says Silva. "But there's a problem."

"What's the problem?" asks Fenton.

"Those are the last two available Hummers we can requisition without, how should I put it, stealing," explains Silva.

"Do we have anything comparable? Any SUVs or Jeeps, something like that?" responds Fenton. Silva looks left and right of the screen.

"Ah, no. I mean, it's not like anything new is rolling in off the assembly lines," he responds with slight annoyance. Fenton is equally annoyed.

"Fine, just...keep me posted," Fenton barks back, shutting off the video chat before Silva can respond. He turns his attention back to the maps on the wall monitor, watching both red dots steadily progress forward on opposite ends of the same destination. The stylus effortlessly slipping through his fingers.

▲ ▲ ▲

While most executives operate from their exclusive floors at "the Mick," Chief Information Officer Nathan Lamb rules autonomously from the Manhattan Island Datacenter. Appropriately called "the Brain," it's located on Broad near the southern tip of Manhattan island, occupying the former Internap data center in the heart of the financial district.

Initially housed in one building, post-asteroid impact saw expansion into the next-door multi-purpose office building to bolster and consolidate it all in one central hub - financial data, citizen records, population management, communications, surveillance, transportation, etc.. Every aspect of daily life on Manhattan Island monitored, recorded, downloaded, analyzed, and forecasted through these facilities.

Lamb, a Silicon Valley wunderkind who started his first virtual reality gaming start-up in his basement at age fifteen, has been the mastermind behind the expansion and advancements made at the center. In his virtual reality world-building, he was able to measure and monetize the action of every player and brought this same hunger for data crunching to the financial sector in his early twenties. Wall Street insiders had never seen such advanced economic modeling. Lamb was no longer interested in running a company, he wanted the keys to the world economy.

The timing was poor, as six months into his raid of financial markets across the globe, the third and final attempt to redirect the asteroid failed. Currency quickly became irrelevant, so he wisely repositioned himself as the information caretaker of whatever Manhattan would be post-asteroid impact. For the first few years, Lamb was content to focus on unleashing his virtual reality data mining expertise on the population of Manhattan, anticipating and extrapolating within an inch, ounce, and second of every citizen's existence. He knew what every resident wanted, and the maximum credits he could squeeze out of them as they ground away at their daily life.

Having always forged his own path, he bristled at attempts by the board to conduct oversight on his end of the island, considering it an attack on his sovereignty. He turned his obsessive attention to the board members themselves and sharply sussed-out their various indiscretions, focusing on

Lloyd Rust. The latter was senior only to Elton Vinick in terms of respect and experience.

Unfortunately for Lamb, Vinick lived a guarded life in seclusion, protected from Lamb's invasions. Rust was not as lucky, thanks to his preference for barely legal debauched off-hours companionship. While not inherently damning, considering brothels operated freely in the city, it was his penchant for particularly violent encounters, running counter to his genteel daily mannerism, which caught him in Lambs web.

It was Rust who would end up his coerced advocate to be appointed to the board, but an opening would need to occur in the Chief Information Officer chair, one Lamb was able to manufacture with slithering ease. With no compensation for board members and executives, everything available freely as an executive perk, there was no chance of nefarious financial activity such as embezzlement or insider trading. He would need to find another trapdoor to drop his target through.

Lamb's predecessor, Michael Bauer, was a competent and well-liked CIO. Lamb despised him, if only because the nuts and bolts dirty work he had been doing since childhood was utterly foreign to Bauer, a white-glove, country club executive through and through. Though they were on cordial terms professionally, Bauer found Lamb a persistent pain and mostly left him alone to run the day to day operations at the data center, busying himself with the corporate side, which was of no interest to Lamb.

When Lamb finally launched "Operation Destroy Michael Bauer," the malfeasance pickings were slim, closer to none. Married, with no children, he didn't have a wandering eye and spent most of his free time at home on his executive floor at the

Mick reading history books and playing a variety of self-taught instruments. Once Lamb expanded his scope, cracks revealed themselves, and he had an opening to exploit - Mrs. Bauer.

As she had no official position on the island, Barbara Bauer spent her days alone in their executive floor suite with a growing self-prescribed chemical addiction to alleviate depression and bipolar hypomania. The fact that her husband was not on a daily regimen of pills was the greater anomaly. Most Manhattan residents ingested something to stay sane, focused, happy, pain-free, or numb to whatever other ailments could be solved via a daily tablet, injection, or inhalant.

All Lamb had to do was access the island pharmaceutical records database and alter the pills delivered weekly to the Bauer residence, gradually decreasing the tricyclic antidepressants to negatively impact the serotonin and norepinephrine levels in the nervous system. In little over a month, Mrs. Bauer endured a paranoid, manic episode so profound, she awoke confused in the middle of the night convinced her husband was a cannibalistic Free Zoner and promptly cracked his skull with a marble-based table side lamp.

With Bauer incapacitated and an open seat on the board, Rust promptly nominated Lamb to fill the position. It was met with a unanimous if wearied vote in favor, his reputation as brash and arrogant preceding him. He immediately made his presence felt, backing down attempts at board overview of data center activities, while simultaneously expanding the reach of the facility, including the previously restricted military networks. Within a year of his CIO tenure, the Brain was now in full control of all aspects of Manhattan island.

Lamb increasingly saw Vinick and the board as nothing more than relics of the pre-asteroid world, inefficient and gluttonous empty suits. Everything they believe they brought to the table as executives Lamb saw as a waste of ones and zeroes he could manipulate. Still, Vinick was the well-guarded key he would need to unlock to eradicate this irritant, so he had patiently waited until an opening presented itself. And now he had one.

♟ ♟ ♟

In the Hummer, Bishop carefully loads shells into the ten-round cartridge for the CheyTac M20 sniper rifle. With a range of fifteen hundred meters, his plan is basic - find an elevated position a half-mile out from the residence, confirm Wolcott's presence, neutralize any guards patrolling the area, then move in with the tranquilizer gun and subdue the target.

Parked two miles south in an overgrown switchgrass field, a slow approach will take time, giving him an estimated arrival between 2:30 and 3:00 PM. He'd prefer to move under cover of night, but waiting extra hours is not an option, having lost time on the detour through Boston, and already closing in on the twenty-four-hour mark of a forty-eight-hour operation.

Exiting the vehicle, he straps on body armor and covers himself head to toe in the black fatigues. He collapses the barrel of the rifle and loads it back into the duffle bag with the tranquilizer gun, several extra cartridges, his pistol, a thermal blanket, an energy bar, and a bottle of water. Slinging the duffle bag over his shoulders, he straps it on like a backpack, locking the handles at his chest with a metal carabiner chain link.

As he marches towards the elevated knoll a mile and a half ahead, Bishop reflects on how long it has been since he attempted a shot of this distance. Half mile shots in the desert with zero visibility issues, a ballistic computer measuring barometric pressure and altitude, and even basic wind measuring tools were doable, even though he was not an expert marksman. With a totally unfamiliar off the shelf rifle and scope, the seeds of doubt were starting to gnaw away at his confidence, never mind the ever-present tremors of withdrawal.

The solution is to move in closer, but the lack of elevation and good cover makes such an approach less attractive. He trudges through the neck-high leaves of grass, his boots crunching the light covering of snow upon the hard January ground below him. His eyes open and ears uncovered, he hears no noise, the eerie silence of open land absent life of any sort. Why anyone would retreat this far north was beyond comprehension to him.

After forty minutes, he finally reaches the knoll, more of an unnatural mound from what he could tell. With the yellow construction vehicles rusting nearby, he surmises this was once a municipal department of transportation drop-off for unearthed dirt and rocks from regional construction projects. The dirt mound left unattended had acquired a sickly covering of grass and weeds, providing enough coverage for Bishop to unpack and find a vantage point.

After setting up the rifle on its stabilizing feet and lying down into position, Bishop brings the house into focus on the scope. Ten minutes of surveillance and no movement. He takes this as a sign to refuel, cracking open the energy bar from his bag, downing it straightaway while depleting the water bottle in quick succession.

He decides to do a quick equipment check, pulling out the pistol, checking the cartridge and chamber. He opens the black case containing the dart syringes and loads one into the CO_2 tranquilizer gun, returning it along with the pistol to his bag. It is then he hears the crack of thunder in the distance and realizes a storm is on a quick approach, charcoal clouds darken an already half-lit sky. While cold, the temperature hovers at the precipice of snow and rain. An hour from now, he might be covered in white flakes, but as the storm approaches, he hears the oncoming freezing wet rain splatter the ground.

From the duffle bag, he grabs the waterproof thermal blanket, big enough to cover his entire body head to toe and most of the rifle, leaving only a few inches of the barrel exposed. He is not happy with the reflective silver material making him stand out like a big silver dollar, but the distance and lack of sunlight make detection negligible.

As the pellets loudly pound his cover, he again scans the house for movement, observing no lights or people.

Maybe they were gone?

Maybe they relocated?

Maybe this was never the right location to begin with?

Maybe I'm screwed?

Thanks to the pounding sheets of ice pouring down, Bishop doesn't hear the footsteps creep behind him, weaving their way through the abandoned construction vehicles and up the backside of the hill. It is not until he feels the burning sensation in his right buttock that he realizes he is not alone. Twisting in confusion, he sees a dart syringe poking through the blanket into his rear quarter, the same type of dart syringe he just loaded into his tranquilizer gun.

As his eyes get heavy, he looks back and spots a hooded figure closing in, dressed in familiar fatigues, just as the lightness goes dark.

CHAPTER 10

Sandra Nolan looks up at the illuminated floor indicator above the elevator doors in her executive suite, then back down on her phone, typing intensely. The numbers click through the thirties and forties, closing on the fifty-fourth floor. The doors split open, and inside stands a weary-eyed Robert Fenton.

"Follow me," she says with a glance at Fenton, making her way to and through the stairwell door. He follows as told, annoyed but expecting the curt exchange, which has become the norm recently. They march up two flights of the stairwell to the exit.

"Leave your phone here," she says, placing her device on a metal ledge to the right of the doorway. He does as instructed, and they both walk out onto the roof. She watches the door shut completely.

"What are we doing up here?" he asks, ignoring the cold current whipping around them.

"I'm sharing information with you that I was sworn not to

share with anyone," she says. Fenton is curiously taken aback.

"The target is not just a doctor. It's his son. Marion Wolcott is Elton's son from his first marriage. He used to be a citizen here but left, some sort of long-standing family issue between them."

"That's a helluva issue. Why didn't he share that information upfront?" wonders Fenton.

"I don't know," responds Nolan. "He didn't go into much detail, but we might have a bigger problem."

"What could be bigger than this?" he blurts before considering the question. Her pause and obvious struggle to start immediately worries Fenton.

"I'm copied on a daily report, it's sent out programmatically to the board and need-to-know types to monitor the current population numbers, make sure we're not exceeding the threshold, everything is in balance according to whatever the Brain algorithms dictate," she explains. "It also gives details on any additions or subtractions. Everyone is tracked, so if someone dies or leaves the island, they're on the report."

"I'm copied on that report, but I don't give it much more than a passing glance. What caught your attention?"

"It's not what. It's who."

"Okay, who caught your attention?"

"We can go a week or so without an addition or subtraction usually, sometimes longer. The report sent today includes the name Kell Sanders. Do you know who that is?"

"Kell Sanders?" he mulls over.

"I did some checking," she says, "because it's not often a sixteen-year-old kid just disappears. His mom is Regina Sanders." The name registers alarm with Fenton.

"She was deployed today, this morning. Her son went missing

right after that?"

"She's not the only one," she states. "I went back through previous reports in the last two weeks and started checking on relatives of people who had fallen off the citizen list since we started this operation. Bishop Dawes' wife is off-island, so we have nothing on her, but six of the previous seven all had a family member, a child, a spouse, a parent, who went missing, usually the same day, as they were deployed."

"Oh my God," Fenton says with horror. "We... I compiled the asset list based on our ability to leverage a family member with citizenship debt to get them on board the mission."

"Somebody," says Nolan, stepping in close, "has access to that list, and knows when assets are being deployed. Someone is monitoring our communication and abducting them. Who and why?"

"Insurance," he says, knowing she's already reached the same conclusion. "They don't want the mission completed, so if they grab our leverage, they can use it against us. Have any of these people reappeared, shown up as active citizens again?" He almost doesn't want an answer. Nolan, clearly shaken by the implications of their actions, simply shakes her head "No."

"There's only one person who could do this," says Fenton angrily. "He's wired into everything."

"And he's the one who has been leading the anti-Vinick group on the board," she responds. "I knew he was gunning for CEO; I just didn't realize how truly dangerous he is."

"It means Lamb has men working for him," Fenton surmises. "He's got an extraction team moving people off-island rapidly. Undetected."

"We have to assume everything is compromised, our phones,

our computers, surveillance is everywhere," she says. "But we can't let on we know."

"Since Bishop and Sanders are both active," he reasons, "we have to assume Bishop's wife and Sanders' son are both still alive. And we have to keep it that way."

♟ ♟ ♟

Tessa lies parallel to the cold concrete floor in a plank position. Her legs stretched straight out behind her, she balances on the tips of her toes, supporting her along with her elbows as she holds the thesaurus and scans the pages.

"Did you know a synonym of truck is barter?" she says. "A verb, to trade goods or services. That's weird. You ever hear that before?" A long audible sigh from the hallway outside the door; inquires of this nature from Tessa are not new.

"How do you even use it in a sentence?" she asks "I'd like to truck with you for that sweater. Would you be willing to truck for these bottles of clean water? Doesn't sound right."

"You're not using it right," says the voice from the hallway. "It's an idiom."

"A what?" she responds, knowing full well what an idiom is.

"You know, like an expression," he says. "You never heard anyone say 'I ain't got no truck with that?'"

"No," she answers.

"It's like, you won't deal with someone," seeking to explain as she hears his walkie-talkie crackle to life, unable to make out the distorted conversation.

"Yeah, I'm on my way," he says, rising from his chair, footsteps taking him down the hallway. She relaxes to the floor and pushes herself up on her feet, then over to the door with her ear to the dirty window. The footsteps gradually disappear down the hallway. She listens intently, and for a moment, there is silence before the footsteps return. Only this time, she hears a second pair of boots and some sort of repetitious squeaking noise. As they grow closer, she can hear the guard and another man, probably Ward, talking in the hallway as they approach. *What the hell is that noise?*

They finally arrive at the door, and she hurries into a far corner as Ward instructs. The door opens, and out of the corner of her eye, the mystery is solved as the guard pushes in a large metal two-wheeled dolly currently carrying an unconscious teenager strapped down at the chest, waist, knees, and ankles. They lower the dolly to the ground, unlocking the straps holding them in place.

"You're going to have a roommate for a while until we get things sorted out," says Ward. "Same boat as you, so feel free to give 'em the lay of the land when they wake up."

The two men exit the room, shutting and locking the door behind them. No visible wounds she can see, he or she didn't put up a fight, or like her, have a chance to.

"Can I get some water in here for when the kid wakes up, maybe some food," she says aloud. She can hear the two men talking outside the door, but there is no response. "Hello, water?"

"Yeah, just a minute," shouts Ward, off-put by the interruption. She creeps to the door and puts her ear as close to the window as possible without standing in front of it and giving away her position. The muffled voices come into aural focus.

"Signal has been stationary for four hours," says Ward. "It's still active. We gotta wait it out, but we don't make a move until he says so. Got it?"

"Yeah, okay," says the guard, uninterested in the details. "But this is messed up. It supposed to be one at a time. That's what we're getting paid for. We should have another guard down here."

"Trust me, this kid is no fighter," says Ward with a chuckle. "You actually worried about these two? Do I need to get someone else to sit their ass in that chair all day?" She doesn't hear a response. "That's what I thought, now get the kid some water."

She hears footsteps as Ward marches off to wherever he disappears to for most of the day. She circles the prone teenager, waiting on the guard to return with the water.

A few moments later, boot steps approach, so she returns to the corner into position. The door opens slightly, and two lidded mason jars are pushed in, the door shutting behind them. Tessa picks up the jars and compares the off-color tint and visible debris.

"Is this safe?" she asks aloud to no response as the guard silently returns to his chair. She sits down cross-legged, her back up against the wall, and picks up the thesaurus, opening it, but not reading.

The signal has been stationary?

What does that mean?

Is he talking about Bishop?

What happens if the signal stops moving for too long?

What happens if they lose the signal?

If he's gone, are they going to let me go?

Not likely, she deduces—too much of a liability.

If his signal disappears, so will she.

♙ ♙ ♙

Tessa spoons up the last of the grits-like muck from the plate in her hand. It feels like a few hours have passed since her new roommate arrived, and other than a few deep sleep twitches and jerks, has remained unconscious. With no clock to reference, she doesn't have a good grasp of how long she was out to compare.

Stripped of footwear like herself, she casually examines the clothing choices. Well-worn socks with a hole or two in the toes, army green cargo pants with plenty of frayed edges, a faded grey fleece sweatshirt, the words long since washed out, just the outlines of an O and S remain of some sort of college name.

She sticks a few fingers in her half-full mason jar and flicks the water at the teenagers' face. The body shifts slightly. She flicks, again and again, a deep breath, and a lazy hand falls on the face, feeling the droplets. A final flick. The body rocks from side to side, eyelids slowly part. She waits and watches as they confusedly survey the room, unsure of everything, finally settling on her.

"Are you thirsty?" she asks. They sit up, bracing themselves with one arm, rubbing their face with the other.

"Where am I? Who are you?" their dry throat croaks.

"My name is Tessa, and I don't know where we are," she responds. "I'm going to take a guess, your dad is ex-military, works some sort of island security job?"

"No, my mom," they answer, surprised by her inquiry.

"Did she recently tell you she would be gone for a while on a mission?" she asks.

"Yeah, how did you know-"

"My husband is on the same mission, and there are men who

have taken you and me hostage because they don't want that mission to succeed. Do you understand?" she explains, waiting for the information to process. "What's your name?"

"Kell."

"Short for?"

"Nothing, just Kell."

"Alright, just Kell."

Kell slowly rises. First on knees, then feet, the thin near six-foot frame stretches out unsteadily.

"How old are you, Kell?" asks Tessa.

"Sixteen," Kell responds. Looking over the concrete room more carefully.

"Wow, you're tall for sixteen. You play ball?" she asks, trying to lighten the mood.

"Sometimes, for exercise, not exactly my thing," he says, still assessing the space. "There's a court in our building."

"I've got some water and some food, or what they're calling food," she tells him. "Care to join me?" She pats the ground next to her along the wall. He shuffles over to the spot, stretching his legs and arms as he squats down.

"You don't seem too freaked out, that's good," she says. "It's best not to panic in situations like this, good on you for not panicking. You live on the island long?"

"Nah," he says, scooping his first taste of the plate of mush. "Like a year. We were down south before that. People who got scared died quick, you know? So, I don't get scared." He smells the shimmery plate of muck. "Oh, this smells terrible."

"I'd suggest some water, but it's not much better," she jokes. She leans, motions him to lean in as well.

"I'm not staying here, I'm getting out," she whispers, looking up at the ceiling air duct vent. "And I've got a plan." The smallest curl of a smile appears on the corner of Kell's right cheek.

♟ ♟ ♟

Lamb reclines in a cushioned metal frame chair attached to the wall by a three-axis metal arm. His virtual reality visor, a custom build of his design, rest comfortably on his nose and temple, wired directly into the chair along with the pair of black haptic gloves he uses to manipulate the invisible virtual space.

The entirety of Manhattan Island's data storage has been virtualized by Lamb. Eight to ten hours a day he spends in this chair, in this room, on the top floor of the Brain. No one else enters, the biometric recognition security limited to him alone. And with good reason.

From this room, his access is not limited to only data and security cameras. Every electronic device is hacked and appropriated for surveillance, providing a live audio and video feed of almost every inch of the island. Over time, he has rebuilt every street, every building, and every room virtually within his surveillance program. The omnipotent system continually monitors the world and adjusts accordingly.

It is from this perch Lamb watches the entire city. He walks in their presence as a ghost, listens to their conversations, invades their most private moments. It is also where he relentlessly, obsessively, observes Sandra Nolan for hours at a time, perched in her presence without her knowledge, trying to gain access to the hidden world of Elton Vinick.

Thanks to the live feed via her laptop camera, he watches her eat dinner across from her assistant Zach, a not untypical evening occurrence. He sees her phone vibrate and receive a new text message, which simultaneously appears on Lamb's screen.

Fenton: Sanders 3 hrs out from Bos - 7:02 PM
Fenton: Bishop hasnt moved in 4 hrs - 7:02 PM
Fenton: Write off Bishop MIA? - 7:02 PM
Nolan: Not til signal gone - 7:03 PM
Fenton: Agreed - 7:03 PM

In his virtual field, he swipes right to left, opening a menu of options. He selects CONTACTS and scrolls to find "Ward Whaley - Security." Tapping on the name with his right hand, it appears: a virtual instant message box. He grabs the Fenton/Nolan exchange with his left hand and drops them into the open text message. He folds the message box in half and throws it off-screen. "Text Message Sent" flashes and dissolves.

He's been at it for too long, fatigue and twitching boredom setting in. Lamb lifts the VR glasses off his face; red indentations encircle his bloodshot eyes. He stands up out of the chair, setting down the glasses, rubbing his eyes and painfully stretching out his arms and back. He hasn't left the chair since he returned from the morning board meeting seven hours ago. Most days, food is an afterthought, and today is no different.

The dimly lit square room is utterly barren except for the VR chair and equipment, black surfaces illuminated by small floor-mounted lights. He steps to the door, placing his hand on a piece of rectangular glass flush with the wall with a dim red glow. The security program recognizes his fingerprints, the rectangle switches from red to green, and the door silently splits open to a sterile hallway, painted cinder block walls, and industrial halogen bar lights overhead.

Dressed in running shorts, a gray t-shirt, and cheap plastic flip-flops, he reaches a second doorway, applying his hand to another scanner before entering an elevator. Another fingerprint scan and a blank panel lights up with floor level options. He selects Level 2, and the bullet elevator car drops lightning-fast through the building, stopping with imperceptible deceleration. The doors open into a marble-floored lobby. Lamb exits with his focus on his phone and an electronic earpiece pulled from his pocket.

He inserts the earpiece into the canal and rounds the corner to a doorway, an overhead sign reads "Executives Only." Doors whisper open, and he enters to an ornate dark wood-paneled foyer. Behind a desk, the concierge knowingly nods as Lamb walks past into a dining room filled with business dressed middle management types at a dozen tables. As he makes his way through the room to a half-circle booth in a dark corner, the conversation volume gradually lowers, some out of respect, most out of fear.

Though designed for four, there is a lone table setting in the center. He slides in as a waiter urgently approaches carrying a tray with a glass of water topped with a lemon wedge and a bowl of mixed fruit.

"What can the chef prepare for you this evening, Mr. Lamb?" asks the waiter. Lamb is more focused on his phone than the question.

"I need some protein," he responds with half attention.

"The chef has a portabella mushroom burger topped with garlic aioli, tomatoes, and arugula paired with rosemary sea salt frites," responds the waiter. "And your choice of vegetable."

"That's fine," says Lamb. "Steamed carrots."

"Very good, Mr. Lamb," says the waiter making a quick exit. Lamb grabs a small handful of blueberries from the fruit bowl and drops them into his mouth while flipping through screens on his phone, finally landing on his contacts screen.

While the rest of the world, and most of the island citizens, scrape and claw for low quality genetically modified and lab-created synthetic sustenance, the corporate hierarchy Lamb enjoys enables access to a vast indoor organic aeroponic farm occupying multiple floors in both the Mick and the Brain. With animal stock depleted to resourceful rodents, a vegan diet is no longer a fad for the health-conscious or ethically conflicted.

The technology of aeroponic farming, or air culture growing via water vapor sprayed on the dangling roots and lower stem, had been around in the mid-twentieth century. However, commercial microchip-controlled aeroponic chambers were not on the market until the early 1980s. After NASA began experimenting, developments in pathogen-free seed stocks and high-density companion planting pointed the future toward aeroponics for food production around the world. Had it not been for the interruption of the asteroid, a global farming revolution could have taken place. Only those with uncanny foresight like Elton Vinick were able to purchase the stocks of various aeroponic chamber manufacturers and acquire their inventory.

Lamb scrolls through the contacts and selects, the phone rings in the earpiece.

"Tell me about your progress today," he says aloud, the tiny microphone built into his earpiece picks up his voice. He unwraps the cloth napkin table setting, glistening silverware lies beneath. He casually examines the fork first, then the spoon, for flaws and watermarks while listening.

"My timeframe was very generous, you did agree to it up front, correct?" he asks mockingly. "Is it possible you're not up to the task? Did you overestimate your abilities?" Nearby diners shift uncomfortably in their chairs, overhearing but not wanting to appear they are listening in on this side of the conversation. He picks up the knife, catching his reflection in the pristine blade.

"I brought you in because you said you could get the job done, and we have yet to meet a single milestone, not a single one," says an increasingly agitated Lamb, his voice rising. "Twenty-four hours became forty-eight. A week became two. Three months became six. And we are not one inch closer." He places the knife back down into the napkin.

"NOT ONE," he roars into the phone. His fist slams the table, rattling the fruit bowl and glass. Several people dining at tables in the nearby vicinity rise and scurry out, leaving a ring of abandoned seats around him. The waiter approaches with a towel and quickly wipes the spilled water from the table, retreating promptly. Lamb inhales deeply to calm his anger, exhaling slowly.

"Give me a revised timeline," his voice lowers but seethes. "Scratch that, are you capable of completing this? Yes or no? Your answer now." He receives the answer he did not want and terminates the call on the cell phone. Scrolling back through his contacts, he locates another number and dials.

"The project is on hold again," he says, "Hit the same wall as the last one, I've never seen anything like it. Thoughts?" He watches the waiter approach carrying a tray with his order, placing the dish carefully in front of Lamb mindful of the phone on the table.

"It has to be a closed network, we're going to have to put someone physically on the inside to get access," he begrudgingly admits. "I'm certainly not getting in, it's gotta be someone he already trusts who has his confidence." He picks up one of the French fries and bites. He savors the salt for a moment before nearly spitting it out.

"Her? Are you kidding?" he asks in bemused shock. "Tell you what, you make that happen, you can be CEO. I'm not joking, you get her to flip for us, and you're the next CEO of Manhattan."

▲ ▲ ▲

Bishop's groggy eyes ease open, natural sunlight beams through arched patio doors and windows. Tessa kneels over him; her hand rubs his cheek. He can see her mouth moving, but the sound is muffled. He tries bending his arms to touch her but can't. He looks left and right, his limbs uncomfortably outstretched.

Wake up, she says.

Wake up.

Wake up.

He's hearing her now, the audio comes in more and more clearly, but he doesn't understand. *I'm looking right at her; she can see I'm awake.* His cheek is warming up, her hand rubs harder and harder, her voice gets louder and louder.

WAKE UP.

His system properly shocked like a jumped dead battery, Bishop readjusts. He looks back again at his arms to see his wrists handcuffed to a metal bed frame. A hand slaps him hard across the face.

"Ollie, that's enough," says a voice in the room.

"Sorry, doc," says another voice with a southern drawl Bishop can't quite place. "Sometimes it takes a bit of force to wake them from the slumber." Two overhead light bulbs shine brightly above him, making it difficult to pinpoint the location of the voices, or if there is anyone else in the room.

"Why don't you give us a minute?" says the first voice.

"Sure thing, doc," says Ollie. "Holler if you need me." He exits, and Bishop hears something being dragged across the room. Looking to his left, he is finally able to make out a figure pulling a wooden stool next to the bed. A gray-haired, middle-aged man sits down.

"So, the good news is, you've completed your mission. Well, the first half, I guess," says the seated man. "I'm Marion Wolcott, the man you have been sent to find and bring back to save the life of Elton Vinick. Congrats."

"Uh, thanks," says Bishop. "I get the feeling the second half of the mission might be in jeopardy."

"Yes and no," says Wolcott. "Let's just say in your lingo, mission parameters have changed. The fairytale you were told that I am needed to save the life of Elton Vinick, that my medical expertise will grant you your freedom and the freedom for your..." he holds, waiting for Bishop to fill in the blank.

"My wife," Bishop responds.

"For you and your wife, well, that never existed. The truth is, I'm nothing but spare parts for Elton. Being his only living heir, my liver, lungs, heart, blood, and whatever else he wants, are just replacement parts for his naturally decaying body. Of course, if I were to produce a child for him, then he'd have access to stem cells. But that's another discussion."

"Wait, you're his son?" he confusedly asks.

"Yeah, let that marinate for a minute," Wolcott responds. "Kill your only child so you can live a few more years. For him to reproduce so, he can dissect the offspring for a mythical fountain of youth. I'd like to say that's the worst thing about my father. But to be honest, that doesn't even make the top ten list."

"So, what's the new mission?" Bishop asks skeptically.

"A small team will be heading back to the island," says Wolcott. "We are going to infiltrate the island, apprehend my father, and make him face up for what he has done."

"Nobody can infiltrate the island," says Bishop. "Trust me, I know, I worked border security."

"Exactly," says Ollie, re-entering the room. "And your mission was to return Dr. Wolcott safe and sound, which is what you're going to do. Only, you're going to have a few extra friends long for the ride. Ain't that right, Arch?"

"That's right," says a voice entering from the hallway, who walks up to the bed and extends a hand attached to a heavily tattooed arm.

"Arch Takeshi, good to meet ya," he says. "Oh, sorry, didn't realize you were still locked up. Does he still need to be locked up? Are we good yet?"

"That's up to…" Wolcott pauses. "We actually don't know your name."

"Bishop Dawes," he says. "So, wait a sec. You two guys, you were the ones that made it here before me, right?"

"Yep," says Arch.

"Guilty," says Ollie.

"What is it? What made you abandon your mission and side with him?" asks Bishop. "This family stuff isn't enough, what's really going on here?"

"There are so many lies," Arch responds. "I honestly don't know where to start."

"Why not start with the big one," says Ollie. "Everything else is second place compared to that one."

"Because it sounds crazy if you just jump to the big one," Arch retorts.

"What's the big one?" Bishop asks impatiently. Wolcott looks at Ollie and Arch, annoyed they started down this road so soon.

"The asteroid," says Wolcott with a sigh, "was not misfortune, not an act of God, not an unstoppable freak cosmic accident. It was caused by, planned for, and profited off of by men like and with my father."

Bishop stares at Wolcott, then Ollie and Arch, to register the reality of what he has just been told. If this was poker, he would be pretty sure they were each holding a full house.

"Hold on a sec," says Bishop, laying his head back on the mattress and staring straight up at the ceiling. "I just gonna need a minute to process." His head spins, the death and pain and suffering of the last ten years overwhelm his gray matter.

"Also," he adds, "I'm going to throw up."

11

Bishop raises his nauseous head from the bucket between his legs. While the revelation from Wolcott is upsetting beyond comprehension, his current state is thanks to the diacetylmorphine withdrawal. Just over twenty-four hours since his last dose, the shakes have moved from his extremities to his stomach and head, driving up a high fever and covering him in sweat. Wolcott enters the room holding a syringe.

"I'm not going to lie, this isn't going to feel good," says Wolcott. "I give this to Arch and Ollie as well, and they hate it. Ollie almost punched me the first time. And last."

"Just get it over with," spits out Bishop between dry heaves.

Wolcott pushes up Bishop's shirt sleeve and dabs his arm with an iodine-soaked cotton swab before inserting the syringe and depressing the plunger.

"What are you injecting me with?" asks Bishop.

"Little concoction will help calm your stomach and nerves until we can wean you off the junk," responds Wolcott. "What you really need is some sleep. If you can put in a solid six to eight, you'll feel a helluva lot better."

"I'm going to need a bit more detail if I'm going to join up with your little rebellion," says Bishop, wiping sweat from his brow.

"Like I said, get some rest," Wolcott says as he gets up. "There's a mild sedative in what I gave you, just enough to help you relax. Talk with Ollie and Arch when you wake up, they'll go over everything."

Bishop can already feel it kick in, but fights it, grabbing Wolcott's forearm.

"You're not walking out of here until you explain," implores Bishop. Wolcott brushes Bishop's hand off and sits back down.

"Okay. My father and I were estranged for most of my life," Wolcott starts with a sigh. "Even though we lived in the same city, I was nothing but an unpleasant reminder of a previous life. A lesser life. After the asteroid, I moved down south for a while and stayed with some extended family. Eventually, everything fell apart, just like everywhere else. Initially, I went to Atlanta, thinking I might be able to get hired there, but the waiting list is years long. I made the trek back to Manhattan last year with a convoy of desperate folks. Elton had secretly flagged the citizenship application list if, by chance, my name was added, he would be notified. He pulled some strings and got me in right away, faster than anyone else. When he did, it was awkward, I knew he had an agenda, but he's very charismatic. He's played the wise old man card for a long time. I fooled myself into thinking he wanted a relationship. It wasn't the case."

Wolcott stands and slowly paces the small bedroom, giving an occasional glance out a window.

"He knew he was having serious health problems, but he

didn't trust outside medical staff to fully examine him," explains Wolcott. "He was worried about a leak; he can be very paranoid that way. I did it, and I asked to see his medical records, which he kept on his private computer, off-network from the rest of the island."

"After reviewing his records, I got... curious. I wasn't looking for anything specific, I just wanted to learn more about the man, find out who my absent father was, what he was doing all those years. The personal records were minimal, some photos, not much else. I ended up in a huge file of business documents, and a name appeared - Solear. Does that name ring a bell?"

"Can't say it does," says a weary Bishop.

"Solear Industries was the company that bought Manhattan. They had dozens of companies and divisions. One of those divisions, which was aerospace projects, built the focused laser used in the defense system that tried to stop the asteroid," says Wolcott. "But one of the other projects involved the asteroid mining industry."

"You're getting outside my area of expertise, doc."

"Let me backtrack a bit. I learned a little when I was digging through the files, and this is about all of it, so stay with me. Most asteroids and planetoids are made up of very familiar elements - nickel, iron, cobalt, aluminum, and such. Stuff that doesn't warrant mining since it's plentiful on earth. 975 Perseverantia, one of those planetoids, was different. Spectral analysis showed the presence of samarium."

"Let me guess, samarium is valuable," quips Bishop.

"Yes, and it has a wide range of applications," explains Wolcott. "It's used in nuclear power plant fuel rods, military stealth technology, precision-guided weapons, quantum computing, cancer medication."

"Energy, military, health care - those are big hitters," says Bishop.

"And all under the Solear corporate umbrella. They wanted to mine the planetoid for samarium," says Wolcott, "Of the few asteroid mining companies which had managed to get off the ground, nobody had ever ventured out too far, nor had they attempted to extract from a small planetoid of that size. They were trying to separate the samarium deposit when it splintered off. If they had stopped there, it would have simply drifted off into space. But they didn't. They purposely redirected the chunk of the planetoid towards earth to save their mission, which cost several billion dollars at this point, in hopes of slowing and stopping it on approach, which is where the laser came in. Obviously, that didn't work."

"How the hell did none of this get out?" says Bishop angrily.

"How would anyone know?" responds Wolcott. "They were millions of miles away; space agency monitoring is all near earth. Beyond that, there's just too much sky to keep an eye on. But don't focus on the asteroid, think back to that time. There were almost three years of plans and failed missions to stop the asteroid. Do you know what Elton Vinick and the Solear board did during that time? They figured out a way to turn the end of the world into a business opportunity. Used predictive modeling to estimate food shortages, occurrences, and locations of natural disasters, which governments would fall on what timetable, which industries, and more importantly, cities would be ripe for acquisition and which to abandon. They turned the end of the world into a hostile takeover of humanity."

Bishop leans back in the bed, resting his head on the pillow.

"Not gonna lie, it's a lot to take in," he says, rubbing his eyes. "Did you save all of this info on a hard drive or something? If the four of us are going to march in there, we've gotta have proof to back it up."

"No," sighs Wolcott. "I confronted him with it, we argued, threats were made, I got out of there. It happened fast; I wasn't smart enough to back it up on an external hard drive. Before I left, though, I made contact with someone who can help us, someone high up with access to Vinick."

"Who?" asks Bishop, half awake and losing consciousness.

"He works in IT security. Nathan Lamb," responds Wolcott.

⁂

Tessa and Kell lie on their backs on the cold concrete, the only light seeps in under the locked door, casting the floor in an eerie glow. A new guard rotated outside their room some time ago, but it has been an hour, maybe two, since either of them heard a sound. The only noise comes from the overhead ventilation systems, pumping in warm air. It's loud, the sound of loose fittings rattle as the ducts shimmy and shake, expanding and contracting with the changing temperatures.

She clocks the loud and warm cycles at approximately ten minutes. With the current cycle set to end in the next minute as she flips silently onto her stomach and crawls on her hands and toes to the door. Placing her ear as close to the tiny gap between the door and the floor as possible, she waits for the warming cycle to end and go silent. When it finally does, she closes her eyes, takes a deep breath, and holds. Although it is faint, just above her heartbeat, she can hear the light snore of the guard outside, asleep in the metal chair just a few feet away from her on the other side.

Tessa exhales slowly and slips back next to Kell.

"He's out," she whispers. "In ten minutes, the heat will kick back on, and it will be on for ten minutes. That's our window. Above the chair is a light bulb hanging from a chain. I tested it; it'll support our weight. I'll go up first and unscrew the vent cover. It's going to be tight up there. When Ward, the guy in charge, leaves for his office, he goes to the left. Hopefully, this will lead there, that's where all our stuff will be. Either way, we're leaving. You ready for this?"

"Yeah. How are you going to get the vent cover off?" asks Kell.

"With this," she responds, tugging on the zipper tab of her pants. She squeezes the slider between her thumb and forefinger, and with the other hand twists the zipper tab, bending the arms enough to snap it off the slider.

"There are two screws and two hinges," she says under her breath. "I'm going hand the screws down to you, we can't let them fall and make any noise, okay?"

"Got it," he responds.

"When we move through the vent," she explains, "try to keep your weight spread out. Don't bunch up or pull your legs too close. It will make more noise. Stay a few feet back from me. If we get too close to each other, the weight might bring us down."

"Okay," he says with a gulp. "But how you gonna get those screws out with just that."

"I got it, don't worry," she responds. She rises to her bare feet and stretches her arms, legs, back, and neck, waiting for the sound of the heating system to kick back on. When the sound of rushing air and creaking metal returns, she silently steps back onto the chair and clenches the zipper tab in her teeth. She grips the metal light chain and undertakes her ascent, one hand over the other, her fingers interlace the links.

She reaches the ceiling and looks down in the dark to find Kell standing directly below the ventilation cover as instructed. Wrapping one leg around the chain, she releases her left-hand grip and finds the clasp on the back of her necklace, undoing it with two fingers, scooping the jewelry into her free hand. She unthreads the cross and slips the necklace chain into her pant pocket.

From her mouth, she removes the zipper tab and manipulates the cross through the square opening on the end. With the makeshift screwdriver in her fingers, she touches the ceiling and feels for the vent cover, finding the metal edge and then the first Phillips screw head. She inserts the flat end of the zipper tab and, with her fingers tightly gripping the cross, twists counterclockwise. The rusty screw doesn't budge, so she pauses, then wiggles it gently back and forth. Slowly, there is movement, the screw unspools in fits and starts until the final thread is free.

Tessa carefully cradles the screw and her makeshift screwdriver into her hand, lowering them down far enough for Kell to reach up and grab the screw from her. She repeats the same process for the second screw. When complete, she carefully opens the vent cover, allowing the unoiled hinges to creak open slowly and quietly, masked by the heating system hum.

After dropping the second screw down to Kell, she pockets the zipper tab and cross, and reaches up into the vent shaft, gently running her hand along the interior edges, feeling for a good grip. When she thinks she's found the right angle, she releases her other hand from the chain and dangles from the vent shaft opening.

In one sharp and smooth chin up, she lifts herself in, head and shoulders squeeze through the narrow opening. Another nimble movement, she readjusts, her arms spread-out inside the shaft, using the walls to propel her up and in. Unable to turn around, she backs up over the opening slightly, stretching her arm out enough to give Kell a thumbs up.

He quietly lays the screws on the ground and follows her path up the chain and into the blackness of the vent shaft. With only an inch or so on either side of their shoulders, and about the same above their backs, they shimmy slowly on their stomachs as the warm air whistles past them, using fingertips and toes to push forward a few inches at a time.

Tessa revisits her mental clock and surmises they have less than a minute before the heating system shuts down. Unsure of where exactly they are, she looks back at Kell and sticks her foot out, which brushes the top of his head, catching his attention.

"The heat is going to turn off soon," she whispers forcefully to him. "Get comfortable, we're not moving for ten minutes. No sounds, no moving, no talking."

"I got it," he responds. They both gingerly lower their entire bodies onto the metal vent, creaking as their weight shifts. As they both settle, the heat systems abruptly stop, and the eerie quiet calm returns, broken only by the sound of their breathing.

While this is not the ideal location, she closes her eyes and silently repeats the mantra given to her decades ago when she started transcendental meditation. In high school, her basketball skills were evident but raw, paired with nervous anxiety and a violent temper, which lead to multiple on and off the court incidents, causing her to miss a significant portion of her junior year due to suspensions.

Her basketball coach, a former PAC-10 conference all-star with a short stint in the WNBA, was laughed off when first suggesting meditation and yoga to sharpen focus and calm her anxiety. With her mind singularly focused on blankness, the confines of the ventilation shaft currently encasing her body melt away.

Kell tries his hardest not to panic.

Before gaining entrance to the island, he and his mother spent several years wandering the Midwest for shelter and food, doing their best to avoid any sort of organized gangs. Confrontation was death, so they became skilled at disappearing, only engaging when all other options were exhausted. Drainpipes, abandoned appliances, anywhere they could find a few hours to stay hidden from the mobilized mobs on the hunt.

The ten minutes pass smoothly for Tessa, less so for Kell, who is anxious to move. The heat rushes through the vent once again, and their slow crawl continues onward. With no light, Tessa feels for vents and openings in other directions, finding none for several minutes.

Where the hell is this leading?

Her mental clock tells her they've already gone five minutes inching forward before her hand brushes across what feels like another vent opening. She gently pats around the corners; her fingers find footing and trace the rectangular shape of a vent cover like the one they just escaped through. She looks through the vent but cannot see anything other than the dim light peeking underneath what looks like a door.

With the screw heads on the opposite side of the vent, and the hinges inaccessible, she pauses for a moment. *How the hell do I get us out of here?* She feels around the sheet metal and finds the welded corners diagonally from each other, forming the two L-shaped pieces. She crawls up just ahead of the cover.

"Kell, move up here towards me," she says. When he does, she guides his hand to their left. "Put your feet, here, and your back against the opposite side. We need to break the weld enough so I can get my arm around underneath and unscrew the vent cover."

"If I break the weld, won't we fall through?" he reasons.

"Well," she considers his point. "As long as it's only a few inches, it should hold, I think. I just need a gap big enough to slip my arm through."

"You sure about this plan?" he responds with appropriate concern.

"If you have a better idea, I'm open to it," she says.

"Nah, let's do this. Hopefully, it's a room full of pillows," he jokes. She lets herself laugh just a bit at the suggestion.

"Ready?" she says, getting in position. Kell does the same. "On three...one, two, three." With their knees in their chests, they simultaneously press their legs and backs into either side of the air duct. The sheet metal bends, pushing outward while condensing inward as the walls are stretched. The weld holds momentarily, they bear down as the space becomes more and more confined. After a few long seconds, the first weld snaps, gradually opening a gaping breach, and both their legs dangle over.

"Holy shit, it worked!" Kell says louder than he should.

"Yeah, but that was loud. Guard might have heard us," Tessa warns. "Stay here, keep the hole open for me. I'm going to drop down and find a light."

She slides her legs and torso over the edge being kept open by Kell, and slowly lowers her legs down, using one foot to feel for footing. She finds none and changes her plan. She reaches around the ceiling and locates a metal chain like the one in her cell. Taking hold, she slithers down far enough her foot reaches a flat surface, what feels like metal on her bare toes. She drops her other foot and releases her grip from the chain, lowering herself to a crouch and feeling out her surroundings. She finds the edge, moving off and onto the concrete floor, just like in the cell she just left.

Light trickles in just below the door she gingerly moves toward. Upon reaching it, she slides her hand up and around the door frame, locating what feels like a light switch. She flips it up, and the light bulb attached to the metal chain flickers on, illuminating the room in a soft glow. Looking up, she notices the ceiling is open, unlike her room where the air duct was enclosed. She motions to Kell to climb down, and he follows her path, slipping through the mangled ventilation shaft, down the chain to the desk.

As he does, she surveys the room. Behind the unoccupied metal desk in the center of the room are two large, black, metal cabinets. Tessa maneuvers to them and grips the handles on the first cabinet. Unlocked, the cabinet door glides open. Inside, her coat and bag hang from hooks, her boots sit at the bottom.

"Is this yours?" she says, pointing to another coat and pair of boots.

"Yeah," Kell responds, climbing down from the desk. She grabs her bag and opens it, finding her Jagdkommando knives and sleeves tucked inside along with everything she had brought to the trading market. She puts on her boots first, then grabs the knife sheaths and slides them on her wrists, tightening the straps before locking them into place. While Kell puts on his boots, she places her coat and bags on the desk then moves over to the other cabinet.

It opens to reveal a cache of weapons - long rifles, automatic and semi-automatic machine guns, pistols, a tranquilizer gun, and an army green metal box marked **HANDLE WITH EXTREME CAUTION**. She knees down, pulls it out and opens it - inside are several small glass bottles laying in foam support. She picks one out and reads the label: Kolokol-1. She looks up at Kell, putting on his coat.

"Are you ready to get out of here?" she says. He looks in the cabinet and selects a Glock 9mm pistol with a laser sight attached under the barrel along with multiple six-round clips. He inserts a clip, pulls the slide, and chambers a round.

"Hell yeah I am," he says. With belongings retrieved, they make their way to the door. Tessa slowly turns the doorknob, careful to make as little noise as possible and peels it open a crack. Eyeing the hallway outside, she sees the guard asleep in his chair. She opens the door enough to slip through, the hinges creak slightly, but not enough to wake him.

As she approaches his position a dozen feet away, she pulls a rag from her jacket pocket and unscrews the cap on the glass bottle. Six feet away, she pours the contents of the bottle onto the cloth, careful not to inhale the fumes. The sound of her boots on the concrete subconsciously registers with the guard, his eyelids flutter, body shifting in the seat. Before he can wake, she shoves the doused rag over his nose and mouth. For a moment, the shock wakes him, but the Kolokol-1 does its job on him the way it had on her, quickly knocking him out.

"Grab his keys and open the door," she says. Kell unhooks the keychain dangling from his belt and opens the door to the room they just escaped from. Tessa grabs his arms, Kell his legs, and they drag him into the room, depositing him before closing and locking the door.

"Now what?" asks Kell. Tessa looks left, back to the office they just exited, then to the right, and points.

"When they brought you in, you were on a dolly," she says. "There are no windows anywhere, so I think we're underground. There has to be an elevator."

She leads him down the hall past several more doors to a hard-left turn. The overhead fluorescent lights flicker as they reach the corner. Tessa peeks her head around for a look, finding nothing. At the end of the hall, a large metal gate protects the entrance to a service elevator.

They make their way down the hallway to the elevator door, Tessa unclasps the latch from the wall and collapses the accordion gate to the right, then grabs the handle and lifts the door upward, revealing a twelve-foot by twelve-foot space. They step inside and check out the control panel.

"B and G. Basement and Ground," says Kell. "Guess we don't have many options." Tessa lowers the elevator door back down.

"Be ready, we don't know what we're walking into," she says. He nods, the Glock in hand at the ready. She presses the Ground button, and the noisy, slow upward ascent of the elevator is triggered. Tessa flicks the strap release on each of her sheaths, the Jagdkommando knives slip down and into her grip. They exchange a tense glance as the elevator jolts to a stop at the end of its short cycle.

Kell steps forward and grips the door handle, lifting upward. They both step back to the sides of the elevator car as the door rises, dim light trickles in from below, increasing as the door opens. More concrete floors, another empty hallway, same fluorescent lighting.

"Any idea where we are?" whispers Kell.

"No," she responds. "But we gotta move." She looks left and right, spots a door with an unlit overhead EXIT sign and points to it.

"There," she says, and moves cautiously towards the door. They reach it and stop.

"Let me," says Kell. He brings the Glock up parallel to his eyes and presses the exit door bar handle downward gently. It opens, and he peers out, the barrel of the gun pointing the way. He pauses, looks back at Tessa. She can see the confusion on his face.

"What is it?" she asks. He pushes the door open further and steps outside, cold January air fully engulfs them.

"Look at that," he says, motioning up. She looks up and sees a sign - Jungle World. She steps out into the cold midnight. Only a hazy moon above illuminates their surroundings.

"I think I know where we are," says Tessa. "This is the Bronx Zoo."

12

"Thank you for meeting me for breakfast," says Lloyd Rust, sitting down at a frosted glass topped rectangular kitchen table, placing his phone down next to a bone-white plate and stainless-steel silverware. Across from him, Sandra Nolan takes her seat. She looks around the Chief Financial Officer's residence, the floor below her own.

"Something's different, did you change the paint color?" she says, as a member of the staff fills her coffee cup, then Lloyd's.

"Uh, yes. Some months back," he responds. "I had a new couch made for the living room as well, quite comfortable." A tray of assorted fruits and muffins is placed on the table.

"Would you like something prepared," he says. "They can whip you up an omelet, perhaps?"

"This is fine," she says, placing a blueberry muffin and a ladle full of berries on the plate in front of her. Lloyd nods to the wait staff and they depart, leaving the two of them alone. Sandra breaks off a piece of the muffin top and eats it.

"It's been a while since we had a chance to speak privately, away from board business," says Lloyd as he stirs his coffee while pouring in the creamer. "I know Elton places a great deal of trust in you. I'm hoping I can do the same."

"Is there an issue you want to discuss?" she says.

"Yes," he responds, placing the stir stick on the table. "Nathan Lamb."

"Oh, my favorite person," she says with an unamused chuckle. "And what would you like to discuss about Nathan?" Lloyd shifts uncomfortably in his chair, which Sandra notices.

"He's an annoying prick," he says, looking to his phone.

"On that we can agree," she responds.

Where's he going with this?

"But he's not dumb, I think we can both agree on that," his voice strengthening. "Are you aware Elton's son reached out to Nathan before he left the city?"

"No," Sandra responds, curious.

"Elton kept the fact that his son was living in the city from you, just like the rest of us, didn't he?" he probes.

"He kept some personal issues to himself," she responds defensively. "But I've known him half as long as you have, and you know he has never been someone who shares details of his private life."

"What about his professional life, do you think you were fully in the loop?" he asks.

"I'm sorry, I don't think I want to answer your questions, Lloyd, unless I know why exactly you're asking them," she says, her casual posture stiffening.

"It's Solear," he snaps. "Specifically, the asteroid mining project."

"One of many start-ups. I don't remember them all," she says with growing agitation. "What does this have to do with Elton's son and Lamb? And know I'm asking this with very little patience remaining."

"Before I lay out all my cards, so to speak," he says as he stands up from the table, "I want you to know I was once in your position. I sat and listened to a story so ridiculous, so at odds with the reality that I perceived, I was in total denial for days, a week even. But deep down, deep in my subconscious, or gut, or heart, whatever you want to assign it to, something took hold and would not let go. And the more it stayed there, the more it gnawed away at me, and the foundations of what I perceived to be true began to shake." He pauses to take a drink with a trembling hand.

"Elton and I have been colleagues and rivals at different points in our professional lives," he continues at a slow pace around the table. "He was just ahead of me in college, but our paths always seemed to cross. The universe either wanted us to collaborate or kill each other. We did quite a bit of both, financially speaking. Elton is many things. A master negotiator, uniquely perceptive, strong-willed, unflinchingly confident in his abilities. All the things you know, because you have been on his side of the table. But he wants to win at all costs. He has no sense of proportion. Compromise is a failure to him. If he isn't crushing his opponent, he believes he has shown unearned mercy. His perspective is of someone who looks at life as a zero-sum game, with no regard for the stakes, and anyone who gets in his way, God help them. You know this, you've seen it. He likes to pretend he is a spiritual being, Eastern philosophy, or some nonsense. It's window dressing. You can refute it, but you know it's true."

She stares at Lloyd, silently looking him up and down.

Lamb is pulling the strings here; nobody wants to go up against Elton. He must have Lloyd up against the wall, something bad.

He waits for a response, but she gives him nothing, biting a small strawberry to the edge of the stem. She wipes her hands on a napkin and pushes her chair back from the table.

"I think I'm done here," she exhales, rising to her feet. "Whatever's got you in a tizzy, count me out. You know where I stand, if you're going to try to shake me, you better come with something better than your gut." She makes her way to the door; Lloyd grabs his phone from the table and follows.

"Please, please listen," he begs, catching her at the door.

"We're done, do you understand?" she barks at him.

"The asteroid happened because of him. Because of us. And Elton's son found out. It's why he left, it's connected, and Elton has all the files on his personal computer, off-network. Nobody has access, not even Lamb, and he's everywhere," he says, glaring at his phone. She notices the overt gesture.

"Elton is responsible for the asteroid? What you are saying is insane and impossible."

"Is it? Who came out ahead? Elton did. Not just ahead, he won. At everything. He runs his own city, he is a king, total control, total power."

"That's doesn't mean…"

"When has Elton not been willing to take advantage of any flaw, any crisis, and turn it into a gain? He bought politicians with campaign contributions and changed laws, influenced foreign policy, repealed regulations. He always had that power, and you know that. You were a part of it. I bet you helped draft that legislation."

"We're done, you understand me? We're done," she barges past Lloyd and out through the doorway.

"It's not going away," he says as she marches off towards the elevator entrance. "Now you know, and it's going to stick with you."

She presses the elevator up button, it opens immediately, and she steps inside.

"It's going to stay with you until you do something about it."

The elevator doors close between them.

♟ ♟ ♟

Bishop stretches his arms and legs, feeling as though he had slept for days, not hours. It had been a long time since he noticed genuine hunger pangs, but his stomach is currently in desperate need of nourishment. Hearing voices from another room, he slides his bare feet onto the old wooden floor as he surveys his surroundings. No sign of his weapons or gear. Other than the bed, the room is empty.

He steps out into the hallway and follows the lines of pine hardwood to a staircase, which he tries to descend quietly but is immediately betrayed by the creaking boards. An outdated, worn floral pattern wallpaper wraps around the landing down the second half of the flight to the first-floor hall. Bishop walks past a small formal dining room, a sitting room with a brick fireplace in disrepair, before finally reaching the kitchen, where Takeshi and Ollie sit, staring up at him from a round wooden table.

"Grab yourself some breakfast off the stove," says Takeshi while Ollie sips from a coffee cup, both eyeing him cautiously.

"You've probably got a few questions, eh?" Ollie says with a bit of glee.

"Yeah, a few," Bishop mutters as he walks to the stove. Diced yellow potatoes brown in a skillet on low heat next to the second skillet with scrambled eggs. On the counter, a loaf of homemade bread is already sliced while a coffee maker gurgles.

This looks like real food. Where are they getting this stuff?

He pulls a plate from the open overhead cabinet and loads it with two slices of bread and hefty scoops of the offerings, then fills a mug with coffee and walks to the table, settling down to eat. He grabs a fork from a cylinder of utensils and digs in, lost for a moment in the unfamiliar taste of palatable food.

Oh my God, this is good.

"Better than those dog shit MRE's you were eating, huh?" says Ollie. "Not my best work, but you play the hand you're dealt."

"Where did you get fresh eggs and potatoes?" gushes Bishop, stuffing his face with another fork full, "I haven't had food like this in forever."

"After you eat, we'll take you into town, you can get the lay of the land, see what's what," says Takeshi. "We're gonna meet up with the doc and his people."

"His people?" blurts Bishop through a bite of eggs and potatoes.

"You think the four of us are it?" chuckles Ollie. "The city ain't like anything you or I have seen in years. They got their shit together."

"Well, that's great and all, but getting back to Manhattan won't be easy."

"We're working on it, couple of different plans in the hopper," says Takeshi, being purposely vague for the moment.

"What you need is a helo," says Bishop without hesitation. "Something that can manage the trip without a refuel and take some lumps." Takeshi and Ollie perk up.

"What'd you do before? Army?" asks Ollie.

"UAVs at Creech. Before that, motor transport mechanic at Barstow," says Bishop. "Serviced every vehicle on the west coast outta that place."

"So, you're familiar with a Sikorsky CH-53 Sea Stallion?" Ollie inquires, giving Arch a glance that raises an eyebrow.

"That's awfully specific. Yeah, why?" responds Bishop. "You got one lying around? That would be... wait, you do, don't you?"

"It's roached," interjects Takeshi. "Went down years ago in a neighborhood, sitting in somebody's backyard on top of their swing set. Don't get excited."

"Just let me take a look at it," says Bishop. "Those are some tough birds."

"Yeah, sure," says Takeshi, his memory suddenly jogged. "You ever make it up to Miramar?

"Oh yeah, serviced the 130s, Sea Knights, F18s, all their rides," responds Bishop. "Which group were you?"

"Thirty-eight, first squadron," Takeshi responds. "I was a UAV maintenance tech."

"No kidding," smirks Bishop. "Small world."

"Oh jeez," Ollie remarks with feigned indignation. "Can we wrap up this little reunion and get on with it?" Bishop scoops up the last bite of food and empties the coffee mug.

This food is unbelievable.

"I'm taking some of this for the road."

⚠ ⚠ ⚠

The sun rises behind the clouds on a dreary Maine winter morning as the Jeep cruises down a two-lane country road sparsely lined by nineteenth-century farmhouses. Every day is overcast, just the shade of darkness changes. Wipers clean a cold, wet mist from the windshield. Takeshi drives, Bishop, once again in possession of his belongings, rides shotgun, munching on a slice of toast. Ollie stretches out in the back seat, eyeing Bishop with one hand on his waist holstered pistol. Bishop takes notice.

"Is there a problem?" asks Bishop.

"No problem," responds Ollie. "But we still don't know you yet, despite the pleasantries. Pardon me if I remain vigilant." Bishop looks over at Takeshi.

"He always like this?" Bishop inquires. Takeshi chuckles.

"Just wait," quips Takeshi. "Once he likes you, you're going to wish he was just staring blankly at you."

"Great," says Bishop, glancing at Ollie before fixating on the road ahead. Takeshi guides the Jeep from the country back roads through abandoned suburbs, passing the familiar sights of gutted and burnt-out strip malls, residential homes, and crumbling infrastructure. Picking up Route 222, rusted and collapsing overhead signs for the Bangor airport and I-95 come and go. All too familiar to Bishop, the remnants of a world still present but relinquished to mother nature.

Ten minutes later, they make a left onto Main Street running parallel to the Penobscot River and head north to the city center. It's here where Bishop perks up. No shells of neglected automobiles line the roads. No debris or garbage is strewn about. No storefronts battered by looting and anarchy. Under a light dusting of snow in the below-freezing temperatures, this could be "Anytown, U.S.A." before the asteroid. Bishop has seen nothing like it in years.

A few turns onto State Street and then Harlow, he spots men on horseback in winter military fatigues with a variety of long rifles slung over their backs in front of a notable brick and concrete building. Up the steps, he notices the words Bangor City Hall above the arched doorways as the Jeep comes to a stop. He looks up and down the street and sees people dressed in winter clothing, walking along the sidewalks going about their business as if nothing was amiss.

It looks almost too normal.

Like the asteroid never happened here.

"Confused yet?" says Ollie, slapping Bishop on the shoulder. They open their doors and exit the Jeep. While the pall of the sun blocked sky hangs overhead, Bishop immediately notices the lack of toxicity in the air. He takes a deep breath, holds it, and exhales.

"Why is this place so.... nice?" asks Bishop.

"C'mon, time's a-wastin'" says Takeshi, already walking towards the concrete steps in front of City Hall. Ollie and Bishop follow, moving between the horse backed sentries, who eye Ollie and Takeshi with familiarity while Bishop gets the once over.

Up the steps into the building, the warmth smacks Bishop in the face. Takeshi and Ollie stroll up to a middle-aged woman seated behind a folding table while removing their cold weather gloves and knit hats.

"Good morning, gentlemen. How can I help you today?" says the woman, with an unusual level of chipperness.

"We're here to meet with the mayor, I believe Doctor Wolcott is already here," says Takeshi. Bishop looks around the hundred-year-old building, cracks in the ceiling look to have been patched recently. The woman speaks into a walkie-talkie.

"Frank, the rest of Doctor Wolcott's group is here, shall I send them down?" she says into the speaker.

"Yeah, send them down," responds a static male voice.

"Thanks, Frank," she says before turning her attention back to them.

"Down the hall, all the way, then a right," she points. "Office is on the left. You have yourselves a good day now."

"You as well," says Ollie with a flirty wink and nod, and the group moves down the hallway, the rubber soles of their boots squeaking on the marble floors. As they pass by open doors, Bishop glances in each, finding people behind desks working alone or in groups around tables.

This all looks way too normal.

They turn the corner down another hall to a closed door, the top half frosted glass. In the wooden midsection, a removable plastic sign reads "Mayor" with the second half covered by a piece of a paper, with the word "Remeny" written in thick black ink. Takeshi raps his knuckles on the wooden frame, and a moment later, the door opens, thanks to Wolcott.

"Good morning, gentlemen. Come in," he says, spotting Bishop behind the other two. "Did you sleep okay? Feeling better?"

"Yeah, thanks Doc," responds Bishop, eyeballing the room as they enter. Nearest to the door, an older woman, white hair pulled back in a bun, and a knitted shawl over her shoulders stands by a chairless conference table alongside a short but stout male in his forties with a heavy beard and a holstered six-shot pistol. To their left on the wall is a map of the city of Bangor covered with Post-It notes, illegible scribbles on each. Opposite the door is a large window overlooking bushes and a vacant parking lot. To the right is a large wooden desk, probably as old as the building, backed by a wall of what looks like hundreds of old books.

"I see we have a new addition to the group," says the woman. "What's your name, son?" Bishop approaches the table.

"Bishop Dawes, ma'am." He sticks out his right hand, and she returns his offering, placing her left hand over his. "Good to meet you, Bishop. I'm Mayor Remeny. This is Frank Bloom, our sheriff." Frank nods as Bishop takes a step back to look over the table. On a large swatch of butcher paper, a crudely drawn map of the United States is sketched. Fourteen black stars are distributed across the map in the locations of the current corporate-owned cities, a red dot marks Boston, and a green dot indicates Bangor.

The three stars in Texas - Houston, Dallas, and San Antonio, are circled together along with two stars indicating Tulsa and Oklahoma City, Oklahoma. The name "Jasper Reynolds" is written in the middle of the circle. It takes a moment to place it, but Bishop recognizes the name.

"Isn't Jasper Reynolds that crazy oil tycoon who kept running for President?" he asks.

"That's right," says Mayor Remeny. "Now he and his energy consortium are in control of five cities, and they're looking to expand." Bishop looks over the map.

"Our best guess," interjects Takeshi, "Boston is the first strike eastward. A random gang couldn't mass that sort of firepower, but five cities could raise an army."

"And a full-on assault of Manhattan without a forward operating base would be near impossible," says Ollie. "Boston is prime real estate for an advance, plus whenever they feel like it, they can swing up here and stomp out the socialist do-gooders on their hippie commune. No offense." Remeny laughs at the description while Bloom smirks.

"What this comes down to is an old school pissing match between my father and Reynolds, who was also a stakeholder in Solear," responds Wolcott. "Elton's been content with his little fiefdom, but Reynolds has always had grand aspirations."

"Damn, the chessboard keeps getting bigger and bigger," says Bishop as he steps away from the table to look at the wall-mounted map of Bangor. He stops with his nose nearly touching the wall to analyze the scribblings on each note.

Hydro - third shift super

Hospital - two nurses & E-M-T

Police - new vehicles

Fire - repair hydrants (see list), second station next year

"Wow, you're doing it, huh? Running the city out of this office," remarks Bishop.

"No," Mayor Remeny responds. "This is just a to-do list. The people run the city, we just let them know where the openings are and try to match them up with a job."

"What if they don't want or aren't trained for one of these jobs?" he inquires.

"On the job training is available, I guess you would call it mentoring, but plenty of people are needed to keep the city running," she says, walking over. "There are farmers, various trades are needed like plumbers, electricians, metal fabricators.

You don't have to do one of these jobs, but you do need to work to get the water running and electricity turned on. Despite our reputation, we are not some end of the world sanctuary. We won't force people to work, and we will take pity on those in need, the elderly, sick, disabled. We're not going to throw people away like trash like they do in the cities, where your only value is the wealth you produce and the products you consume. If I sound like some sort of tree-hugging hippie, so be it. But if you're able-bodied, you're not getting a free ride."

"And how's that working out so far?" he asks.

"We're about as far away from the rest of the world as you can get these days. If people find us, they came a long way to do so. Most don't want to turn around and go back, not after what they've seen and been through." She turns and walks back to the table. "But enough about our little city, let's get back to the more pressing issue - Elton Vinick."

"I've worked up several incursion plans with Ollie and Frank, none are ideal at the moment," says Takeshi.

"What about the Sea Stallion?" Bishop interjects.

"We don't even know if that thing will lift off," says Takeshi.

"Give me twenty minutes to look it over, if it's salvageable, I can get it in the air. Besides, you'll never get past the gates with a ground assault. Every bridge entrance has gunners, remote activated anti-personnel mines, spike strips, the works. And that's the welcome mat. Then you've got to deal with the porthole snipers up the wall and the big guns up top. You want to get in, it's gotta be by air."

"But what about those tower guns?" argues Ollie. "What are we dealing with?"

"20mm Gatlings, radar-guided, nine-kilometer kill range.

Nasty bastards. And there are a few dozen of them," responds Bishop. "But they have one weakness. They're remotely operated. Kill power to the control center, and they're useless. Can't even be fired on location, terminal operation only."

"Great, anyone got an EMP weapon lying around?" snarks Takeshi.

"Wait, I do," says Ollie, shocking himself. "My Hummer is equipped with an EMP and some kind of cloaking system."

"Huh," says Bishop. "I got the cloak, but with an active denial system instead. What about you, Takeshi?"

"I didn't get any cool shit," he says, feigning disappointment. "Guess Silva doesn't like me."

"They're expecting me to come back with you," says Wolcott. "We'd have to drive back into the security compound and detonate the EMP to knock everything out, but then we'd lose the ability to signal the helo team to approach."

"The three of us have driven the tunnel system to get out, we should be able to time the drive to estimate when the EMP would go off," responds Bishop. "Trick is, the pulse will just shut everything down, but the system will reboot within a few minutes. If the helo team doesn't hit that window..."

"We'll be sitting ducks," quips Takeshi. "So, let's make sure we have this timed down to the second."

"Well, this is getting real interesting, ain't it," laughs Ollie. "What's the plan if we actually make it in, or is that too much to ask?"

"Assault team moves on the headquarters to grab Vinick," says Takeshi, "Wolcott and Bishop rendezvous with Lamb, hopefully, he'll have the intel."

"And my wife," interjects Bishop. "The deal was, I bring back

Wolcott, I get my wife onto the island. I know where she is. If I don't, they'll be suspicious."

Takeshi puts his hand on Bishop's shoulder, looks him straight in the eye. "Hey, you're not the only one who has someone to get back to. My wife is working off her debt, just like me. We're both free if we come through. Only Ollie here is doing it for himself 'cause no one can stand him."

"He's right," says Ollie. "They didn't have personal leverage on me, they just offered me a shitload of credits and a cushy job. I'm not one to sit on my ass all day, but I do like credits."

"Gentlemen," says Mayor Remeny. "It sounds like we have the start of a plan. This is not my area of expertise, so I'll leave you to work out the details. Frank will get you to the site of the helicopter, and God willing, it can be utilized. Bishop..." she walks over to Bishop and puts a hand on his shoulder.

"I want to thank you for doing this," she says. "Be safe, and please take care of my boy."

"Your boy, ma'am?" he asks.

"Marion," she responds. "My son."

12

"What the hell?" Ward spits out as he rounds the concrete corridor, eyes on the empty guard chair outside the makeshift cell. He hurries his pace to the door and snatches out his key chain, sifting the ring to locate the correct one. Hurriedly finding it, he unlocks the door and grunts in with his shoulder to discover his guard sprawled out unconscious on the floor. He kneels at the guard's torso and slaps his open hand across the cheek.

"Ow, what the…" the guard recoils, rolling over as he snaps awake.

"What happened?" Ward demands. The guard blinks at him, confused and unsure.

"Goddammit."

Ward steps back and surveys the room, spotting the open vent cover in the ceiling. He darts out, heading straight to his office, bursts through the ajar door, flips on the light switch, and spies the split open overhead vent shaft along with the open cabinet doors. He inspects them both. Gone are all the prisoner's belongings. His face conveys the knowing dread.

He's going to have to call Lamb.

From his pocket, he pulls out his cell phone and slowly exits his office, finds Lamb in the contacts, and reluctantly pushes the call button. While doing so, he unzips his heavy winter coat and removes the 9mm pistol from its holster.

"Why are you calling me this early?" asks Lamb, clearly having been woken from sleep. Ward reaches the cell doorway, looks in on the guard sitting upon the ground, still groggy.

"Sir, the prisoners incapacitated the guard and escaped sometime in the last six hours," he says with a wince. Silence for uncomfortable seconds. No response from Lamb, so he decides to continue.

"Sir, my best guess is the woman will attempt to return to her apartment since it is the rendezvous point with her husband midday today," he states. "I'm going to contact my additional assets and assemble a team to reacquire her and the boy." More silence from Lamb and the call disconnects. Ward is about to holster his pistol when the phone vibrates back to life. He answers it.

"Kill that idiot, please," says Lamb.

"Yessir," responds Ward, who in one clean motion aims and fires at the guard, the bullet enters through his forehead and explodes out the back of his skull, coloring the concrete wall and floor in a thick red spray.

"And Ward," he says. "You won't get a second chance."

⚑ ⚑ ⚑

Traveling at dawn provided Tessa and Kell cover during their long trek from the Bronx Zoo back to her Walton Avenue apartment. The circuitous route meant slow going thanks to the various gangs controlling a gerrymandered collection of neighborhoods. With a suitably armed or armored vehicle, the kind which said *Don't Mess With Me*, it was possible to drive through gang territory, but on foot with a single handgun between them, Tessa knows better.

Traversing the city from memory, she takes them far north first into the West Bronx along the Harlem River, away from the largest gang in the area operating out of the Webster Avenue towers in Claremont Village. Thanks to the island tower guns and sharpshooters along the Manhattan island wall, most Free Zoners long ago abandoned the area, allowing them to move south freely as night dissipates into a foggy overcast early dawn.

They move through the overgrown forest, previously known as Joyce Kilmer Park, to take up a position along Walton Avenue across from her apartment building. The green space, where parents once took their kids for outdoor recreation or dogs for a walk, is now a dumping ground for garbage and abandoned cars relocated from the street. When someone long ago actually cared about clearing the street.

Her concern now is how to get into the building. An informer, either working in the building or an outsider sent to track her, had provided her whereabouts to Ward and his guard so they knew when she would be at the Yankee Stadium trading market. She cannot just stroll back in and up to her apartment, but the clock is ticking. The forty-eight hours' deadline will expire this afternoon, and Tessa needs to get back in the apartment for Bishop's return.

Although the building is secure, it is not impenetrable. Since things like building fire and safety codes are non-existent, the Italian Brothers have made egress a simple proposition - one door, heavily guarded for each building. Every other doorway is sealed. The familiar pair of steroid-enhanced guards will be securing the front door with their tripod gun and enough bullets to last many lifetimes.

Tessa doesn't have many friends on the outside, but she had connected with Gertrude, the elderly woman living in the apartment next door whose residency stretches back to the early 1980s. When Tessa moved into the apartment, three months passed before she met Gertrude, who rarely stepped outside due to security concerns. Because of the familial relationship, she repaid her nephews with home-cooked meals prepared almost daily in her apartment. They would send a courier to her room with whatever groceries were attainable, and hours later, she would call for the couriers return with her best approximation of spaghetti Bolognese, pizza Margherita, or gnocchi with peppers and onions.

In getting to know Gertie over time, and the fundamental need to connect with another human being, Tessa, on occasion, would sharpen knives for her while Gertie cooked. She told her about her childhood in the New York City of the 1970s and of her immigrant parents. They spent their entire life operating a twelve-table, thousand square foot Bronx trattoria, of trips back to Sicily, which succumbed to rising post-asteroid seas and no longer existed. Tessa counted Gertie as her lone ally in the Free Zone and will now need to call upon her friend for help.

While Tessa hides in the park overgrowth, Kell trudges toward the front door of her building with precise instructions to ensure he does not get mowed down by gunfire. The entrance has two sets of glass doors, reinforced by steel bars. The same bars cover the first-floor windows around the building. As directed, Kell approaches with his hands open and in the air, satchel over his shoulder, reaching the locked outer door. Spotted well before he reaches it, the guards remotely unlock the first set of doors, and Kell enters. The doors shut and lock behind him, placing him in a ten-foot by ten-foot foyer surrounded by the glass doors in front and back, glass walls to the left and right. A guard flips on an overhead speaker and talks into a handheld microphone.

"State your business," blares the speaker.

"I have a delivery for Gertrude DeMauro from the market."

"Does it require payment?" asks the guard.

"No, I was told to give to the front desk, that's all."

"Place the package on the floor and exit," says the guard, unlocking the door behind Kell. He does as instructed and walks back to the park, making sure not to look back as the guard re-locks the first set of doors. The second guard retrieves the small faux-leather purse, once a street vendor knock-off of some expensive brand, now Tessa and Kell's ticket inside.

Returning to the front desk, the guard opens the bag and glances at the handles of a variety of knives of mixed sizes and materials. Metal handled steak knives, rubber handled butcher knives, wooden-handled paring knives, and more. He shows these to his counterpart, they both shrug wordlessly, and he makes his way down the corridor, up the stairs and down the hall to Gertrude's apartment door. His knock is firm but respectful of her connection to their employers. A moment later, she unlocks and answers the door.

"This just came from the market for you," he explains, holding out the purse. She takes the bag and opens it, peering inside.

"Well, okay," she says. She wasn't expecting a delivery, and Tessa has been maintaining her knives for over a year. *Maybe these are from Tessa? I haven't seen her in a few days.* The guard nods goodbye before she can inquire further. She closes the door behind him and locks it before taking the bag into the kitchen and placing it onto the weathered tile countertop. Gingerly, she grips the handle of each knife and removes it from the bag, spacing them out. She groups them by type, noticing not all the knives seem to be in good condition or even adequately sharpened.

On the underside of the four paring knives, she feels roughness in their wooden handles and turns one over to inspect. She finds, in crude carving, two slashes (//) and the letters Y-O-U-R. Curious, she feels each of the wooden blade handles and finds more roughness, more carvings. She inspects each, and arranges them in the following order:

/ - OPEN
// - YOUR
/// - WINDOW
//// - TESSA

Gertrude, though not spry, shuffles as speedily as she can to the pair of windows in her apartment overlooking Walton Street and surveys the street below and across to the park. She sees nothing and moves to the single window looking out on the alleyway between her building and the next up the block. Unable to see the sidewalk between the two buildings, she unlocks and opens it, cold January air gusting in as she peers down to find Tessa staring up at her next to Kell.

"Tessa, what are you doing down there, dear?" she asks.

"I need help getting in, and I can't go through the front. Can you help me?"

"Of course, what do you need me to do?" Gertrude responds.

"My friend is going to help me up."

Gertrude takes a step back as Kell puts his back to the brick wall and squats, placing his hands together, fingers interlocked. Tessa steps up and puts one foot into his hands as he boosts her up high enough, so she can grab the decorative brick ledge of the window. He lifts his arms, his muscles straining under her weight and the backpack of supplies over her shoulders, and raises her up another few feet, enough for her to grab hold of the actual windowsill. From there, she pulls herself up and in, tumbling onto the floor in front of Gertrude. Tessa gets up, taking off her bag and placing it on the floor.

"How are you going to get your friend up?" asks Gertrude.

"Do you have any large towels or blankets?"

"Sure," she says. "Right over here."

Neatly folded over a chair is a queen size grey wool blanket Tessa grabs and unfurls. She lays it on the floor and rolls it tightly until it becomes one long tube. She takes it over to the window and lowers one end down.

"Let me know when you've got it." A few seconds later, Kell tugs at it, and she stops lowering, putting one foot up on the wall to the right of the window. "Okay, start climbing."

Kell plants his left foot on the brick and pulls himself up the wall, hand over hand. Tessa struggles to counterbalance his weight, she can feel the wool in her hand wanting to slip but grips it with every ounce of strength her exhausted arms can muster. Finally, she sees a hand reach up to the windowsill, and then another. She immediately drops the blanket and grabs onto his wrists. He twists his hands to grip her wrists, and they work in tandem to pull him over and into the apartment, both wearily collapsing to the floor.

"Who's your friend, dear?" asks Gertrude.

"Kell, ma'am." He stands up and turns, grabs the bottom of the window, and slides it down into the closed position, locking it at the top.

"Well, I don't mean to be nosy, but it seems like you two might be in some trouble," says Gertrude with knowing charm. "How about I get you both a glass of water, and we sit down for a bit."

Tessa gives Kell a nod of assurance, and they both walk over to the living area, appointed with a low wooden coffee table and four upholstered sitting chairs, each of distinct design and fabric. They sink into chairs opposite each other, fatigued from their morning excursion. Gertrude appears with a tray and two glasses of water, which she hands to eager outstretched hands, then places the tray down on the coffee table and takes a seat between them. After downing half her glass, Tessa explains everything, starting with her abduction in the Yankee Stadium market to how they ended up outside the window.

Being a native of the Bronx, Gertrude's kindly grandmother demeanor conceals a woman who has survived the blight and desolation of the worst New York City had to offer. She fought off multiple muggings throughout her life, battled and beat cancer, shrugged off the advances of local low-level mobsters for protection money, and was generally considered an unshakable rock of the neighborhood. Despite the rough resume, even she is taken aback by Tessa's story, more than once gasping audibly.

"Oh dear, they're going to be coming for you," says Gertrude.

Tessa smirks. "I'm counting on it."

♟ ♟ ♟

Ward, along with three well-armed mercenaries sporting matching Kevlar vests, holstered pistols, black fatigues, and shaved heads, pull up to the apartment buildings along Walton Avenue in a Marine Growler, a four-seat light utility vehicle. A distant cousin of a consumer-grade Jeep, only this one is topped with a 40-millimeter grenade launcher. They disembark, one grabs a green duffle bag from the open rear of the truck, and Ward leads them toward the front glass doors.

The guards inside spot them and one immediately unlocks both sets of glass doors. Ward and his men push through with calm urgency, eyeing the desk and the hallways split off left and right.

"Anything?" asks Ward.

"She ain't been back here yet. I can open up her room, and you can wait for her there if you want."

"Have you had any visitors in the last hour or so? She might be traveling with a kid, mid-teens. Tall, skinny," says Ward.

"Well, there was a kid who came from the market, dropped off some stuff for one of the residents. But he was here and took off a half-hour ago."

"What did he deliver?" inquires Ward, suspicious.

"They were like, cooking knives. You know, for cutting up food. They went to an old lady, she's a cook."

"Take me to her now." Ward fires back.

"Wait, you don't understand. She's family to the brothers. You can't just barge in there." Ward considers the information for a moment.

"The old lady, where is her room in relation to Tessa's? And what floor" Ward asks.

"Uh, next door. They're neighbors on the second floor." Ward turns to his men.

"We're going up. Remember, we need them alive. Pass out the masks," Ward instructs. The merc with the bag unzips and grabs gas masks, distributing them out to the group. He hands a silver canister the size of a pop can with a large ring dangling from one end, a tear gas grenade, to Ward.

"After we breach the target's room, you two will move in with me, and we'll sweep the apartment. You're keeping eyes on the old woman's place, got it?" All three mercs respond as directed. He turns his attention back to the guards at the front desk.

"Room number," Ward barks, not a question but an order.

"Twenty-six, down that hall, up the stairs."

Following Ward's lead, the group moves down the hallway to the stairwell, taking two steps at a time before they reach the second-floor door. Ward opens it a crack and peers through. His eyes follow the wall and doorways, all in disrepair covered in yellow halogen glow from the overhead lighting.

The group exits the stairwell and steps down the hall, passing rooms marked "22" and "24" on the left, "21" and "23" on the right. They reach the last two rooms, and the merc with the bag drops it front of Tessa's door, removing a small metal box connected via a cord to a black L-shaped tool with a round, metal cone at the end.

The merc slips on goggles and a pair of heavy gloves and flicks a switch on the box, then depresses a trigger on the tool which produces a small but intense burst of blue then yellow then orange flame - a plasma cutter.

He raps the door gently with his knuckles. No response to the clanking. He applies the flame to the edge of the round doorknob base, burning open a half-inch hole in the door, which he traces around the handle until it completes the circle. The doorknob falls towards the floor into the duffle bag without a sound. The merc turns off the plasma cutter and places it back in the bag, sliding it away from the door. He looks to Ward, who nods to the group - the signal to put on their masks. They all comply.

Ward grips the tear gas canister and slips it into the hole, pushing forward until the knob on the other side slips out and falls to the ground with a clank. He then grabs the ring with a finger and pulls, releasing a cloud of tear gas into the room. Some of it seeps through the space between the canister and the hole in the door—some curls under the door like morning fog along a river. Ward keeps count in his head, waiting for the thirty-second mark as the incapacitating agent fills the rooms of the apartment. Finally, the canister supply exhausts, and Ward steps back.

All four draw their pistols.

Pushing on the door, it creaks open a few inches before stopping thanks to a thin chain link, which he cuts through with a pair of wire cutters the merc hands him out of the duffle bag. He touches the door again, gives it a nudge, and it swings in, revealing a dingy gas cloud-filled room. Ward maneuvers into the narrow hallway first, taking small, deliberate steps, followed by the pair of mercs. The third, as instructed, stands just outside the door with eyes focused on Gertrude's door across the hall, while periodically glancing down the corridor as more gas spills out and dissipates at his feet.

Ward continues forward to the small closet and bathroom

ahead, flipping on light switches as he goes, but no lights turn on. He grabs a stout metal flashlight from his pocket and holds it just above his pistol, which is raised to eye level. The mercs follow cautiously behind; as he opens the closet door, a merc closes the main door behind them.

Ward steps forward into the bathroom doorway and runs his hand along the wall inside the room, groping for the next light switch. As the two mercs, one behind the other, step closer to Ward, they peer into the kitchen through the archway.

They do not notice that above them, perched silently on the chandelier, awaits one of their targets - Tessa.

Outfitted in her gas mask, her feet lean carefully forward on the round base of the circular metal fixture, shaped like an upside cone. What was once ornate, with hundreds of dusty crystals dangling via small hooks to create a luminescent entryway, had been long ago stripped to its simple tubular frame along with all the lightbulbs. Obscured by the fog of the tear gas, she watches as Ward and the first merc walk right under her as she crouches in the small space between the top of the chandelier and the ceiling. She waits for them to move just far enough past her to give her space to land when it is time to spring the trap.

Ward continues to fumble for a light switch in the bathroom, not knowing the light activates via a chain pull to the right of the vanity mirror along the left wall, a quirk of the hundred-year-old building design.

Tessa makes her move.

She flicks the snap on each leather sheath housing the Jagdkommando knives under her wrists and lets them slowly slide forward until the grip is in her palm. Bouncing her eyes between Ward and the mercs, she rotates the knives from a forward grip to a reverse grip and leans forward, allowing her body weight to carry her off the chandelier to the floor.

Ward hears a loud thudding noise from the hallway behind him and turns around, not believing at first what he is seeing through the slowly dissolving tear gas fog. Tessa had positioned the Jagdkommando knives directly above the head of each merc. The expertly sharpened blades had found the seam where the frontal bone and the parietal bone meet about halfway on top of the cranium, splitting them apart and into their respective lobes down into the brain stem, killing both instantly.

Ward watches in horror as their limp bodies slide off the knives and slump to the floor.

Before he can swing and aim his pistol at Tessa, she darts to her right through the archway into the kitchen. Ward gives pursuit just as the door to the bedroom slams shut. He races after her, failing to check the blind spot on his left in the living area, where Kell, also outfitted with a gas mask, fires two shots from his laser-sighted Glock into the back of Ward's left and right thighs. He loses his grip on his gun and flashlight as they tumble away out of reach.

Hearing the shots, the merc in the hallway dons his mask and bursts in through the front door, stopping immediately at the sight of the two mercs lying prone on the floor with pools of blood spreading around their heads. He carefully steps over them, pistol raised ahead of him, as he turns and investigates the kitchen. He spots Ward across the room, down but moving. Ward waves furiously while yelling something muffled by the gas mask. Kell raises his Glock again and squeezes the trigger, putting one round into the left temple of the last mercs head, who plummets to the floor in a lifeless heap.

Killing did not come easy for Kell.

Although he and his mother had survived in some of the harshest conditions before finally making their way to Manhattan, they had not done so with a trail of bodies behind them. Unlike some who treated survival as a zero-sum game, Regina had tried to impart some level of basic human decency in her son, while also training him for the worst-case scenarios. Kell had ended a life before, at only twelve years old, when a pair of bandits put a knife to his mother's throat. He was shaken, but not broken by the experience, and swore he would only do so again if he or his mother's life was in jeopardy.

For helping him escape from the concrete prison cell Ward had placed him in, he now counted Tessa as someone he would pull the trigger for if necessary.

Ward pounds the floor in frustration and agony as the bedroom door opens. Before him stands Tessa, both Jagdkommando knives still in the reverse position and covered with blood and brain matter. She kneels and wipes them on Ward's back as Kell approaches, Glock steady on Ward. She raises both arms upward, and the knives slide back into their sheaths, which she snaps to secure them in place. She looks up at Kell and nods. Ward notices and closes his eyes, believing he is about to be put out of his current misery.

Instead, Tessa grabs the back of Ward's shirt collar and Kevlar vest and drags him into the bedroom, where the two sets of windows have been opened through which the tear gas escapes.

She pulls him across the room, Kell following with the Glock, all the way to the window, putting his face parallel to the sill. She waits, staring at Ward, who is trying not to grimace until the air is clear. Kell removes his mask and takes a deep breath, then

Tessa does the same before ripping Ward's off with far less concern.

"Why don't you just kill me?" Ward asks through gritted teeth. She leans in, examining his front of confidence betrayed by fear.

"Because you're going to introduce me to your boss."

14

Meeting with Mayor Remeny at Bangor City Hall is a revelation for Bishop, and the ride from downtown Bangor out to the suburban development referred to as Bangor Gardens fills in some of the blanks thanks to Deputy Bloom. On their route northeast through the Broadway District past St. Joseph Hospital, Bloom gives the nuts and bolts explanation of how they have managed to not just survive but return to something resembling civilized society without the benefit of a corporate takeover.

The eastern coast of the United States was spared while a tsunami engulfed the west with twenty-foot-high waves, killing millions and taking months to partially recede. At the same time, parts of southern California also experienced devastation when the Salton Trough Fault, which acted as a buffer to the San Andreas Fault, could no longer carry the seismic strain and buckled, disappearing Los Angeles forever into the ocean.

Like the rest of the globe, Bangor suffered the same unprecedented freezing temperatures. In the year following the impact of the asteroid, deaths from starvation and exposure accounted for thousands of fatalities among the metropolitan population of 150,000.

Harold Bloom, Frank's father, was mayor at the time and instituted several measures that prepared the stage for the population's survival. The first was to convert the Bangor Mall into an extensive indoor farming complex using a similar organic aeroponic farming setup utilized on Manhattan island and other corporate cities around the country, albeit a far more makeshift operation. With the atmosphere full of dust and other material, the sun was erased, a worldwide polar night lasted an entire year, slowly giving way to the daily atmospheric soup.

Farming via traditional methods spanning thousands of years was abruptly over.

In years two and three, almost half the population abandoned the city in search of a warmer climate, their departure success rate diminished by the day as gasoline availability promptly dwindled to nothing. Many were caught in violent windstorms plunging the temperatures to the negative thirties and forties, freezing them in automobile sarcophagi. As the gloom partially lifted midway through year five, closer to the present constant overcast, temperatures rose enough to allow for regular daily travel. However, movement at night continued to be urged against.

With the collapse of the federal and most state and local governments, unable to respond to the nationwide famine and abandoned by security forces, then-Mayor Bloom and his staff steeled the remaining community with an honest assessment of their chances. While the corporations walled off their cities and carefully managed and manipulated their populations through debt and fear of exile to the Free Zone, Bloom took a more utilitarian approach. The community depended on each other but could no longer utilize currency as a means of exchange. As a lifelong economic conservative with more progressive social views, he couldn't stomach moving toward socialism but was left with few options.

The Bangor hydroelectric plant and solar wind farm were both nationalized, or whatever the equivalent is for a small city when there is no longer a nation, along with the area hospitals. To maximize energy distribution, residents were encouraged to move as close to the city center as possible, which doubled to improve ridesharing, as only electric vehicles were now in use, as well as bond the community in a unified struggle for survival.

Bloom and his administration cobbled together a list of critical infrastructures requiring staffing, such as the mall agricultural center, the hospital, and the water and hydroelectric plants. The elementary and high schools attempted to carry on for the sake of providing normalcy to the remaining school-age children. The local University was converted into a skills development center for adults whose careers no longer existed, such as insurance sales, post office workers, most service employees, and the like. Although the mayor believed no one should be forced into labor, he made it very clear - one able-bodied adult from each household needed to work in critical infrastructure facilities. Those who declined would no longer receive the benefit of free electricity, water, and food the rest of the residents counted on for survival. For those who were unable to contribute, whether by age, injury, or some other reasonable circumstance, the college dormitories were set up as a communal living space.

Years five, six, and seven were, by all accounts, miserable.

The world would never be the same, which took a considerable psychological toll. Occasional food shortages or particularly brutal winter storms would kill people within minutes of being outside. The population continued to decline, with the best estimate by year seven of an informal census indicating less than 20,000 total residents.

It was year eight when the first Bangor resident who had left years ago returned, along with a small group of refugees who had been displaced from Atlanta following the mandate for younger and cheaper child labor. It was around this time Bloom, in one of his last acts as mayor, declared Bangor would be open to all newcomers, provided options among the various available neighborhoods for housing, as well as assessed for skill sets and training.

Not long after, a late winter influenza strain would kill approximately a thousand residents, including Mayor Bloom. His final act was to recommend to the citizenry that Pasha Remeny, a close friend and former college professor who had titled Bloom's ear more than a few times during the hard years on socioeconomic issues, be the top choice as his replacement. An open town meeting was held, with various neighborhoods sending representatives who unanimously backed Remeny as the next mayor of Bangor.

Bishop is happy to pass the drive time with the history lesson on Bangor as they pull up to the neighborhood development where the Sikorsky CH-53 Sea Stallion made its hard landing years ago.

Truth be told, he is not optimistic.

He had spent time completely dismantling and rebuilding the gas turbine engines the Sea Stallion utilized and knows their complexity. His hope is whatever damage it endured was mainly to the fuselage underbelly, and the engines are intact. Fueling them will be an entirely different issue.

The street they turn onto appears to have been a relatively new cul de sac, as there were no old-growth trees, only dead saplings who never matured and now stuck out of the ground like fallen twigs. At the tip of the circle, Bloom slows and pulls up into the driveway of a two-story colonial home.

Bloom, Bishop, Ollie, and Takeshi all exit the Jeep and immediately march around the right side of the house. Bishop takes a moment to survey the homes - all marked with large orange X's spray-painted on their garage doors with the letter G in the bottom quadrant. Bloom looks back and spies Bishop scanning the neighborhood.

"Those houses have gas heat, so they're not inhabited right now," he explains. "We've got a team going around flipping as many to run electric heat, but it's a lot of cobbling together parts and building from scratch. When they surveyed this neighborhood a year or so ago, that's when they spotted the chopper."

They continue between the homes to the backyard where Bishop finally gets a look at the helicopter. They weren't kidding, as the mammoth twenty-four-thousand-pound machine appears to have crushed a metal A-frame swing set flat to the ground, with parts of the right legs peeking out behind the rear of the undercarriage. With nothing but an open field behind them where another cul-de-sac is carved out, but no foundations laid, the rotors managed to avoid contact with any structures, a positive in Bishop's mind as he walks around the outside of the Sea Stallion, looking for visible damage.

When he reaches the front under the cockpit windows, he concludes the landing, while semi-controlled, was nose first, as the inflight refueling probe extending out from the left side of the avionics array is crumpled into the ground and is a complete loss. No matter, as they won't be doing any inflight refueling anytime soon. Of more significant concern was the avionics array itself, which is misaligned and partially crushed. Losing avionics will mean losing infrared sensors and terrain-following radar, among other things. Flying at night will be a challenging but not impossible task.

"That doesn't look too good," remarks Takeshi.

"I've seen worse, but if we get it operational, it means whoever's piloting this thing will be flying by sight, because the radar is probably toasted," responds Bishop. "What I'm more concerned about is what kind of juice they were running on."

"Juice?" Bloom asks. "You mean fuel?"

"Yep," responds Bishop, climbing up the side of the Sea Stallion and opening the engine cover. "Unless they ran dry, or it leaked out, these two big tanks should have reserve fuel in them. The problem is thermal stability. Any condensation or bacteria built up inside could kill the engine, but it depends on the type of juice. If we're talking regular old twentieth-century jet fuel, the odds are not in our favor. However, the fleet started moving towards synthetics and biofuels to reduce oil dependency years before the asteroid, so depending on the age of this bird, we might catch a break."

"If its biofuel, they could have added a biocide, which is supposed to keep the tanks clean for long periods. The only way to know is to start it up. If it's a biofuel, we're in business. It'll cough and bark at us, but she'll start up. If it's old fashioned or synth, whatever nasty bits are in there will get sucked in and kill the engine fast. Hopefully, nothing sparks or shorts and blows us to kingdom come."

"So, we've got a one-out-of-three shot," says Ollie. "I got better odds playing craps in Vegas."

"Wait, go back to the part about blowing up," Takeshi interjects.

"Nah, odds are good it won't," responds Bishop. "But just in case, everyone grab some cover around the corner of the house." Bloom, Takeshi, and Ollie do as Bishop instructs, and he climbs into the cockpit and checks off the pre-flight list he completed hundreds of times before. Neither of the jettison switches have been flipped, so he was sure the crew had not dumped their reserve fuel before the hard landing.

Unlike an automobile, there is no key needed to start the helicopter. Whoever had dumped the Sea Stallion had made an effort to completely power it down to "dead cold," meaning all systems were shut off entirely and properly. Whoever parked it might have thought they would be back again but apparently didn't make it.

In scanning the control panels, Bishop notices splattered specks of brown, most likely dried blood. A quick visual inspection of the open cargo and personnel area behind the cockpit reveals an ugly scene. Large puddles of brown on the floor, bullet holes, and burns riddle the walls. There had been a firefight either in the rear of the hold, or shots fired from the outside in, fatally wounding several occupants. From the look of the spray, striking the pilot as well. His best guess was anyone who made it out alive probably sought shelter but never made it back, most likely succumbing to their injuries or the weather.

He turns his attention back to the start-up procedure, switching on the master battery. The control panels come to life, followed by the master avionics switch. As he predicted, radar and infrared capabilities are gone, but the auxiliary fuel tanks show almost full capacity, enough for a trip to Manhattan and back.

He flips the start switch cover to open, places his finger on the FUEL switch, and takes a deep breath. Depressing the button initiates the fuel cycle process and leaves only one button left - START. A warmed engine would start immediately, but since this had been sitting for years, who knows. He holds and winces, hoping particulates don't flood the pistons and explode the engine.

A half-second or so passes, and Bishop hasn't been engulfed by flames, so burning to a crisp is likely off the menu. After a few more seconds, he hears the slow build in the engine as it lurches toward idle, scanning the engine oil pressure and temperature gauges as the RPMs build, slowly rotating the blades above him and on the rear tail.

It's not pretty, but it will fly.

Bishop sees cheering from Bloom, Takeshi, and Ollie and waves them over to his cockpit window. Bloom gives him the location of the makeshift encampment they'll be utilizing for the operation to Manhattan and advises Bishop to follow him. Takeshi decides to play it safe and heads back to the vehicle with Bloom while Ollie climbs into the Sea Stallion and plants himself in the co-pilot seat. Bishop slides on the headphones and positions the microphone in front of his mouth, which Ollie mimics, and flips on the internal communication system.

"Better odds in Vegas, huh," Bishop cracks via the mic as he feels the pedals beneath his feet and grips the cyclic stick between his legs.

"You don't want to hear my odds on this whole insane mission," responds Ollie.

Bishop gives him an uneasy stare then turns his attention back to getting the helicopter airborne, which he does. The sound of the crushed swing set peeling off the bottom of the fuselage where it had sat frozen and fused for years pops and snaps. The concrete anchors poured years ago tear the long metal tubes back towards the earth as it rises slowly above the houses and hovers. They watch Bloom and Takeshi climb back into the vehicle and depart the cul de sac, Bishop engages the stick, and the nose of the Sea Stallion dips slightly as the bulky helicopter lurches forward.

Twenty minutes later, Bishop completes the power down process as the Sea Stallion rests on the tarmac of the former Bangor Air National Guard Base adjacent to the Bangor International Airport. The base was once home to a half dozen Boeing KC-135R Stratotankers, an aerial refueling aircraft slated for replacement in the mid-2000s, but was so effectively stubborn they never actually retired.

Only two remain at the far end of the rectangular concrete slab. Both are missing large sections of their aluminum wings and rendered inoperable, buffeted by a silver octagonal hangar utilized for single-engine aircraft on one side, and a larger white square building on the other, the latter where everyone heads.

Moving through the double doors, Ollie leads Bishop into a large austere entryway lined with glass display cases housing military memorabilia - photos, plaques, model aircraft, and the like. Through another set of doors, they enter what was once a large pilot lounge, filled with leather couches and chairs arranged in a family room style surrounding a coffee table, a dining area with several round tables and scattered kitchen chairs, along with a pool table and bar. Seated at the kitchen tables are two men, one old and one young, talking with Takeshi and Bloom as Ollie and Bishop make their way over. Bloom says something and eyeballs redirect towards Bishop, who instinctively looks behind him as if the attention weren't meant for him

"I hope one of you two has flight time piloting something similar to a Sea Stallion," says Bishop. The older gentlemen, gray-hair receding, immediately speaks up.

"That'd be me, Charlie Fischer. I flew Apaches back in one of our various Middle East interventions, then regionally for a few news stations," he says. Bishop reaches out his hand, and Charlie reciprocates.

"Thanks, Charlie," says a relieved Bishop. "I was worried I'd be the only one who knows how to fly that thing. There are a few quirks we can go over before we depart. Speaking of, what's our departure time?" He looks to Takeshi.

"We need to remove the EMP from Ollie's Hummer and install into yours," he steps up and explains. "Both vehicles are on their way here now. We're shooting for departure at eleven hundred, which puts us under the gun. You think you can get the EMP installed in the next hour?"

"Hopefully less, but what about the return trip?" he asks. "Getting back through Boston is not going to be easy."

"We're working on it. Derek, you want to explain?" suggests Takeshi.

A skinny, bespectacled kid, in a flannel shirt and jeans, Bishop places in his late teens or early twenties, rises and avoids eye contact in a combination of awe shucks and genuine social anxiety.

"We're spoofing the homing beacon in the vehicle based on the route you previously drove," the nervous Derek explains, gripping a computer tablet in on hand. "To whoever is tracking, it will just look like you're heading back at the same rate you came here. It's just a little script I wrote to reverse the geocache in the GPS. We can trigger it from anywhere we want along the route. We can speed it up or slow it down too. If we want."

"We'll haul the Hummer with us and land on a highway outside Manhattan," interrupts Takeshi. "When the spoof signal catches up, you'll take the Hummer with Wolcott the rest of the way. Once you go into the tunnel, we'll lose your signal, so we'll have to work on a countdown for you to deploy the EMP and our assault to begin."

"Sounds like a plan, when does the spoof signal start?" asks Bishop. Derek looks at Takeshi, not sure if he should answer.

"It already did," responds Takeshi. "We kicked off the return trip just after you got the copter operational. We couldn't afford to lose the daylight this afternoon, that's why we need to get the EMP installed and off the ground by eleven. We going to take the scenic route down the coast to avoid any ground contact, so flight time is between a hundred and a hundred twenty minutes which means we'll have a two hour lead on the signal when we make the drop-off and time for final prep for the assault on the Mick. Our drop point is five clicks out from the island. Anything I'm missing?"

Bishop considers the question. He had not expected the wheels to already be in motion but realizes the original forty-eight-hour deadline imposed by Fenton expires in less than ten hours, and with the spoof signal already broadcasting, his arrival assured before the deadline. Now it was only a matter of installing the EMP, making the flight, picking up Tessa from her apartment, and starting the assault on the island.

Before he can muster a question, Derek interjects.

"What about this other signal coming towards us, it's an hour outside the city?" he asks, pointing to his tablet.

"It's whoever Fenton sent to follow-up Bishop," Ollie says. "Guess he didn't want to wait and see if the signal moved again. Oh well, they'll have to find their own ride back."

"We're not going to leave them, are we?" asks Bishop. "You know where their heading, just cut them off and-" Takeshi holds up his hand to interrupt Bishop. "I hear what you're saying, but we don't have the time. The mission has already started, and this is not a part of it."

⁂

Strapped into his wall mounted chair donning the VR glasses, Lamb can feel his face boiling. "Come again?" he asks, not believing what Ward just relayed to him.

"The recovery was a failure. I'm currently being held at gunpoint by the female and the boy, they are in charge now."

"And you called me because?" asks Lamb.

"She has a lot of knives, and I don't want her to use them on me."

"Fair enough," responds Lamb. "Can I speak with…"

"Tessa."

"Yeah, I can talk to her, please?" forcing congeniality through gritted teeth. He hears the phone being handed over.

"Hello."

"I want to tell you first, so you'll understand, no one was ever going to hurt you."

"Where are the others?"

"What others?"

"The ones before Kell and me. If no one was ever going to hurt us, what happened to the ones before us?"

Lamb sighs. "Huh, I guess Ward's been talking."

"You'd be surprised how fast people start talking when you threaten to cut off parts of them, Nathan Lamb."

"Great, you know my name, I know your name. We're formally acquainted. If you're going to kill Ward, well, whatever. Won't do you any good. He's on a need to know basis, and what he knows is basically nothing. So, sorry, better luck next time."

Tessa lets out a little chuckle. "See, that's where you're wrong. He knows, and you know, that my husband is still alive because I'm still alive. If he were dead, you would have gotten rid of me already, because I'm a loose end. But he's not dead. That means he's coming to get me, and when he does, we'll be welcomed onto the island, because he will have brought back the doctor who saved Elton Vinick's life. What do you think will happen then?"

Lamb considers the options, weighing if he should lay all his cards out on the virtual table to save his life, tell her about Wolcott's connection to Vinick, about the files Wolcott had viewed exposing the truth regarding the asteroid and described to Lamb. Would she believe any information from him right now? He has already seen a text, a communication Tessa didn't know about from a little over an hour ago, from Fenton to Nolan notifying her Bishop had started his return, presumably with Wolcott, something he had not yet relayed to Ward.

Or should he just lie?

"While you've been running your mouth, I've already contacted an assault team now en route to your location thanks to Ward's phone, which I'm currently tracking to your apartment on Walton Avenue. I'm telling you this to allow you and the kid to run. Run as far away as possible, and you get to live, but this time the orders are not to capture but to kill. And make no mistake, they won't be as sloppy as Ward and his team of idiots were. So, what do you say, do you want to live?"

Lamb hears only silence for the first few agonizing seconds, hoping his gambit has paid off. His blood goes cold when he hears the laughter.

"You've never done this before, have you? You've never had to survive outside the walls of the island. To fight and to kill to keep breathing. To consider and plan every move as if it might be your last. You think I'm stupid enough to make this call not knowing your contingencies, or more accurately, your lack of a contingency? You don't have an assault team, because Ward was your assault team. He already gave you up so he could keep breathing. You're isolated. You're alone. And now you're exposed. And I'm coming for you."

DISCONNECTED appears on screen in Lamb's VR display. He sits for a moment, his chest pounds from the accelerated heart rate. The virtual world of Manhattan Island laid out in front of him hiccups and distorts in noticeable waves as the panic attack overtakes him.

Destroying the lives of executives in his safe little room via ones and zeroes had provided a false sense of invincibility now crumbling before him. He tears off the VR goggles and haptic gloves and drops to the floor on his hands and knees, his chest constricting as he gasps for air. He takes one long, deep inhale and holds it, releasing at the last possible second and repeats, trying to calm himself down.

He sits back on feet, his legs folded underneath him, and slowly pulls himself together. Climbing back into the chair, he slips back on the goggles and gloves and takes several long deep breaths, exhaling deliberately after each one. Once he soothes himself, he works feverishly through several programs to locate a contact list.

"Hello, sir. I've got an update. We've run into some complications. I'm afraid I might need an extraction. I'm going to recover the data today, but the security team has lost control of the returning assets. As soon as the data is my possession, please have your men ready to go."

Lamb listens intently as assurance is given he will be taken care of, and his service in recovering the data will be rewarded.

"Thank you, I appreciate that," he says as confidence and calm return. "I'll give you an update as soon as I have one. Thanks again, Mr. Reynolds. Talk to you soon."

CHAPTER 15

Arranging the rendezvous in Bryant Park, the only remaining ground-level green space left on Manhattan just south of the Mick, was Nolan's choice. Since the morning meeting with Lloyd, doubts regarding Vinick had permeated her thinking, but she still could not fully embrace the plausibility. She did not trust Nathan Lamb.

She is positive it had been Lamb who has abducted a loved one of every asset she and Fenton have sent out to recover Wolcott, but she did not have tangible proof. She also realized Vinick, whom she considered a mentor and pseudo-father figure, was the most guarded human being she had ever known. Lloyd wasn't a power-hungry zealot like Lamb, he didn't need to lead the board to achieve validation, which made his accusations even more troubling.

As she sits on the park bench inside the towering glass greenhouse built to maintain a consistent year-round temperature, accessible via reasonable one-time fees or a yearly subscription, she spots Lamb on approach. He looks disheveled beyond his usual casual norm, hair mussed in what appears to be a pair of long running shorts under his winter coat, as if he had finished up at the gym but disregarded a change of clothes. He sits down next to her and folds one leg up so his foot can rest on his knee and proceeds to untie and retie his shoe.

"Your breakfast with Lloyd," he starts.

"I assume you were listening in on us."

He switches legs, repeating the sequence. "You have to understand; this isn't about me. I know how I come off, but you can consider what I have to say, and then you can reassess my actions."

"I'm here, aren't I," she retorts coldly.

He turns to her and slightly leans in. "Vinick's son, the doctor, he came to me before he skipped town. He told me he had proof his old man was the reason why when Solear's asteroid mining project broke down, Elton initiated a contingency plan to direct whatever could be salvaged back to earth. That they would figure out how to stop it in the years it would take to arrive. They were in for half a billion dollars, and he couldn't let it go because the upside was trillions. But all that documentation is on Elton's personal device, never been connected to the Island network. So, even with my resources, I can't hack into it, and nobody gets onto his floor. Nobody except you."

She takes a moment to consider the information.

"Look," he continues without waiting for a response. "You don't trust me, and why should you? I'm willing to show you how serious I am about this; I'm going to resign my board position effective immediately and just go back to running things back in the Brain. I don't need the board meetings anyway, hate 'em. I want you to understand this isn't a power play. I'm not out for Vinick's job, that's for a company guy like Lloyd. Suits who like to sit around boardrooms and act busy. No offense."

She looks him in the eye, "Have you been monitoring my communications with Bob Fenton in HQ and kidnapping family members of the assets we've sent out?" Lamb is caught flat-footed by the question and can feel the anxiety rise again within him. He can only affirm the inquiry with a nod and wait for the follow-up.

"Where are they?" her voice lowering but intensifying.

"They're fine, they're all fine," he spits out. "Yes, I have a team that's been detaining the people you dangled as incentives and keeping them off-island until someone came back with the doctor so Vinick couldn't get his hands on him. The plan was to intercept them before they got back on the island and take Vinick, and then once Vinick is removed, let them go. It's not a perfect plan, I know, but we didn't have a lot of options."

"Well, since you probably already know since you've been spying on us, one of the assets appears to have recovered Wolcott and should arrive back late this afternoon."

"Then you need to get into Vinick's computer today," responds Lamb. "Wolcott is only a piece of the puzzle, when he tells you what Vinick had in store, your head will spin. But we need the files on Vinick's computer just as bad, and if he deletes those, all the evidence is gone. You need to secure everything on this external drive."

From his pocket, he removes a small black plastic disc, roughly the diameter of a pinky fingernail and the thickness of a quarter. He squeezes it between his forefinger and thumb, and after three seconds, the disc changes from black to white.

"When you activate this, it becomes magnetic and launches a wireless drop box program. Place it anywhere on the device. All you have to do is unlock the computer, and the program will appear on the screen. It will scan all the files and they'll transfer. Depending on how much data there is, it shouldn't take more than a minute."

"Security wands and pats down everyone who enters."

"I know," says Lamb. "The outer casing shields it; metal detector won't pick it up. You just need a short window of time to get into his computer, find the data, and transfer it. Can you do it?"

She holds the disc between in her fingers and examines it. She cannot, for the life of her, believe it has come to this. Conspiring with someone she despises against her mentor. A man who took her under his wing and guided her career to the highest levels. She has always been at Vinick's side like a Chief of Staff to the President. Her stomach had turned all morning, and this visit with Lamb only solidified her suspicions.

"No," she spits, tossing the device back at Lamb's lap as she stands. "It's not enough. You may have convinced Lloyd, or maybe blackmailed him, I don't know, but this isn't happening." She strides off, heart racing with adrenaline.

"Your parents, Grace and Terrance Nolan," he barks, knowing it will stop her gait. It does.

"What did you say?" she asks incredulously as she turns and slowly walks back.

"I didn't want to have to do this, but this is the ace up my sleeve," exhales Lamb almost empathetically. She sits back down on the bench and glares at him.

"Why do you know their names?" she growls.

"I have access to every bit of security data this island has ever produced. Your parents left Manhattan before the asteroid, right?"

"Yes, they have...had a home in the Adirondacks. They thought the city would be overrun and they'd be safer out there."

"I know, I saw the real estate listing. Twenty acres, a private lake, a greenhouse for year-round gardening, solar array. Nice place."

"What's your point?"

"When was the last time you spoke to them?"

"The day the asteroid hit, just before. They had stocked a fallout shelter with three years-worth of provisions. Plus, they could grow their own food..."

"They didn't make it a year. You know how I know? Because they came back. They came to one of the gates, said they wanted to speak to you, fires had swept through the woods and destroyed the house. They had walked over two hundred miles to get back."

"Bullshit."

"I know this because it happened inside a guard gate with the security camera running. Full audio and video. It's on my phone if you want to see it."

Nolan shakes.

"Why are you telling me this now?"

"The guards didn't call you. Certain names were on a list, a list created by Elton Vinick. It's how his son got in under your radar. If the person showed up at a gate, he and he only was to be contacted. You wanna know what Elton Vinick said?"

She did, but she didn't. She nodded anyway.

"He said, tell them you're sorry, but there is no one by the name of Sandra Nolan on the island."

▲ ▲ ▲

"Holy mother…," remarks Bishop as he watches a pair of tow-trucks drag his and Ollie's Hummer's onto the tarmac near the Sea Stallion. His vehicle looks like how he left it, relatively unscathed from the trip north to Bangor but with a few bumps and bruises. Ollie's, however, is in much worse shape. Correction: it's a wreck.

"How the hell did you drive that thing here?" inquires Bishop.

"Sheer will," responds Ollie.

Takeshi rolls his eyes at the exaggerated bravado. As the Hummer is lowered from the tow truck, Ollie walks over and gives a detailed blow-by-blow account of how the rear of the vehicle was hit not once but twice by rocket-propelled grenades on the tailgate, the second dislodging the rear doors, causing the extra shielding to break off and spidering several of the rear bulletproof glass panels. On the front end, or what is left of it, the engine is exposed, as the hood and most of both quarter panels were torn off when Ollie used the Hummer as a battering ram to penetrate a roadblock on the outer belt around Boston consisting of an overturned semi-trailer, a pair of pickup trucks and a makeshift cinder block wall.

Bishop sticks his head into the back of the wrecked Hummer and surveys the three linked batteries, set-up the same as in his Hummer. He walks back and forth for a minute, comparing the engine set-ups, finding the differences, and tracing exposed wiring to two pieces of equipment inside Ollie's vehicle not present in his own.

"Alright," he starts. "This long tube here, this is the fuselage of a missile Silva partially dismantled and repurposed. That's the weapon core, but it looks like it attaches to this cylinder here."

"Yeah," interjects Ollie. "When I deployed the weapon, the sunroof opened, and that big coffee can looking thing went up and through it."

"Did you lose power?"

"The engine shut down right before the EMP fired."

"It's a built-in defense mechanism. The vehicle is shielded to a degree, but by shutting down all the electronics before the EMP fired, it protected itself from the blast. The batteries would have drained out, and you would have been a sitting duck."

"Good thing Silva was thinking ahead."

"Yes and no," replies Bishop. "Makes it more complicated. To get this all disassembled and then reassembled is way more than an hour."

"How long to just disassemble?" asks Takeshi.

"Best case, forty-five minutes."

"Okay, then get it done. We'll load your Hummer and the EMP on the chopper, and you can do the reassemble in flight en route."

"There's a small problem," says Bishop. "I can't test it, which is kind of important, but also, any undetected electrical surge when installing it could lead to an accidental discharge of the weapon."

"That would be bad, right?" quips Ollie.

"Only if you want to prevent us falling from the sky like a rock," says Bishop.

"Sorry," responds Takeshi. "This is the timeline, we have no wiggle room. We're airborne in forty-five. Whatever help you need, you'll get, but we gotta move."

Derek exits the hangar with a toolbox full of various wrenches and screwdrivers, a wire cutter and stripper, pliers, electrical tape, a circuit tester, fasteners, a power drill, tachometer, and clamp meter.

"This is everything I could find, where do we start?"

Bishop smiles at him and explains the basic construction of the EMP, the missile connected to the batteries, and how the extendable disbursement peers through the sunroof opening. With the battery already drained in Ollie's Hummer and no chance of the weapon firing, Bishop expertly disconnects the power supply and then the wires running along the floorboards to the disbursement arm and dash-mounted control switch, located in the same spot as the cloaking weapon in his Hummer. With Derek's help, they work together to relocate the bulky four-foot-long cylinder into Bishop's Hummer and then work to disassemble the mountings and motor for the disbursement arm. As they unscrew the last bolt from the metal housing attached to the Hummer floorboards, Takeshi, who has been loading gear and weapons into the Sea Stallion, with Ollie, Bloom and Charlie announces their departure in two minutes.

Bishop makes a final sweep of Ollie's Hummer to make sure no tools, wires, or parts have been left behind as Charlie goes through pre-check on the helicopter. The hefty rotors slowly turn as they walk up the lowered rear tailgate. Takeshi stands on the lip of the gate, nodding to each as they make their way in. As the last enters, he shouts inaudibly to Bishop, who completes his double-check of Ollie's Hummer and hustles over to Takeshi and up the metal incline into the belly of the Sea Stallion.

Takeshi slams his fist on the oval wall-mounted button, and

the tailgate raises up, achieving a clear "Closed" register on the cockpit control panel. He walks past the Hummer into the loading bay area behind the cockpit where Ollie, Wolcott, Bishop, and Bloom are all seated and strapped in via shoulder harnesses and finds a seat, placing a pair of noise-canceling headphones over his ears like the rest of the occupants. Charlie announces via the closed-circuit headset mic they are ready for takeoff as Derek, seated to his right in the co-pilot seat, plugs his tablet into an outlet to monitor the progress of the spoof Hummer signal currently in route back to Manhattan.

Now carrying an extra ten thousand pounds of weight thanks to the passengers, equipment, and vehicle parked in its bay, the helicopter creaks and moans. It slowly lifts off the tarmac to a safe cruising altitude before it makes its way southeast toward the Atlantic to follow the coastline back to Manhattan.

Over the headphones, Charlie announces their estimated time to the coast and instructs everyone to stay harnessed in as long as possible due to wind and rain as they travel south. He makes a point to mention "not do anything stupid like soldering wires on a weapon that could kill us all." Everyone gives Bishop a look and some smirks.

"Thanks," he says, waving a friendly middle finger to everyone. "I'll try not to."

"Charlie," says Takeshi via the headset, "we're going to have a slight detour before we head south. One more to join our little wrecking crew. I'll guide you there."

Bishop gives Takeshi an appreciative nod.

Lamb settles into the wall-mounted chair in his office, slipping back on the haptic gloves and VR goggles. His virtual desktop launches, and from a contact list, he grabs a file titled SATUPLINK and splits open using his thumb and forefinger.

In the worldwide nightfall following the asteroid's impact, communication via satellite, the bread and butter of the interconnected twenty-first-century world, was lost. Cellular towers were torn down and repurposed for various needs, while shortwave radio and Morse code made slow but growing comebacks. As the skies improved from pitch black to charcoal to their current consistent gray haze, Lamb had made it his pet project, off the books from the Manhattan Island board, to re-establish a connection with these satellites.

Though over five thousand satellites were orbiting earth pre-asteroid, slightly more than a third were operational, an average level of turnover from aged out models and regular slides into dysfunction. In the passing years, debris in the asteroid's wake had laid waste to hundreds, while others operating with limited lifespans to begin with had gone dark on schedule without replacement. Thanks to the plethora of satellite-based television programming originating from Manhattan, Lamb started bouncing radio signals from an uplink on top of the Brain using repurposed television satellite truck equipment. He found less than a hundred working communication, observation, and navigation/global positioning satellites still operational.

Using global positioning freeware, he was able to create 3-D mapping of the various medium and high-earth orbiting active satellite orbits. He began bouncing signals to gather intel from across the planet. Most of the observation satellites were useless thanks to the near-complete debris cloud cover of the globe, which darkened considerably over Eastern Europe, Russia, and Northern Asia, but electronics and communication monitoring were accessible. It was not long after he was able to tap into local ground communication of the various corporate cities dotting the North American landscape and became aware of Jasper Reynolds's consolidation of Midwestern cities as well as his hostile takeover of Boston.

It was around this time Lamb startled Reynolds by simply calling him on the phone. He discussed a conversation Reynolds had completed just moments before with one of his top military advisors about forecasts for an invasion force on Manhattan to secure what Reynolds repeatedly referred to as "the game-changer." After admitting to eavesdropping on Reynolds for some time, the two men engaging in a frank discussion of what each could do for the other. Lamb offered up the recent revelations of Doctor Wolcott as an opportunity to secure Reynolds a patsy in the form of Lloyd Rust on the Manhattan board in exchange for complete autonomy, while Reynolds could continue to expand his empire.

In the virtual space before him, Lamb reviews the real-time position of the current high-earth geostationary orbiting satellites and maps his best line of communication, linking the Brain to an old National Reconnaissance Office Quasar-project satellite. Once the uplink indicates a successful connection, a countdown clock appears on screen to show the window of time remaining before the satellite orbit will render it no longer viable. Calls with Reynolds rarely last longer than a minute or two, short enough that to reconnect via a secondary option is rarely necessary.

He selects "JR" from CONTACTS and taps the connect button, which brings up a generic display of human figure in place of a real-world avatar. Within the vaults of the Brain lie data files from a variety of defunct news organizations, one of which might have a picture of Reynolds, but Lamb has not bothered to place a face with the voice.

"Mr. Lamb, have you composed yourself following your little panic attack from this morning?" Lamb winces a bit, calling Reynolds after Tessa wound him up was a poor decision on his part.

"I'm fine, and I've been busy. More importantly, Nolan is in, she'll recover the data for us."

"Good job, how did you pull that off?" inquires Reynolds.

"I told her I would resign my position from the board to show her it wasn't about taking Vinick's job. She bought it."

"Thinking on your feet, nice work."

"Thank you. Based on her communications with Fenton in security, Vinick's son is still in route, ETA is between four and five this afternoon."

"Doesn't matter at this point, he's nothing more than insurance now."

"For the board and the city to turn against him, they'll need more than just corporate documents. We need his son to be out in front of this to explain Vinick's actions, both with Solear and what he was trying to do here in Manhattan. People don't know what kind of monster has been leading them."

"Fine and good, but there is still the issue of access for my team. It's the big picture I'm focused on. Elton and his son are the distraction, not the main course."

"It's covered. When Wolcott arrives, Bishop and Fenton will most likely take him straight to Mick to meet up with Nolan, so we must wait for them to confront Vinick. All hell will break loose, they'll call an emergency board meeting, and in the chaos, I'll hack the island security and give your men a red carpet to stroll in on."

"What about your evacuation, will you still be needing an escape route? I'm sure you can catch a ride with my team after they've completed their mission." Lamb can feel his face turn red with anger and embarrassment again.

"Let's table that for the moment. I'm secure here, and with the temporary leadership vacuum, I'll need to make sure Lloyd Rust takes interim control so we can remove Fenton and Nolan, and install loyal security forces."

"Good to hear, Mr. Lamb. By this time tomorrow, we will be onto the next phase of bringing humanity back online from the edge of extinction. When the new history books are written, your name will be among the great men to walk this earth, a rebuilder of civilization, and the start of a new renaissance."

Lamb was well acquainted with Vinick's megalomania. He doubted he would ever meet someone who could surpass such sky-high levels of narcissistic grandiosity. Yet Reynolds's ambition somehow exceeded it; his enthusiasm seemed quaint despite its ruthlessness - he couldn't rule the world if he didn't rebuild first.

CHAPTER 16

Regina Sanders unwraps gauze from the makeshift splint around her tender forearm and wrist. An explosion from a rocket-propelled grenade knocked her Hummer momentarily onto the driver's side and caught her arm in an awkward position, pressing the entire weight of her body onto her left arm. Fairly sure there isn't a break, the swelling and purple-blue coloring of the skin from the base of her palm to halfway up her forearm is uglier than it feels, though it would not be described as pleasant. Best she can figure, based on the reduced mobility of her wrist and fingers, is she has torn some ligaments but nothing more.

She had broken her left wrist on one occasion prior during a high school volleyball game in which she had miscalculated a dive and fractured it on the ankle of a teammate and had sprained it two other times she could recall. Thinking back, her left wrist and forearm had taken the brunt of every injury she had ever endured, though not all the memories were bad. She was masochistically fond of the sprain suffered during the thirtieth hour of labor with Kell. She reacted to a particularly strong contraction with a violent convulse that swung her left arm toward the side of the hospital bed. She thought it would connect with the thin but firm mattress but instead slammed the adjustable metal arm of the tray table she had temporarily forgotten. Perhaps sensing he had overstayed his welcome, Kell was born less than twenty minutes later. Regina's left forearm and wrist securely wrapped with an ice pack and soft cast.

Though light snow has fallen in Bangor, much of it in the field she currently resides in is thinly windswept. Attempts to scoop up and form a decent amount of snow into an ice pack for her wrist is aggravatingly slow. There has been no movement at the house where Wolcott is supposedly located. She decides to take some time to attend the growing throb in her arm when she first hears the faint sound of a helicopter in the distance.

Before she can make visual contact, she knows this is not the four-blade Apache she had encountered around Boston, but a more substantial six-blade model based on the rotational sound pattern currently on approach. The knowledge she had picked up during her time stationed at the Army Forces Command center at Fort Shelby in Mississippi.

She watches as a Sikorsky CH-53 Sea Stallion descends from the murk straight at her position, and decides it is pointless to put up a fight at this point. The beating taken by her Hummer has rendered the countermeasures and drones inoperable. She is down to her tranquilizer gun, a Glock, and an M110 sniper rifle, none of which were useful against what was bearing down on her location. Instead, she reaches into her duffle bag and grabs an energy bar, which she tears open with her teeth since a pinching movement with her left hand isn't an option. As he chomps down, the helicopter makes a circular sweep of the area before setting down in front of Sanders and the Hummer. The fuselage door slides open, and three men exit sans any visible weapons, which piques her curiosity.

As they approach, she instantly recognizes their uniforms, the same she is currently wearing courtesy Robert Fenton and the Manhattan Island Security surplus closet she had visited ten hours earlier. She tosses the half-eaten energy bar back into her duffel as she climbs to her feet. Rather than wait, she makes her way towards the group and meets them halfway.

"Hello, I'm Arch Takeshi," extending his right hand. "Looks like you got banged up on the way in." Sanders reciprocates the handshake, then does the same with Ollie and Bishop as they introduce themselves.

"Regina Sanders, I guess we're all on the same team here. Have you located the doctor?"

"Same team, and we have the doctor on board," responds Takeshi. "But our mission parameters have changed significantly. Why don't we get you and your gear on board, and we can brief you while the doc looks at your arm?" Sanders hesitates, giving them all a quick once over.

"I know, it's confusing," interjects Bishop. "You probably figured we were dead. That's what Fenton and Nolan must think about these two with their vehicles out of commission. But there's more to it, stuff they don't know. What did they offer you?"

"My son and I have debt to pay off."

"We all have people to get back to, and this ride can get us home for dinner, so whaddya say?" Sanders smiles her acknowledgment and hands her rifle to Bishop, then grabs her duffel off the ground and slings it over her shoulder as they make their way to the waiting helicopter.

After boarding the Sea Stallion, they lift off, wet spray kicking out below them. Wolcott examines Sanders's wrist and rewraps the splint while Bishop goes to work reassembling the EMP in his Hummer. To ensure the weapon will fire when needed, he disconnects both the cloaking system and active denial weapon. He builds a redundant circuit to ensure if the first connection to the power source fails, the second will automatically kick in. Usually, this sort of intricate process would be completed within the confines of a room temperature garage with adequate lighting and every tool imaginable at the ready. Instead, Bishop is getting regularly jostled in near-freezing temperatures as the helicopter navigates moderate gusts over the Atlantic, trying to give as wide a berth as possible to Boston without losing sight of the shore. If they drift too far out over the ocean, their lack of radar will most likely send them to a watery demise.

This bounces in and out of Bishop's head as he tries to delicately reconnect the intricate wiring to reactivate the weapon and accurately deploy the firing mechanism. As he twists and caps various connections, he can feel the shake slowly return to his hands, most likely due to the shot Wolcott gave him about twelve hours ago starting to wear off. The pangs of diacetylmorphine withdraw creep back into his fingers, along with the less than ideal temperature in the helicopter. He spots Takeshi, Bloom, and Wolcott talking with Sanders while Ollie leans back in his seat, eyes closed. He puts down his tools and walks over to Ollie and taps him on the shoulder, which elicits a slight squint.

"I need your help; I need a pair of steady hands."

"I'm getting my beauty rest."

"We'll probably all die if you don't help me. But, whatever." Ollie smirks at the remark, appreciating the gallows' humor and stretches his arms.

"Fine, I'll bail you out. Lead the way."

Ollie follows Bishop back to the Hummer, who hands him a soldering gun and explains the mounting of the EMP arm, which will extend through the roof of the vehicle. Even though the temperature inside the helicopter cargo bay is around thirty-five degrees, Bishop drips sweat as the tremors in his hands gradually spread throughout his body.

He steps away from the Hummer back toward where everyone is strapped in along the walls of Sea Stallion and takes a deep, shaky breath before collapsing into an unconscious heap on the cold metal floor.

⚓ ⚓ ⚓

Sandra Nolan faces her elevator doors waiting for the car to arrive to take her up one level to Elton Vinick. She considers her breathing in a way she rarely has. Calming herself, deep inhales and slow exhales. It feels like a hundred pounds are sitting on her chest. The car arrives and she steps in, depressing the familiar fifty-five button, and watches the doors close automatically.

Between the big and long toes in her right foot, she can feel the small plastic disc Lamb gave her, concealed beneath the slip-on athletic flats she currently wears. Her nerves make the disc seem like it is protruding through the shoe and pulsing with glowing heat. The elevator doors open, standing there in his regular spot is Xeno and his guards. She smiles and steps out, raising her arms as nonchalant as possible as Xeno scans with his metal detector.

"Keep seeing more and more of you these days," he quips.

"You know how it is when we get to the end of the fiscal year, and the board is being a particular pain this year."

"Yeah, Lamb especially," he says, running his hand along her legs. "One of these days that mouthy prick will piss off the wrong person. Luckily, I have remarkable patience." She lets out a soft snicker but makes a point not to look at Xeno as he passes over her feet and smiles at one of the guards who does not return the gesture.

Xeno stands up straight, "All set. The nurse was just through, so he might be resting after treatment."

"Thanks, I won't be long," says Nolan as she makes her way down the hall past the gym into the kitchen and living area. She spots Vinick in his chair, rubber tube running into the vein on his left hand as a steady flow of blood moves from the elevated IV bag into his body.

"Were we meeting today?" asks Vinick weakly, his eyes heavy and voice sluggish.

"I was going to let you rest today, but I have news, and I knew you would want to hear as soon as possible."

Nolan scans the room, searching for Vinick's computer.

"Is it about my son?"

"We're showing an asset en route back sometime this afternoon. Assuming they completed their mission and aren't returning empty-handed."

Not spotting it in the kitchen, she turns her attention to the tables and shelves in the living area.

"We can only wait and hope at this point," he says, trailing off.

"There's something else. Commander Fenton and I discovered a plot to interfere with the asset to prevent them from returning with your son." The computer is nowhere to be found. She feels a small sense of relief but immediately purges it, *where did he put it?*

"Lamb, I presume."

"Yes, but he's not working alone. We're still working on his accomplices, but at this point, he believes Commander Fenton and I are in league with him."

"Good, keep stringing him along so we can find out who his conspirators are, we can take them all down together. The world will be a better place without Nathan Lamb in it." She winces slightly at the implication, and Vinick realizes from her expression, he crossed an imaginary line. "Will you do me a favor, Sandy?"

"Sure, what is it?"

"I've got a bit of a chill. Will you go to my room and grab a blanket from my closet? On the top shelf. You'll see them."

Nolan feigns a smile, "No problem. Be right back."

She turns and walks through the living area away from the kitchen and front hall down a corridor to another open doorway. She steps inside the spacious bedroom, itself bigger than most of the multi-occupant apartments in Manhattan, with a king-sized bed surrounded by an array of medical equipment. Locating the entrance to the walk-in closet, she proceeds to retrieve one of the neatly folded blankets from the overhead shelf.

As she exits and makes her way back out of the room, she spots Vinick's computer resting on the dresser to the left of the bed.

Her heart races.

She steps to the doorway and peers out. As expected, no one is there. She places the blanket on the edge of the bed and hurries over to the dresser, grabs the computer, sits down, and unfolds the tablet screen from its keyboard, using the swipe left gesture to activate. In the center of the black screen, the word PASSWORD appears next to a small rectangular box.

Over the many years together, Nolan had managed various business email accounts for Vinick. Half the time, emails of praise or recognition received by employees, meeting reservations, and generic replies to underlings were the handiwork of Nolan, written in Vinick's voice. Before entering, she had considered what Vinick might be using for a password on this computer. His favorite classical music pieces, all which Nolan had performed, had been used in the past. It was merely a matter of figuring out which one he is currently using. If, for example, he is using Mozart's Symphony No. 40, the password would likely be 40GMINORKV550, encompassing the description, key, and chronological composition number in the Kochel catalog of Mozart's works.

But Nolan realizes she has a problem.

While she was aware of Vinick's favorites, her first entry fails with the warning, "Incorrect Password. Two attempts left."

If it isn't Mozart, her next best guess is Bach, his top choice being the Brandenberg Concerto No. 3. She tries NO3GMAJORBWV1048 (BWV being its location in the Bach-Works-Catalogue).

Another failure.

One chance left before the computer will freeze, which will no doubt require a secondary password to unlock the machine for another three tries.

With Mozart and Bach both failures, she contemplates her third attempt. *It must be Beethoven.*

Vinick was fascinated by Beethoven's late third period when he had lost his hearing yet still composed the Grand Fuge, the Ninth Symphony, Missa Solemnis and the composition he revered the most, String Quartet No. 14 in C# minor.

She keys in the phrase NO14C#MINOROP131. The black screen disappears, the computer unlocks, revealing the desktop.

She slips off her shoe and grabs the disk between her toes, squeezing it between her fingers as Lamb showed her. It activates, and she places it on the computer. The magnet adheres, and a rectangular prompt box appears on the screen.

```
SCANNING HARD DRIVE VOLUMES...
HARD DRIVE SCAN COMPLETE...
15.7 TERABYTE...
ESTIMATED TRANSFER TIME 420 SECONDS
PROCEED TRANSFER Y/N
```

She presses the Y key, and a visual representation of files transferring from the computer to the external drive appears along with a percentage complete bar and countdown clock. She watches each excruciating second countdown as the bar creeps closer and closer to halfway, periodically peering over her shoulder at the doorway to the hall. The seconds continue to tick down as the completion bar slowly counts down...90%....95%....99%....100%.

The prompt box flashes TRANSFER COMPLETE - OK TO DISCONNECT, and she peels the magnetic disk from the computer, squeezing it again to turn it off and places it back between her toes. She folds the laptop to the closed position and puts it back on the dresser and smooths out the portion of the bed where she sat before, grabs the blanket off the edge of the bed, and heads to the doorway. When she reaches the opening, she freezes. Standing on the other side, leaning on his cane, is Vinick.

"I think we need to talk, don't you, Sandy?" She looks past Vinick down the corridor and sees Xeno at the end of the short hallway.

"Maybe we do." She feels panic at first but pushes it down. "You have a lot of explaining to do."

"Do I?" says Vinick, turning away.

"Let's have a cup of tea in the kitchen and discuss for which sins I need to answer." She slowly follows behind him. "But don't think your hands are clean, my dear. Just because you didn't pull the trigger doesn't mean you're innocent. You provided plenty of the bullets, and you reaped the rewards."

They walk back out into the living area and into the kitchen, Xeno stands in the hallway leading to the elevator, blocking the only exit. Nolan trails Vinick, who walks over to the stove and pulls out two coffee mugs from an overhead cabinet, fills them with hot water from a kettle on the stovetop, and places them on saucers. He hands one to Nolan, who takes it and sits at the kitchen table, grabbing a teabag from a metal container on the table. Vinick follows and sits across from her.

"So, you were saying how I have a lot answer for?" he quips.

"Solear. The asteroid mining project. You're responsible for all of it. Billions of people died because of you did."

"What WE did," he retorts. "You reviewed the contracts. You crunched the numbers. You had access to everything. You just weren't in the room when the hard decisions had to be made. Maybe I coddled you too much. Maybe I should have let you see the blood along with the sweat, get your hands really dirty. Then this babe in the woods act wouldn't be so pathetic." She is both taken aback and infuriated by Vinick, but also ashamed.

She drank up the promises of wealth and power like anyone would. She coddled thoughts of building the occasional hospital wing or creating college endowments. Believed these balanced the business concerns leading to debilitated environmental regulations, monopolized markets, and toppled financially "unfriendly" third world governments. The only difference this time is Vinick had kept her out of the biggest loop of them all.

"That may be true, but you're lying about your medical condition. What's the real reason for bringing your son back here? You don't need a surgeon."

"This blood they give me, it's a technical match, but for it to work, it needs to be a relation. The ideal situation would be a transfusion maybe once a week instead of daily. A fresh oil change, and when needed, some spare parts. Kidney, liver, lungs, those sorts of things. Stems cells would be useful as well, the advances that have been made with cell regeneration..."

"Spare parts? Stem cells? What the hell is wrong with you?"

"You're getting bogged down in the minutia, why aren't you questioning what is motivating Lamb? You're smarter than this, Sandy. He isn't altruistic, this isn't about exposing me as some monster. Why aren't you asking yourself what his real agenda is?"

"The asteroid wasn't minutia," she growls. "It was genocide."

"We did everything we could to try to prevent it, but a mission failure would have caused economic ripples in financial markets around the globe had Solear and its various subsidiaries gone under. Ten of thousands of jobs lost. The world economy in a free fall. We could never allow that to happen.

We were smart enough to plan for and execute the necessary

contingencies to properly prepare for the post-asteroid world. Had we not been ready, well, I wonder if the whole damn planet would have devolved into a living hell akin to Dante's Inferno. You're just not privy to the entire chessboard the way I am. It's no longer about survival, we're rebuilding society from the ground up. We are protected by our walls now, but those days are numbered, and we will need to expand. All the cities will. It's the new gold rush, the skies get clearer every year, the air becomes more breathable. Either we will expand, or someone else will. I plan on being around for as long as possible, to reconnect and remake this world."

"Dear God, you want to rule the whole world, don't you?"

"No," he spits out defensively. "I'm not a fool. I know my time is limited. By all rights, I should be dead already. Every extra day or month or year I remain upright thanks to the transfusions or an occasional transplant is a day this island thrives. Believe me, there are men out there who want Manhattan for themselves, for its labor, its technology, and its military. It's why your new friend Nathan Lamb is so keen to turn you against me and take me down. He's been given access to the big picture, and now he's working against us, against this island, against what we have built. But I won't let him. I've still got some tricks up my very old sleeves."

Nolan feels the phone in her pocket vibrate. She pulls it out and reads the message appearing on the screen.

"Well, I guess we're about to find out. Fenton has tracked the returning assets signal to less than two hours outside Manhattan. You're about to be reunited with your son."

"I doubt he'll be pleased to see me," Vinick smirks. "I understood his betrayal; his mother had poisoned his mind against me long ago. But you, Sandy, for you to turn against me, I am truly hurt."

Her blood rises, and for a moment, she considers getting up and attacking Vinick but looks at Xeno and thinks better of it.

"You're hurt? That's rich. Is that why you lied to my parents when they came to the island?"

For the first time she can remember, Vinick is stunned into silence.

"Where's your long-winded, self-congratulatory speech now, Elton?" He says nothing as he winces, staring down at his steaming coffee mug.

"When this is over, Elton, remember: you did this. Just you. No board of directors. No shareholders. You."

▲ ▲ ▲

Bishop sits straight up, the cold metal of the helicopter pulses beneath his hands. He looks blurrily around, spotting the familiar faces gathered. Wolcott, squatting next to him, places a hand on Bishop's shoulder.

"How do you feel?"

"Fantastic," quips Bishop.

"Ladies and gentlemen, he does not," says Wolcott.

"What happened?"

"You collapsed. The shot I gave you yesterday had worn off, and the withdrawal knocked you on your ass."

"Why aren't we moving? Are we on the ground already?"

"You've been out for about three hours, we touched down an hour or so ago. I gave you another shot, but the sedative put you out good, so we had to give you another something to get going again." Bishop looks down at his left arms, both sleeves rolled up with tape over gauze in his elbow crooks.

"What the hell'd you give me? I feel like I just drank a pot of coffee. Like, really good, super fueled coffee."

"So, back in the day, some clinical testing was using Ritalin to bring patients quickly out of anesthesia. Luckily, there is a vast amount of unused Ritalin, so we've been filtering them for post-surgery use at the hospital. When you're ready, go ahead and stand up."

Bishop pushes himself to his feet and immediately feels lightheaded, losing his balance for a moment before steadying himself.

"Give me a status report," he says, his focus coming and going. Derek, tablet in hand, clears his throat.

"Uh, me and Ollie, I mean, Ollie and I finished installing the EMP. We think it's operational. Hopefully, fingers crossed. So, that's done. Spoof signal is on schedule, will rendezvous with our location in forty-eight minutes. We are still on for the departure time of three o'clock, I mean, fifteen hundred hours. And, uh, well, there's one other thing."

"There is activity from Boston," interjects Takeshi. "Just south of New Haven, we saw multiple birds in the air. Four Apaches heading south, looked like they were hugging the highway. I happened to catch them on a pair of binoculars, don't think they had eyes our way, so we slipped past them. They were moving slow, probably running protection for something on the ground at only about fifty miles an hour. At this point, if they're coming our way, they're about an hour and a half behind us."

"Where's Sanders?" asks Bishop, looking around. He spots her on the ground talking with Bloom near the offloaded

Hummer and hops down from the helicopter onto the highway asphalt.

"Sanders," he calls out, who spots him and makes her way over. "You made it past Boston after me, how'd you get through?"

"Route 95 the whole way, why?"

"Did you see a convoy of tractor-trailers? When I went through, they were moving trucks from downtown out to 95."

"Yeah, on the southbound side of the 95 loop, before it splits off from Route number one and heads back south, there were probably a dozen trucks with trailers parked there. I figured they were using them for the blockade, like how they had the trailers spread out along the northbound lane, but they still had cabs attached."

"Thanks," he says to Sanders and turns back to Wolcott and the group. "I think your mom was right. I think Reynolds is making his move on Manhattan. And they're moving something in those trucks."

"Unless those trucks are empty," interjects Sanders.

"We need to move up our timetable," says Takeshi. "Derek, what's the rate of the spoof signal coming back?" Derek doesn't have to look at the tablet.

"Right now, it's traveling about forty-five miles an hour," he says.

"Can you increase to seventy?" asks Takeshi. "It will trim some time off, maybe fifteen or twenty minutes. We can't wait around and go up against those Apaches and whatever they've got on the ground."

"Screw the signal, let's go now," says Bishop.

"That will heavily mess with our timetable, we'll need to

adjust," says Derek.

"Bishop is right, we need to get this show on the road," says Ollie. "Get him into the city, he can scoop up his old lady and deploy the weapon before we're in a firefight."

"So, why's everybody standing around?" barks Takeshi. "The Hummer is on the move in five minutes. Everyone else, gear up and back on the chopper."

There is a flurry of activity as everyone opens various duffel bags, divvying out Kevlar chest, thigh and arm sleeves, magazine clips, cold weather hats and gloves, and other gear before climbing back into the helicopter.

Bishop enters the Hummer and starts the engine, which silently comes to life with a hum. Wolcott opens the passenger door and climbs in. They watch as Takeshi approaches the Hummer, leaning over to the driver side window as the Sea Stallion rotors slowly turn behind him.

"Let's synchronize countdown," says Takeshi, raising his arm and accessing the watch on his wrist. Bishop does the same. "In sixty minutes, we will be inbound on Manhattan, EMP deployed, rendezvous at the Mick. Start the countdown now."

60:00...

59:59...

59:58...

CHAPTER

17

Bishop and Wolcott reach the boroughs outside Manhattan on schedule without incident, the Hummer generating stares from the few inhabitants milling about in the cold afternoon. The militarized vehicle is a rich target in the Free Zone, and Bishop is aware they need to make their stop brief. As they approach the apartment building on Walton Avenue, Bishop spots a military-style vehicle parked outside, giving him pause. No resident would leave their vehicle if they had one, parked outside and unattended. There were only two groups who have consistent access to vehicles like this - the military and well-organized gangs.

He pulls the Hummer slowly parallel to the parked vehicle and looks it over. If he was a betting man, he would put his money on the military rather than the gang. It was too clean, gangs liked to mark their vehicles as a warning, like a sports team logo, and this had no markings. Bishop parks the Hummer closer to the entrance of the building and checks his watch.

"My gut says to bring you along, but my head says if folks show up with a tow truck and try to jack our ride, we need someone to deal with them. You think you can handle it?"

"Not gonna lie," responds Wolcott. "I'm not too handy with a gun."

"You don't need to be. This thing is bulletproof, so no one is getting in. You just need to open the hatch and fire a few rounds in their direction if anyone gets the idea this isn't guarded."

"All right, I can do that," says Wolcott, already nervous at the thought. Bishop grabs his duffel bag from behind his seat and pulls out the pair of 9mm pistols along with extra loaded clips. Handing one to Wolcott and holstering one for himself, he explains ejecting a spent clip and inserting a new one.

"Honestly, if I hear gunshots, I'll be back out before you'll be able to reload anyway. This is all just a precaution."

"I know it is, so let's not waste any more time. Go get your wife."

Bishop is out of the Hummer and to the front doors in a flash. Through the glass entryway, he spies a scene he is unsure of and slows as he reaches the first set of doors. He steps inside the foyer and waits at the second set of glass doors. Inside, two tall men in tracksuits, one black, the other red, supervise a group of people hurriedly cleaning what appears to be blood and viscera off the tile floor with mops and sponges, while another group zip-up black body bags. The man in the red tracksuit spots Bishop and leans over the counter to speak into a microphone.

"State your business," he says.

"I'm here to see Tessa Dawes, she's a resident."

"And you are?"

"I'm her husband."

"Okay, she said you'd be here today. I'm supposed to ask you a question, to confirm you are who you say you are," he says.

"Go ahead."

"After you got married, where did you go?"

Bishop smirks to himself. "The Dank," he says.

He hadn't thought of that place in a long time, or not by name. The off-the-strip dive bar in Las Vegas where they had their first date and returned two years later after a courthouse marriage for punk rock karaoke, two-for-one tacos, and cheap champagne. Their joy would be cut short, when the television above the bar, like every television across the globe, cut away from regular programming to carry an unprecedented broadcast by world leaders announcing the discovery of an imminent threat to all life on earth.

A buzzer announces the unlocking of the second set of glass doors, which Bishop pushes through, eyes fixed on the pool of blood on the floor ahead. The two men walk around the mess and approach him in tandem. When they meet, Bishop realizes just how truly tall these men are, as he cannot see over either of their shoulders. Their imposing leg and arm muscles press against the fabric of the tracksuits - these two are unquestionably heavy steroid users. He surmises these two are the legendary Italian Brothers. They introduce themselves - Anthony in red, Matthew in black.

"Please excuse the mess," says Anthony. "The safety of our residents is of the utmost concern. Unfortunately, we had a pair of employees who betrayed our customer service principle, so they had to be retired."

"We want you to know," interjects Matthew, "because of your wife's relationship with our family, the cost to repair the door and remove the corpses from her apartment will not be taken out of her deposit. Consider it a gesture of apology."

Bishop considers probing for more information.

Repair the door? Corpses? What the hell happened here?

He instead thanks them and asks for her room number, then urgently moves down the hall to the stairwell up the second floor to her room. He notices the doorknob is gone but decides to knock rather than enter. A moment later, and she stands before him. The first time they have been face-to-face in the flesh in a year and a half.

All the weathered strength momentarily melts away. Their embrace is vice-like, they can feel the bones poking through malnourished bodies. A long, deep kiss gives way to euphoric giggles and tears.

"The brothers tell me you had some unwanted guests," he jokes.

"You have no idea what the last two days have been like," she says. "Come in, there are some people you need to meet." He happily follows her into the apartment.

"Ok, but we're on a tight schedule. We're leaving in five-" He sees Kell sitting in a chair, gun in hand, watching over Ward, lying prone on the ground, makeshift bandages around his legs and his hands tied. "-what is going on here?"

"Oh, God. Where to start?" she says, mildly exasperated at the thought of recapping the last forty-eight hours.

"After you called me, I went to the trader market and got kidnapped and locked in a cell at the Bronx Zoo by Ward, who is on the floor. He told me your mission had to be stopped. He's working with some guy named Nathan Lamb on the island. The people who sent you sent someone else after you, and then Ward and his men kidnapped Kell here and stuck him in the cell with me. But we broke out and made our way back the apartment. Ward tracked us back here, but Kell and I took care of his team and have been waiting for you. I think that sums it up. Did I miss anything? Kell? Ward?"

They both shake their heads.

Bishop checks his watch.

"Shit, we gotta move. Okay, a lot of information to process, and we'll talk about this more on the ride because it is not all adding up. However, we're on a timetable, we gotta be heading to the island in three minutes, so grab what you need and let's move."

"We're ready," she says, grabbing a packed bag off the bed and tossing it to Kell while grabbing another and slinging it over her shoulder. "But what are we going to do with him?"

"We bring him," says Bishop, kneeling over Ward. "Can you walk at all?"

"Not without help," Ward grimaces.

"I'll give you a hand, but do not try anything, or I'll end you right then and there, clear?"

"Crystal."

Bishop grabs both of Ward's hands and helps him up off the ground. Ward throws one of his arms around Bishop's neck and winces in pain as he tries to walk but ends up in more of a hobbled limp. As the mental seconds tick down, Bishop strains to try to move down the hallway with Ward as Tessa knocks on the door across the corridor. As she watches Kell trail Bishop slowly down the hall, Gertrude opens the door to her apartment.

"I have to go, Gertie," says Tessa. "Thank you for your help today. I wouldn't have survived all this time without you as my neighbor." She feels herself tearing up and fights it.

"Come here, hon." Gertrude holds open her arms, and they embrace a warm familial hug. "You've got a long life ahead of you, I know it. Go do something wonderful."

"I will." She turns and starts to walk away but gives Gertrude a wave and receives one in return, then jogs to meet up with the group as they reach the stairwell to the first floor.

Rather than have Ward limp down the stairs, Kell and Bishop both lift and carry him down, giving his wounded legs a brief respite. As they move down the first-floor hallway to the foyer, they see the clean-up crew mopping and sponging up the last remnants of guards who once staffed the front desk. Bishop pauses to address the brothers.

"I've got something for you guys, a thank you gift. I'll be right back after I get them to the truck."

"No thank you is necessary," says Anthony.

"Still, I think you guys will appreciate this." The group makes their way out to the Hummer where Wolcott waits, relieved to see them make it back without any complications on his end.

"It's gonna be a little tight, was only expecting to have three passengers, not five. There's some space in the back-seat area, it's not the best situation because of the engine, but Ward should be able to lie along one side, and Kell, you'll be able to squeeze in on the other. Tessa, you'll have to ride up front with me and the doc. Everyone say hello to Doctor Marion Wolcott. Son of one Elton Vinick." They exchange quick hellos as everyone finds their place in the Hummer. "Hey Ward, is that truck over there your ride?"

"Yeah, that's mine."

"Thought so, got the key?" Ward reaches into his pocket and pulls out a single key on a metal ring and hands it to Bishop. From behind the driver seat, he grabs the CheyTac M200 sniper rifle along with its magazines and rounds and marches back to the front doors of the apartment. Upon approach, the brothers unlock the doors and Bishop enters, proudly displaying his gift.

"This, gentlemen, is the deadliest sniper rifle ever built, the CheyTac M200. Please take it as a token of my appreciation for giving Tessa a safe place to reside this last year and a half." He hands over the gun to Anthony and places the magazines and boxes of rounds on the front desk.

"This is beautiful," says Anthony, giving the weapon a loving once-over.

"Oh yeah, and if you want it, there's a nice little truck out front. Grenade launcher attached. Here's the key. Enjoy, stay safe."

He tosses it to Matthew, who catches it in a clean swipe, and makes his way back outside through the glass doors to the Hummer, where the group has found their uncomfortable spots inside. Bishop climbs inside and starts the engine.

"Everyone listen up, here's how this is going to go down."

As he weaves the Hummer through the city streets en route to the tunnel back into Manhattan, Bishop explains it all: the drive to and through the tunnel into the garage at security HQ, the EMP weapon, and the assault team in the helicopter relying on them to fire the weapon on time so they are not shot down by the tower gun defenses. The group then exchanges conflicting information about Nathan Lamb, Wolcott claiming he is an ally, instrumental in helping expose Vinick and Solear, and Tessa calling dibs on gutting him like a freshly caught trout for arranging her and Kell's kidnapping.

"Wait a sec," interjects Bishop. "Is your mom Regina

Sanders?"

"Yeah, do you know where she is? Is she okay?"

"She's fine. She's with the assault team. We picked her up just as she arrived in town." Tessa turns to the back seat and exchanges a smile with Kell, who is relieved but tries not to show emotion, though some peek through.

Bishop considers the info he just relayed. "Wait, there should be one more. Arch Takeshi's wife?"

"What do you mean?" asks Tessa.

"Two other guys made it to Bangor before me. They're on the chopper with Kell's mom. Arch Takeshi and Ollie DuBois. Their vehicles both got wrecked, so Fenton probably lost their tracking signal. Ollie didn't have anyone, he said they were just going to bump his rank and give him a bunch of credits. But Takeshi said he and his wife both had a lot of debt to pay off. Where is she?"

Tessa glares at Ward in the back seat. "She's dead, isn't she? You killed her, you son of a bitch." He doesn't flinch.

"I did what I was paid to do, just like your husband," retorts Ward. "Tell her what you did defending that wall, Bishop. Tell her about the people, the families, who tried to sneak onto the island. I used to work the wall, just like him. You don't get to sit around and have discussions about morality. Did I kill some guy's wife? Yeah, and plenty of others. I did what I had to, and I got to go home at night, just like your husband. I have zero regrets. I'm alive. My wife is alive. My kid is alive. They're safe and housed and fed, and it's all I got. You got a problem with what I'm saying, take it up with your husband."

Silence. Tessa and Bishop know Ward is right, and they are as disgusted at themselves, at what they have been forced to become, to survive and scrape out some level of security, as much as they are angered at him for verbalizing it. The Hummer cruises beneath the dilapidated Major Deegan Expressway along Third Avenue.

"We're here," says Bishop, breaking the tension. In front of them lies the Third Avenue Bridge, at the far end the hulking gate and behind it, the guard station and various weapons meant to keep interlopers at bay. "Hopefully, Fenton is monitoring and will notify the guard station, otherwise..."

"Otherwise, we're dead?" asks Kell.

"Exactly."

The Hummer continues along Third Avenue. Green traffic signs once hanging above the bridge in the metal scaffolds have been replaced with large red signs with stay-the-hell-away text:

DO NOT CONTINUE
WITHOUT AUTHORIZATION
TRESPASSERS SHOT ON SIGHT
NO EXCEPTIONS

"I hope you're right," says Tessa, giving Bishop a worried glance. He reaches for her hand and gives it a gentle squeeze. They pass beneath the signage toward the gate. Along the edges of the five-lane road lie the framework of various vehicles, all smashed and scorched from surface-to-surface missiles and heavy artillery.

It does not go unnoticed by anyone in the vehicle.

"They haven't killed us yet. That's a good sign, right?" remarks Wolcott. Bishop smirks in agreement as the Hummer slows to a stop outside the wall gate, multiple surveillance cameras focused on their location. For an agonizing moment, there is nothing—finally, the sound of large gears turning, metal and concrete shifting. The gate opens.

"Piece of cake," says Bishop, able to exhale again.

Crossing the threshold, Bishop glances at the guard station ahead. From it emerges a dozen heavily armed and armored soldiers, one of whom throws up a hand stop sign while the others encircle the Hummer. Behind them, the gate closes.

The guard approaches the driver's side door, and Bishop slides open the metal porthole.

"Please extend your hand through the opening for an I.D. scan," states the guard in an elevated voice. Bishop does as instructed and using a mobile chip scanner places Bishop's finger on a small rectangular piece of glass the size of a cell phone. On the scanner, the text DAWES, BISHOP appears with an image of his face, his island I.D. number, current address, and security clearance level. He brings the device to his ear.

"Sir," says the guard, peering into the vehicle, "we have I.D. confirmation on the vehicle, it's Bishop Dawes. Also in the vehicle are a female and male in the front seat, and two males in the back seat. Okay, sir. I will." He slides the phone through the porthole to Bishop, who takes it and puts it to his ear, shooting a bemused look to Tessa.

"Hello?"

"Glad you made it back in one piece."

"Thank you, sir. It is good to be back. I have Dr. Wolcott with me, safe and sound."

"And your wife as well, I'm told."

"Yessir."

"I'm told you have to additional passengers, care to explain?"

"I have Kell Sanders, the son of Regina Sanders. I believe you know who she is, sir."

"I do, I do," says Fenton, caught off guard. "What about your fifth."

"Sir, I've got Ward-," he cups the phone, looks to the back seat.

"What's your last name?"

"Whaley,"

"Ward Whaley says he used to be one of yours. He's injured."

"He was. That's... odd. Well, you've put together an interesting group. Guess we should bring you in and have a talk about it."

"I agree, sir." He hands the phone back to the guard, who, after receiving instructions, gives the signal to the other soldiers to return to the guard station.

"You know your way through the tunnels?"

"I do."

The guard steps back and gives a clear sign to the rest of the soldiers, who lower their weapons and clear a path for the Hummer. Bishop accelerates toward East 129th Street, turning onto Lexington Avenue and finally to the ramp, taking them to the garage door at the entrance to the tunnels. He checks his watch.

"Dammit, we are late."

"How late?" asks Wolcott. The garage door to the tunnels slowly rises.

"It took me ten minutes to get through the tunnels last time. We've got about seven and a half."

"Then drive fast!" exclaims Kell.

"Hang on." With the door open fully, Bishop guides the Hummer down into the tunnel, murky sunlight disappears behind them as they slip into the halogen lighted concrete tube once home to the New York subway system.

Flooded and severely damaged following the asteroid, rail cars, tracks, and other useful pieces of metal were repurposed in the above-ground repair of existing structures and construction of new buildings wherever space allowed. The tunnels are now the sole domain of executives and security personnel, who use it to traverse the city undetected by the general population.

Surveillance cameras track Bishop's progress as he pushes the Hummer as hard as possible through the narrow passages. Most who drive these did so at a consistent sub-thirty mile an hour pace, accounting for sections of low lighting and the uneven makeshift roads. At a clip of almost fifty, he loses his right rearview mirror, thanks to a protruding drainpipe. The Hummer skids to a screeching halt past a connecting cross tunnel, which will take them the final stretch to the last door outside the main security garage where Silva and Fenton handed over the Hummer.

As they reach the final gate, Bishop rechecks his watch. One minute until the deadline, then the assault team liftoff and make their five-minute flight to Manhattan. He flashes his headlights at the gate. Finally, the last door starts its slow ascent. The metal panels creak upward far enough; he can accelerate into the garage. Waiting ahead are Fenton and Silva, who is thrilled one of his vehicles actually made it back, clapping and giving Bishop and enthusiastic thumbs up, shouting to the mechanics in the area, "That's right! That's one tough bastard right there!"

Silva's face contorts from unbridled glee to concerned confusion as the Hummer comes to an abrupt stop before reaching the vehicle repair bay, the sunroof panel opens, and a dish mounted on a metal pole pokes through.

"Wait, what the-" Before Silva can finish his thought, the entire garage goes pitch black and silent. Air vents go quiet, powered tools drop dormant, emergency lighting fails to kick on.

"What the hell is going on?" yells Fenton, suddenly disoriented and feeling around for something to grab onto as if he just fell into unfamiliar water above his head. He grabs the phone out of his pocket, thinking he can use it as a light source, but it is drained dead.

"That was the EMP stick," says Silva, feeling his way around on the floor. "I only put that in a few vehicles we sent out. We put the active denial system in Bishop's ride, this doesn't make sense."

"Bishop. Bishop! What the hell is going on?! What are you doing?!" Fenton blindly finds a tool cart and fumbles around trying to find a hammer or some sort of weapon. It's then he feels a hand grip his forearm and hears the cart kicked away.

"Sorry sir, we don't have time. I'll explain on the way," says Bishop, wearing infrared night vision goggles. Around him, also outfitted with goggles and armed with pistols, Tessa and Wolcott grab Silva and the half dozen mechanics in the area and guide them into the nearby locker room.

"We're going to the Mick. We need to go see Elton Vinick," says Bishop.

"Why did you deploy an EMP? You just crippled the island defenses!" spits out Fenton.

"An inbound Sikorsky Sea Stallion carrying an assault team will be landing on the roof of the Mick in less than ten minutes to neutralize Vinick's security detail. On the chopper are Arch Takeshi, Ollie DuBois, and Regina Sanders."

"Arch and Ollie are alive?" Fenton is both shocked and

relieved at the news. "Look, I'm on your side here-"

Tessa interrupts. "What do we do with Ward?"

"Put him in the locker room, he's not going anywhere."

"I'll grab Kell and guide him through," says Wolcott.

"Thanks," says Bishop. "So, you were saying, you're on our side, huh? What does that even mean?"

"Nolan and I figured out what Nathan Lamb has been up to."

"There's that name again. Keep walking."

"Lamb has been working against us. He was monitoring the assets we were sending out and then kidnapping their family members, we assume in the event if any of you made it back, to force you to hand over the doctor. Eventually, Vinick would run out of time, and Lamb would make a move to become CEO."

"Well, you got part of the puzzle, but not the whole thing. Ward was running the snatch and grab for him, but it is not only Lamb who wants the island, we think he's colluding with someone named Jasper Reynolds who is consolidating power out in the Midwest. He's got five cities under his control, and he's using Boston as a forward operating base for a strike against the island."

"Dear God."

They reach the emergency stairwell, Tessa, Wolcott, and Kell trail just behind, and climb the steps.

"It gets worse." Bishop tells him about Takeshi's wife, and it momentarily stops Fenton in his tracks.

"When we find Lamb, I'm gonna kill him," blurts Fenton.

"Get in line," says Tessa.

They reach the ground level and move through the door into the main hallway, the same main halls Bishop has exited every day for the last year and a half to the outside world. He stops the group just before the final door.

"We need to get to Vinick's computer. Wolcott saw information linking Vinick and Solear to the asteroid. They caused this, now it's up to us to finish it. Can you get us into the Mick?"

"It's not that simple. Nobody goes up without an appointment," explains Fenton. "Everything has to be pre-authorized to get off the ground floor. Even I can't override the procedures."

"How many guards?"

"Two on the interior doors, two on the front desk, plus another dozen on the ready."

"Is that all?" Bishop blurts with exasperation.

"And both front desk guards have access to a kill switch to disable the elevators until released by Sandra Nolan. That's if your EMP didn't take out the building power already."

"The range was purposely minimal, designed specifically for the security computer center to take out the tower guns. Let's move. Should have been clear of the Mick"

Bishop pulls off his mask, Wolcott and Tessa follow, as he pushes through the exit door onto the street. As they step out, they see confused and disoriented people everywhere, staring at their blank cell phones, cars stopped, building front's dark. Bishop checks his analog watch.

"Choppers in the air, they should reach the Mick in six minutes."

"So how do we get to the Mick?" asks Wolcott. "The EMP took out all of our transportation options." Bishop looks around the area, seeing everything at a dim standstill.

"We run."

18

Lamb frantically scrolls via his VR screen through a list of security cameras, cell phones, computers, and every other electronic device with visual or audio capability. Sometime in the last minute, a power outage had struck everything between 34th Street and Canal Street, rendering a large chunk of the lower portion of Manhattan Island invisible.

The bottom tip of the island, where Lamb is safely ensconced in the tower of the data center, is unaffected. Power outages, though rare, were not unheard of, yet this was more. Personal devices are impacted, handhelds off the grid. More importantly, the blackout has struck the underground headquarters of island security, rendering the ring of tower guns encircling the island on top of the wall inert. Aside from the guards with automatic rifles in portholes along the wall, the island is effectively defenseless.

Someone, he concludes, has detonated an EMP specifically targeting island security, and someone, in his mind, is most likely

Jasper Reynolds.

Unable to find a single audio or visual feed from the impacted area, he shifts his focus, re-establishes a satellite link, and via his contact list dials Reynolds. It rings for an agonizing half minute before Reynolds accepts the call.

"Wasn't expecting to hear from you so soon."

"Something is happening here, have your men arrived?" asks Lamb in shrill panic. "Are they attacking the island? What the hell is going on?"

"Calm down, for god sakes. Last report I received; the convoy is still en route. Now compose yourself and explain."

"Okay. About a quarter of the island has lost power, it's a complete blackout. But it's not a supply outage. Everything in the area, from handheld devices to vehicles, which includes the island security headquarters, is out. It's like an electromagnetic pulse weapon was discharged."

"Well, that just made our jobs a little bit easier, don't you think?"

"Yes and no," says an exacerbated Lamb. "With security feeds down, I've lost most of my eyes and ears. We're trying to avoid chaos and panic in removing Vinick."

"I could give a damn about chaos and panic; you just make sure my men get in and complete their mission, or else you will be left behind in the rubble. Do we understand each other?"

Lamb stiffens, his blood up at Reynolds's tone.

"I don't think you understand me, Jasper. Without power, the tower guns may be down, but so are all the access tunnels I was going to open. Your men are going to be parked out there with no way inside, sitting ducks on the bridge once they're spotted by the snipers."

"From what I'm told, our convoy will be there in the next thirty to forty minutes. You have until then to get this situation under control." Reynolds disconnects the call. Lamb closes the contact list on his screen and, via a series of animated gestures, recalls a program titled MOSAIC.

"Mosaic, activate all devices and render."

RENDERING INITIATED...
RENDERING... 50% COMPLETE...
RENDERING... COMPLETE.

"Mosaic, apply vantage via One World Trade Center."

Lamb's VR display switches from a black screen with lines of computer text to a digitized recreation of Manhattan from the top of One World Trade Center. Using hand gestures, he can rotate three hundred and sixty degrees, zooming in and out down to the ground with high definition quality. To the south, perfect real-time imaging of the southern tip of the island. As he swings north, an immense void appears where the EMP detonation and its subsequent wake darkens the display.

He moves into and above the void, looking down like GPS satellite mapping. As he pans out, he notices a circular edge to the blackout zone, curving northward through the East Village to the banks of the East River, then back in between Kips Bay and Murray Hill, clipping the Empire State Building into Chelsea.

Utilizing a digital compass caliper application, he draws an outline of the circle, crossing west over the Hudson River, south through the wasteland formerly known as Hoboken and back east just below the Holland Tunnel.

A near-perfect circle, no doubt an EMP was deployed, but where?

"Mosaic, recall previous render and overlay in incomplete data."

RECALLING... RECALLING...
RECALL COMPLETE.

He watches as the void is filled in by a still composite of life. Along the edges, movement exits and enters, disappearing and appearing via the void. Utilizing the compass, he locates the center point and drills down the image to the street level and below, stopping in the security headquarters garage.

It went off inside security headquarters.

That doesn't make any sense.

He zooms out back up to the top One World Trade Center. He twirls the image like a top, contemplating the scenarios in which an EMP would be detonated inside the island security headquarters when an aerial image catches his eye. From a distance, it looks like a helicopter, which Reynolds just said were thirty to forty minutes out from the city. He squeezes the screen between his fingers and zooms in on a large transport helicopter moving slowly over the northern end of the island and watches intently.

Who the hell is this?

It glides over Lenox Hill and Midtown before banking right and settling over the Mick. He zooms in closer as the helicopter lowers onto the roof of the island headquarters, touching down on the gravel and cement. He watches the rear cargo door lower. The side door slides open as armed men exit take up positions behind air vent shafts and other obstructions.

"Launch facial recognition program."

Blue circles appear around the head of each person on the roof, several turning red: NO MATCH FOUND.

Three light up green:

Arch Takeshi / ID # 549-674-210-775
Oliver DuBois / ID # 823-449-309-090
Regina Sanders / ID # 189-773-630-519

"But, they're...dead."

⚑ ⚑ ⚑

It takes Bishop, Tessa, Fenton, Kell, and Wolcott ten minutes to weave their way on foot through the confused pedestrians and stalled traffic to the edge of the EMP blast radius ending somewhere in the middle of the west thirties along 8th Avenue. In the distance, they can hear the Sea Stallion rotors chopping air on approach to Mick rooftop.

As they make a right around the corner onto West 42nd Street, they see the helicopter descend onto the roof and break into an all-out sprint for the last block and half, slowing to an inconspicuous burning-lung jog before reaching the glass walls of One Bryant Park.

"Huddle up," barks Bishop, and they form a small circle. Fenton eyes him with amusement. "Sorry, sir."

"No, go ahead."

"With the island security feed down, there's a good chance the front desk doesn't know about the chopper yet. Sir, you take the lead. We need to keep them from sending reinforcements to Vinick's level."

He slings the duffel bag off his shoulder and unzips, revealing three tranquilizer guns, his own, plus two he collected from Ollie and Takeshi. He hands one to Fenton and one to Tessa. "Let's stagger our entrance. Sir, you first. Tessa and I will follow shortly after. You two wait out here until we wave you in. Everyone got it?" They all nod in agreement, concealing tranquilizer guns in jackets.

"What are we going to do, ask them to not send guards to the roof?" asks Fenton dismissively.

"There's two, correct?"

"Keep them occupied, Tessa and I will improvise."

"Improvise?" says Tessa. Bishop shoots her an 'I'm making this up as I go along' shrug.

Fenton walks off first, passing in front of the grand glass-walled windows and finding the front entrance he has been through dozens of times before. Clean, angular lines of the airy foyer push all traffic to the bank of illuminated security desks currently staffed by a pair of veteran personnel well known to Fenton. On either side of the desk are large rectangular, arched openings leading to a bank of elevators protected by keycard and metal detector pass-through stations. His heels click loudly in the mostly barren space, ricocheting off the tiled floor and walls, calling attention to his urgent approach.

"Commander Fenton, we've lost contact with the island security feed and-"

"I know, I know," he says halfway to the desk when he hears the glass door behind him open to the street and two pairs of shoes slowly sauntering in while making idle chit chat.

"There's been a security breach. I need to brief Sandra Nolan immediately."

The guards look at each other confused.

"Sir, we've had no communication from her or anyone above. If you wait just a second, I'll contact her." Bishop and Tessa casually move closer to the desk, his arm around her like an everyday couple on a leisurely park stroll.

"Goddammit, this city is under attack, I don't have time for a phone call."

"With all due respect, sir, it's protocol. Now, if you'd just let me-" tranquilizer darts pierce the necks of the two guards, who grab at them while falling to the ground. Fenton turns around to see Bishop and Tessa reload their tranquilizer guns.

"Let's move," says Bishop, who turns and waves to the front windows and is immediately spotted by Wolcott and Kell, who hurry through the front door and rush to the front desk. Fenton circles around the sleek granite countertop, drops to a knee next to the downed guards, and unhooks a security badge from each, tossing one up to Bishop.

Everyone gathers at the desk.

"On the other side of the wall," Fenton explains, "through the gates are dozens of elevators. It's a large room with roaming guards on a lazy patrol keeping an eye out for anything unusual, so I'll go through first. The guards will recognize me and won't think anything of it. I'll secure the first shaft on the right, it's about twenty-five to thirty feet through the security gate to the elevator doors. Come through one at a time, don't bunch up and don't run. If they get suspicious, they will shoot. If they're close enough, we can hit them with the tranquilizers, but the range on these isn't great."

"Seems easy," quips Bishop.

"One more thing. The elevators are controlled via a computer on this desk board. The guards inside don't know the desk guards are out, so if they do get suspicious, they'll radio the desk to lock down the elevator. When they realize the desk guards are down, they'll try to do it themselves. If they're on the other side of the room, they won't make it in time. This is a fast elevator, will get us to the top floor in about twenty seconds."

"What happens if they stop it, can we still get out?" asks Wolcott.

"They'll lock it down and dispense a gas sleep agent. It's the airborne version of what's in our guns."

"So, let's not let that happen," says Tessa.

Fenton walks to the security gate farthest to the right and lays the card onto a glowing red glass screen triggering the switch to green. Latches unlock, and he steps through the metal detector and into the elevator bay room, the lightweight polymer of the tranquilizer gun not registering. He looks across the enormous chamber and spots the two guards standing almost dead center, about forty yards away, conversing. One notices Fenton, and he gives them a casual wave on his way to the first elevator door on the right and depresses the UP button. He watches the floor numbers methodically drop from the mid-twenties to zero. The doors split open a second later.

He steps inside the car and places his finger on the "Open Door" button, keeping his eye on the security gate as Wolcott steps through and walks towards him. Wolcott keeps his eyes on Fenton the entire time, breaking his gaze only to check an imaginary watch on his wrist. As he crosses the threshold into the elevator car, he steps to the back and emits a loud exhale of relief.

Fenton watches nervously as Kell and then Tessa steps through two gates at the same time, trailed by Bishop, who has unexpectedly switched his clothes and is wearing the uniform of one of the guards from the front desk.

"Bishop and your goddamn improvising," spits Fenton.

Fenton hears footsteps on approach from one of the guards from the middle of the room.

"Hey, what's going on there?" asks one of the guards.

"All clear," announces Bishop, tranquilizer gun in his right hand, concealed along the length of his thigh. Fenton winces, peeking his head out enough to spot both the guards on slow approach towards Bishop, Tessa, and Kell, halfway to the elevator opening.

"Hold on a sec," yells the other guard in a booming voice.

"Keep walking," murmurs Bishop. He turns his attention to the guards, still moving forward.

"Guys, I'll be back down in a sec. Let me get these people where they're going." The guards look at each other, nod, and draw their firearms.

"STOP!" one yells as they both break into a sprint.

"RUN!" barks Bishop, swinging his tranquilizer gun around and firing, missing both.

Kell and Tessa both make it to the opening as Fenton reaches outside the elevator car and fires his tranquilizer gun, striking one the guards in the stomach who stumbles, then falls flat and unconscious. The second guard continues forward, firing at Bishop, the bullets exploding the tile walls behind him.

Tessa steps to the threshold and fires her tranquilizer gun, hitting the guard in the torso as he fires off the last few rounds in his clip. Bishop awkwardly dives into the elevator car as Fenton depresses the "Close Door" button. Bishop pains to get to his knees, clutching his side just above the waist. Blood seeps between his fingers, the bluish-gray uniform darkens.

"Why aren't we moving?" asks Bishop

"You're shot," responds Fenton.

"Let me see," says Wolcott, who kneels at Bishop's side to untuck the shirt. Tessa clutches Bishop's hand and kisses it.

"You're okay," she says. Her eyes say otherwise.

"I know, but we need to get up there before other guards shut down the elevators," says Bishop.

"You're right." Fenton pushes the button for floor fifty-four, the elevator ascends.

"Looks like it's in and out," says Wolcott. "Entrance and exit wounds. I don't think it hit anything vital."

"What are you doing, that's not Vinick's floor."

"We can't walk into a situation with a man down. Nolan will help us, and if they lock down the elevators, there is an emergency stairwell between fifty-four and fifty-five Nolan has access to."

The elevator decelerates as it reaches the fifty-fourth floor. Fenton puts his hand to his mouth, signaling quiet as the doors open. He reloads the tranquilizer gun and slowly exits the car.

"Hello? Sandra? Zach?" From down the hall by the kitchen and dining area, he sees Zach poke his head out.

"Commander Fenton? Were you scheduled to visit today?" Fenton steps out from the elevator.

"Where's Sandra? There's a situation-" Zach steps out into the hallway wearing a stained cooking apron.

"She's been upstairs meeting with Vinick, haven't seen her in a couple of hours. What situation-" Vinick motions for everyone to exit the elevator. Tessa, Wolcott, Kell, and Bishop, who is covering the bullet wound with his hand, his fingers already soaked red, all march out.

"Uh, who are all these people?"

Fenton leads them into the dining area where Wolcott positions Bishop to sit on the table, his feet on a chair.

"Come with me. Do you have a medkit?" asks Wolcott.

"Sure, just a sec." Zach rummages through kitchen drawers, finally locating a small plastic First Aid kit he tosses to Wolcott.

"How do you feel?" asks Wolcott, grabbing Bishop's wrist for his pulse. "Faint? Nauseous?"

"Believe it or not, this is not my first time getting shot."

"I don't doubt it," quips Wolcott. He cleans the entrance and exit wounds with antiseptic wipes, applies large squares bandages to each side of the injury before wrapping his entire abdomen with gauze to secure them.

"You're good to go, for now. We can clean it and stitch it up properly later."

"Okay, Dr. Wolcott, Kell. You're staying here until we clear the top floor of security, or the helicopter team does. Vinick has his own detail, they always stay on the floor. We only have the three tranq guns, so it'll be us three. Questions?" Zach raises his hand, but Fenton ignores him.

"No? Good. Let's go."

Bishop grimaces as he hops off the table, Tessa puts her arm up to stop him.

"Are you sure you can do this?"

"You're not going up there without me." They kiss, her hand caresses his cheek. She can see him wincing from the pain but won't let her go. Not again.

Fenton reaches the elevator door and pushes the up button, but nothing happens. "I figured. The elevators are offline, we take the stairs." He leads them down the hall to the stairwell door and presses his hands on the open bar, Bishop and Tessa directly behind him. As he is about to push open the door, they hear a loud explosion up above.

"The outer door breach," says Bishop. "It's started, the assault has started."

♟ ♟ ♟

One minute earlier, Ollie applied improvised explosives to the stairwell door on the roof. Having carefully removed the Semtex from the three Hummers, Silva's self-destruct option of last resort. He reformed the tractable material into a series of thin strips six inches long and an inch in diameter. With no doorknob or visible hinges from the outside, the only way through was literally through. He applied the clay-like material to the cold metal door in an oval pattern big enough to enter. From the damaged nose radar and guidance unit of the helicopter, he tore out and linked together a chain of wires reaching to the battery of the Sea Stallion. He then split the wire, applying one half to the positive lead terminal, then the other to the negative, at which point thanks to the electrical charge caused the Semtex to tear open a hole in the door.

Ollie, Sanders, Bloom, and Charlie take up armed positions behind aluminum air vent shafts, pipes, odd obstructions, and the helicopter waiting for the sign from Takeshi, who moves into position with his back against the wall parallel to the stairwell door, ten feet from the frame.

He inches closer and uses the rearview mirror off one of the Hummers to peer inside the makeshift opening. At the same time, he raises his right hand in the air in a fist, indicating a freeze of all movement from everyone. As the smoke clears, he inches closer and closer, the opening comes into focus, but there is nothing but black punctuated by flashes from a malfunctioning hallway overhead light.

Three small, round dark green objects fly through the opening onto the rooftop gravel.

"Grenades!" shouts Takeshi as he dives away from the door. Everyone ducks behind their cover as the grenades explode in the middle of the rooftop, knocking a few people onto their backs but without serious injury.

"Ollie!" yells Takeshi.

"On it," he replies. "Let's send some gas their way."

Sanders and Ollie duck back into the cargo bay of the helicopter. Sanders, her injured arm in a sling, pulls an M79 six-shot grenade launcher from a gun rack and tosses it to Ollie, followed by a tear gas canister. Ollie loads it, aims, and fires the projectile through the opening into the stairwell. Smoke billows from the hole. Takeshi and Ollie exchange a glance via the temporary calm, which shatters thanks to automatic weapons fire from two guns through the opening onto the rooftop.

Windows in the helicopter spider and shatter. Rounds tear through the flimsy air vents as everyone drops to their stomachs, trying to get underneath the fire. Arms and shoulders catch ricochets the Kevlar vests don't cover, yelps and cries of pain rise from around the rooftop.

"The hell with this," grunts Ollie. "Gimme three live rounds!" Sanders opens a rectangular metal box latched to the floor. Inside, secure in foam protection like an egg carrier, are a dozen 40mm grenades. She tosses them one after another to Ollie, who loads the shells and fires them off in quick succession into the stairwell openings. Three successive explosions - flames and smoke burst through the slapdash entrance in a crimson-black plume. Ollie tosses the grenade launcher back to Sanders in the cargo hold, draws his 9mm, and aims it at the door as he hustles across the rooftop to Takeshi along the wall left of the opening.

"I think we woke 'em up," says Ollie, with odd glee. Takeshi glares at Ollie and shakes his head in disapproval.

"We know those guys, that was overkill."

"Hey, we tried to do it the nice way. They did not oblige."

"Everyone, on me!" shouts Takeshi.

Derek, Charlie, Sanders, and Bloom scurry over to Takeshi and Ollie, backing up against the wall. Takeshi steps out and looks them over. "Who's hit? Anyone serious?" He walks up to Derek, who is covering his shoulder with his hand.

"It hurts, but I'm okay." His grimaces say otherwise.

"Let me see." Takeshi peels back Derek's hand. A round, red spot permeates his sweatshirt below the shoulder blade just inside the Kevlar strap. He pulls Derek forward, looking for an exit wound but sees none. "You're staying."

He tells Charlie to attend to Derek's wound back at the helicopter, Derek begrudgingly walks with Charlie back to the chopper.

"Okay. I'll take the lead. Masks on, there will be lingering gas and smoke. Keep your goddamn heads on a swivel."

Pistols and rifles at the ready, the four line up in a column and one-by-one step through the Semtex torn hole into the stairwell. Upon entering, they turn on their individual barrel mounted flashlights. The scene is gruesome.

At the top landing, blood and viscera cover the brick walls. The gunmen who had fired on them were hit with three consecutive close-quarter explosions pulverizing them to a fine paste. As they step over chunks of arms, legs, and torso, then descend the first half flight of the stairs.

More bodies, more blood.

When they reach the mid-story landing to make the one-hundred-and-eighty-degree turn, the slumping dead bodies are mostly intact, killed by shrapnel and the crushing force of being thrown into cinder blocks: cracked spines and skulls, horrifying internal injuries.

Bloom, unfamiliar with the brutality of war up close, heaves and vomits at the overwhelming sights. As Takeshi and Ollie reach the fifty-fifth-floor doorway, they find a still breathing Xeno, whose mechanical arm has been torn off but is still clutching his 9mm pistol. Takeshi throws up a fist, indicating an immediate stop for all. He and Ollie drop a knee before Xeno.

"I... know... you..." says Xeno, glaring at Ollie, laboring as blood trickles from a large gash in his forehead.

"Goddammit, Xeno." spits out Ollie. "Why couldn't you have just...dammit, Xeno. Are there any more?" Xeno affirms with a nod, then lifts his good arm, holding out a walkie-talkie.

"We don't want any more bloodshed," says Takeshi, his natural big-voiced bravado gives way to an empathetic tone. "Tell your men to stand down. We're here for Vinick, he's not worth the fight."

"He... is... to... me....," says Xeno defiantly. "But not them." Ollie understands immediately. The arm giving Xeno purpose came from one of the many Solear divisions. A beneficial pairing of advanced medical technology and military interests intersecting, utilizing psych profiles of veterans to find the perfect willing and malleable candidates, in service to the protection of Elton Vinick.

Xeno labors to curl his arm and bring the walkie-talkie to his mouth, so Ollie takes it and does it for him, depressing the talk button.

"This is... Sergeant... Xeno Reed... ordering a... cease-fire on the fifty-fifth. Lay down all weapons. I repeat... I am ordering... a cease-fire. Weapons...on the ground." Ollie releases the talk button, and Xeno breaks into a coughing fit, spitting up blood and bile.

"Is it all clear up there?" says an echoing voice from beneath them.

Takeshi stands and looks over the metal railing down the stairs to the floor below. Looking up at him is Fenton, then Bishop and Tessa. He gives them a less than enthusiastic smile.

Ollie opens the stairwell door into the fifty-fifth floor. He looks out, up and down the hall. Guards stand around, rifles on the floor as ordered. Fenton calls to Wolcott and Kell, and the group makes their way up the stairs to meet Ollie and Takeshi.

As Fenton, Bishop, Tessa, and Wolcott make their way up from the fifty-fourth floor, Kell pushes ahead and hurriedly weaves around them.

"Mom! MOM!" he yells up the staircase. Sanders tears off her gas mask.

"I'm coming, Kell," yells Sanders from halfway down the rooftop staircase, racing down the steps. At the fifty-fifth-floor landing, Kell and Regina Sanders arrive at the same time, her uninjured arm raps Kell's back in a warm embrace. Everyone, for a moment, feels emboldened by the reunion surrounded by the just inflicted carnage.

"Are you okay, mom?" asks Kell.

"I am, I am now. How did you get here?"

"That guy Lamb, the one you thought was helping you. He's not," says Kell. "He kidnapped me, and Tessa too. We escaped."

"Hold on," interjects Takeshi. "What do you mean he took you?" Tessa steps forward.

"Lamb had a team kidnapping the family members of anyone sent out to try to retrieve the doctor. He's was going to use us to stop the doctor from being turned over to Vinick."

"So, you were held prisoner together?" asks Takeshi.

"Yeah, he was using a basement at the Bronx Zoo."

"Did you see anyone else there? Another woman?"

"Besides the guards, it was just us two. We didn't hear or see any other prisoners."

"You're sure?" says Takeshi. She nods, her heart sinking. "Because my wife-" Ollie puts his hand on Takeshi's shoulder.

"Hey, we'll find her. I'll help ya," says Ollie.

Tessa gives Bishop a deliberately worried look.

"Ollie's right, for once," says Bishop. Ollie rolls his eyes. "Let's go through that door and finish this."

"Okay," says Takeshi. "Commander Fenton, good to see you. How do we want to do this?"

"Good to see you to Arch. Ollie, not so much."

"Hey," protests Ollie.

"It's not far to Vinick," says Fenton. "Regina, why don't you take your son down a flight and hold tight? Find Zach, he has a medkit. Have him call a medical team for Xeno. In the meantime, see if you can help. I know you have some field med experience."

"Will do," says Sanders.

"Takeshi, Ollie, Bishop, Tessa, Doctor Wolcott, you're with me."

Fenton pushes through the stairwell door, the rest of the group follows cautiously. He leads them down the hallways, they pass guards who have laid their guns on the ground and nod as they pass. A few turns, they reach the gymnasium and finally arrive in the kitchen and living space.

A large screen television shows a feed of the current Manhattan Island news broadcast, the scroll reads-

BREAKING: BLACKOUT CRIPPLES LOWER MANHATTAN

Studio talking heads speak to a remote live reporter on the pedestrian-filled street. Vinick is seated in his med chair, glaring at his monitors while Nolan sits at the kitchen table reading something on Vinick's computer. She sees Fenton and stands up.

"What's happening?" she asks. "We heard the explosions and gunshots."

"Is Xeno dead?" asks Vinick, distracted by his multiple screens.

"He's banged up pretty bad," responds Fenton. "We've got people helping him." He turns his attention back to Nolan. "Did you find it?"

"I did," she says. "Everything on the Perseverantia project is on this computer." She walks forward to the group.

"Sandra, these are our assets, Arch Takeshi, Ollie DuBois, Bishop Dawes, his wife Tessa, and this is-"

"Doctor Marion Wolcott," says Sandra, extending her hand, which he reciprocates. This finally pulls Vinick's attention away from the monitors.

"Marion. Son. Come here, won't you?" Wolcott looks at the group, then walks over to Vinick.

"Elton."

"It's so good to see you again, son." Wolcott leans in.

"Everyone knows everything," says Wolcott. "You can cut your father-son act."

"I'm afraid you're very wrong about that. Aren't I right, Commander Fenton?" Fenton grimaces.

"He's right. Sandra, there's a bigger picture. Lamb is playing us. You were correct, he was behind all the disappearances, he was using them as collateral to stop them from returning with Wolcott. But it's not about Solear, that's just his excuse to remove Vinick."

"We have it on good authority he's working with someone named Jasper Reynolds," interjects Takeshi. Sandra rolls the info around in her head for a moment.

"I haven't heard his name in years," says Sandra, turning to Vinick.

"For a short period, he was a board member of Solear. You met him once or twice."

"That's not all," interjects Bishop. "Boston isn't gang-controlled. It's Reynolds. He's got five cities out west under his control, and it looks like he's expanding east. This is his next target."

Vinick lets out a huge sigh and sits up, grabbing his cane to brace himself as he stands and walks over to the group.

"You're still not seeing the whole picture. He took those cities by force, one by one," explains an annoyed Vinick. "But here, instead, he's trying some elaborate coup d'état. Have you stopped and asked yourself, why is that?"

They all consider the question and look around to each other, searching for an answer.

"He's right," says Fenton reluctantly. "The walls built around this city aren't much different than any of the others. We're an island, so it gives us a bit more protection, but..." He trails off, struck by a new thought, and following it.

"But what?" asks Ollie.

"Oh God, I know why," says Fenton. "I know why he won't attack the city straight on." Everyone stares in anticipation. He looks to Vinick, almost as if to ask permission to reveal the information.

"Go on," says Vinick.

"Nukes. We have nukes. Lots of them. Enough to turn his cities into dust."

19

Lamb views the incoming phone number, seamlessly transferred from his hand-held device to his VR display, but has a hard time registering the information. He has never previously received a personal call from Elton Vinick, and yet there it is before him. He pushes the green ACCEPT button.

"Hello?"

"Nathan, how are you? It's Elton Vinick." Calm and smooth, the unflappable Vinick via what sounds like a speakerphone.

"I'm fine. To what do I owe the pleasure?"

"Oh, I'll cut to the chase. Your partner in crime, Jasper Reynolds, is he trying to steal my nuclear missiles?"

"I don't know...what are you saying?"

"You remember, don't you? You designed the remote launch terminal in security headquarters years ago for the submarine parked in the Hudson River. Ring a bell? One of our many purchases at the Pentagon going out of business sale. We didn't want to keep a crew in there, so you rigged together a remote launch terminal in the event anyone got the bright idea they would attack our city. Commander Fenton, what is the current armament status?"

Lamb hears Fenton take a step forward, clear his throat.

"The USS Wyoming still has its original armament, twenty-four Trident II ballistic nuclear missiles as well as a full capacity of MK-48 torpedoes. Also, there are one hundred and fifty-four Tomahawk warheads in multiple variants at the ready."

"Thank you for the, uh, comprehensive breakdown, Commander Fenton. Now, Nathan, I'm sure Jasper Reynolds has more than his share of toys, but what he doesn't have, and what he clearly wants, are my nuclear missiles. And why is that?"

"Are we really going to play this game, Elton? You know why he wants them, same as you."

"No, that's where you're wrong. We have never attacked anyone. We have them strictly as a deterrent, while Jasper keeps adding to his portfolio, one city after another. Quite the opposite of what we're doing here. So why don't you tell us the truth about what Jasper wants."

"You know what he wants."

"I want to hear it from you. Why did you join up with him? What's his vision for our fair city?"

"He wants to put the world back together, Elton. And you know what, I agree with him. You have your little empire, but the world is bigger than that. And that's what I want to be a part of, not your director of I.T. So yeah, I worked with Jasper, worked to stop your son from coming back, which, by the way, you're welcome Doctor Wolcott, who I assume is around there somewhere. If I hadn't intervened, Elton would be chopping you up for parts. So, you're welcome."

"Welcome?" interjects Takeshi angrily. "You kidnapped our families as bargaining chips. Where the hell is my wife?"

Lamb takes a long breath.

"I'm not proud of all the actions I've taken, but I did what needed to be done to expose Elton Vinick and-"

"Where is my wife?" Takeshi reiterates with deepening rage.

"When your signal went offline, it wasn't like we could just return them to population, they would have revealed what was happening."

"Did you...did you kill my wife?"

"There's no point in discussing this. Jasper has an army on the way. This will all be over soon. I'm leaving this hellhole; the winter is unbearable."

"You're a dead man," says Takeshi, his voice cracking. Lamb can hear Takeshi being consoled and led away from the phone. He hears footsteps approach and a deep breath.

"I told you," says Tessa. "I'm coming for you."

Lamb frantically disconnects the call, shaking and panicked. He scrolls through his virtual Rolodex of programs, lands on DRONES, click it. A list of ACTIVE/INACTIVE options appear. He selects the first ACTIVE from a list of a dozen and highlights it. To the right, a LAUNCH option appears, and Lamb selects it.

On-screen, a rectangular box appears with a live camera feed from the drone currently atop the Brain. A virtual control panel appears in the form of what looks like a child's handheld remote control. He grips it using his haptic gloves, using his left thumb on the elevator/rudder control rod and his right thumb on the aileron/thumb control rod.

He pilots the drone up and away from the Brain, finding the top of the wall circling Manhattan and following it north along the East River. After a minute, he reaches the Third Avenue Bridge leading to the Free Zone boroughs and exhales in relief.

Across the river waiting before the bridge are a dozen tractor-trailers flanked on the ground by Jeeps with mounted fifty caliber machine guns, Humvees with surface-to-surface missile launchers, protected by four hovering Apache helicopters.

This will all be over soon.

▲ ▲ ▲

"Where is he? Where is Lamb?" whispers Tessa, her hand on Takeshi's shoulder as he fights back tears. "I'll go with you, and we'll gut the son of a bitch together."

"Wait," says Bishop, cautiously interjecting. "I want to end him as much as you do, but we've got to deal with the bigger problem."

"He's right," says Takeshi, composing himself.

"Lamb isn't going anywhere. We know an assault force is coming. Based on how fast they were going, they're probably already outside our door."

"They are," says Sandra. "Hector Silva just messaged me, he left security headquarters, is out on the street. Guards near the Third Avenue Bridge have reported four helicopters, a dozen tractor-trailers, but they're not moving. It's like they're waiting for orders."

"It's the EMP," says Fenton. "When it went off, everything locked down. None of the bridge gates will open until the security system is back up and running again."

"But the blast should have fried the whole system," says Bishop. "That's the whole point. It's not like flipping a switch will turn it back on, it's supposed to disable it."

"You're right, but you're also wrong," says Fenton. "The security mainframe went down, but as a defensive tactic. It's designed to detect an attack, like an EMP blast, and instantaneously seal the immediate perimeter. It was built in what's called a Faraday cage, it's like a giant box which can absorb the blast. But for it to work, everything connecting it to the power supply outside the box gets cut off."

"So, we need to tell Silva to reconnect the power supply so we can activate the security system and the tower guns?" asks Bishop.

"No, there are only two people with access to lift the lockdown, and we're both in this room." Fenton nods to Nolan.

"Hold on a sec," says Ollie. "Right now, Lamb is locked out of the security system, right?"

"That's right," says Fenton.

"So, if you do unlock it and turn the juice back on, what's to stop him from immediately getting into the system, killing the tower guns and opening the gate to let those tractor-trailers in?"

"Shit, you're right," says Fenton. "If we keep the power off, the only way he can open the gate is by manual override at the gate itself, and there is no way he's leaving the Brain. It's the only place he's safe right now."

"If we do nothing," says Takeshi, "those Apaches have enough firepower to put a serious hole in the side of the island."

"Correct," says Nolan. "Doing nothing doesn't end this. The remote launch terminal for the sub, that's also locked down in the security cage?"

"Yeah, what do you want to do?" asks Fenton. "Take it for a spin?"

"No," Nolan responds. "Lamb has to be communicating with Reynolds, coordinating all this. If we can get the power back on, I want to let him know we're prepared to defend ourselves."

"Sandy, hold on a minute," interjects Vinick. "Be very careful about threatening Jasper Reynolds if you're not prepared to back it up. Are you prepared to use nuclear weapons against him, against his people?"

Everyone remains silent for a moment to weigh the gravity of the situation.

"I... we will do what we need to," says Nolan.

"I guess I don't have a say in this," spits out Vinick. "After all, I'm still the CEO of this island, aren't I?"

"As the deputy CEO and head of island security, I am relieving you of your duties, Elton," shoots back Nolan. "I am naming myself interim CEO until the board can be convened, and a new CEO is selected. Or, like you said, we can turn it over to the people to decide. Either way, you're done. Please go sit in your chair and play some chess until we decide what to do with you."

Vinick, stunned and sulking, shuffles slowly back to his med chair. She turns her attention back to the group.

"We have three tasks ahead of us: number one, Commander Fenton. You need to return to security headquarters, reactivate island security, and prepare the Wyoming for launch capability. Number two, we need to send an assault team to get to Lamb. We cannot, I repeat, cannot kill him," argues Nolan to frustrated faces.

As much as she wants to give the order, she suppresses the darker impulse.

"However he is communicating with Reynolds, we need

access. Once we have launch capability, then we can force Reynolds to back down."

"And if he doesn't?" asks Bishop.

"Then number three - we vaporize Houston."

CHAPTER

20

Lamb reroutes the drone away from the Third Avenue Bridge and Reynolds' waiting forces back south to the Mick. As it approaches, he sees the group re-enter the helicopter via the lowered rear cargo door, the top and rear rotors gradually powering up. On the rooftop, he spots Fenton with Takeshi, Ollie, Bishop, and Tessa at the same time they eye the drone.

Before he can react, Ollie unholsters and aims a pistol, firing off two rounds, the second of which strikes the drone, sending it tumbling out of control to a nearby rooftop where it crumbles on impact.

He switches back to the MOSAIC program and locates the live feed of the helicopter, currently being captured by curious onlookers via cell phones. Enough time has passed for those outside the EMP blast zone to have begun moving into the blackout radius, making the circular nature of the explosion jagged, chipping away, and in some cases, completely bisected the area depending on the path of the entrant.

The helicopter eventually settles over what was once the Whitney Museum of American Art and descends onto the top of the parking garage. The facial recognition program scans and recognizes Hector Silva from the citizenship database. Out the sliding side door of the chopper hops Fenton, who along with Silva, disappears into the building.

They're going to try to reactivate the security system.

Lamb considers the ramifications.

Even if they get the system back online, he can still hack the tower guns to disable them, and then remote open the Third Avenue bridge gate. It occurs to him Fenton and Nolan must realize this as well when he notices the helicopter not returning to Mick or heading north to confront Reynolds' forces, but instead heading in the direction of the Brain.

They're coming for me.

He frantically pulls up his contact list and locates the main security office for his building.

"Hello, HELLO, who is this?" shouts Lamb.

"Mr. Lamb? This is Todd Palmerio, current shift lead for Brain security. What can I do ya for?"

"Todd, I need to warn you. There is an inbound helicopter carrying terrorists to our building. They are going to try to infiltrate the Brain and overtake my office. Pull all your men from the building and repel them, do you understand?"

There is quiet. Lamb can hear a hand clasping the phone receiver and muffled voices.

"Mr. Lamb, this is Todd Palmerio again. I'm afraid I can't do that."

"What do you mean you can't do that? I am the senior executive member present in this building, am I not? There is a terrorist threat-"

"Hold on right there, Mr. Lamb. Before your call, I received a priority one security communication from Sandra Nolan stating you had been relieved of your position, and an urgent recovery team was en route to retrieve you for questioning regarding a breach in our security network. Now, I know you understand that I report to her, not you."

"Goddammit, she's in on it-"

"Excuse me, sir. But as she provided the proper authentication of her credentials, I am duty-bound to carry out her orders. If you would not mind sir, it would expedite whatever issues you are having to present yourself at the front desk when the recovery team arrives, rather than us having to extract you from your office forcefully."

Without replying, Lamb disconnects the call and immediately attempts to contact Reynolds. Unsuccessful, he accesses the drone program and launches another, this time speeding up the East River just outside the wall until it reaches the Third Avenue Bridge. With no communication ability, he can only stare at the army Reynolds sent, waiting impatiently for the gate to raise. Then it occurs to him - the helicopter crews are communicating with each other and the ground via radio.

Lamb enters a quick search parameter into his computer - radio frequencies. This gives him a shortlist of channels and their types - civilian, government, military, and others. He drills the list down to military channels and then, in a separate window, opens the operating system on the drone.

His control of the drone is based on radio waves, he realizes, and he can turn his drone into a broadcasting station if he locates the correct frequency being utilized by Reynolds' team. Rather than repeat himself over and over on each frequency, he records a message to simultaneously send over the military frequencies he has selected:

"This is a message for the assault team currently awaiting the gate to be lowered outside the Third Avenue Bridge. My name is Nathan Lamb, and I have been working with Jasper Reynolds to assist in your breach of Manhattan Island. You must launch an assault on the gate at once, island security is in disarray due to an electromagnetic pulse. Please acknowledge receipt of this message."

He plays the recorded message over all available military radio frequencies and, after a moment, spots movement outside one of the vehicles on the ground. Two soldiers have a brief conversation before one pulls the walkie talkie from his belt and speaks into it.

"Hello, who the hell is this? Over."

Lamb finds the specific frequency being used by the soldier and dials it in, creating a live transmission.

"My name is Nathan Lamb, and I am the head of island I.T. Your window of opportunity is closing rapidly."

"You keep saying that name like I am supposed to know it. I don't. Over."

"I am the person who will guide you through the tunnels to access the submarine from which you will offload the twenty-four nuclear missiles. Does that ring a bell? Over."

"You want us to attack the gate? Over."

"Yes. Your Apache helicopters are armed with Sidewinder missiles, correct? You can punch a hole if you target the same area repeatedly. Do you understand?"

"I understand. But please note if we expend our sidewinder

allotment, and those tower guns are reactivated, we are in intensely deep shit. Over."

"Those tower guns will not reactivate. However, I need you to dispatch one of your Apache's immediately to the south end of the island. There is an inbound assault team on a helicopter intending to remove me from my location, at which point I will no longer be able to guide you through or keep the tower guns offline. Do you understand? I need that assault team taken out."

"I'll see what I can do. Red Rider, are you hearing this conversation? Over." The pilot of Apache furthest left gives the soldier a thumbs-up sign.

"Want me to go take a peek inside? Over."

"If you spot another bird in the air, you know what to do. Over."

▲ ▲ ▲

After the EMP blast and getting stuffed, unfairly in his opinion, into the basement locker room, Silva did not wait around as instructed. Keeping his ear to the door, he waited for the voices of Fenton, Bishop, and the others to disappear before heading out into the main bay to find a handheld acetylene torch he used to construct a makeshift light with an old oily work rag wrapped around the end of a crowbar. It was enough to get him to the stairwell and then surface, where he, with everyone else, wandered in the confusion of what had happened.

Like most people, Silva always kept his handheld cell phone on him, and the one in his pocket was useless. Like most people with citizenship debt, he has more than one occupation. His secondary career is as an independent electronics repairman, most of his clientele being other residents of his overcrowded apartment building. Currently sitting at his apartment were dozens of cell phones, one of which was a clone replica of what he was carrying. As he hustled back to his sub-three hundred square foot home ten minutes from security headquarters, his only hope was the radius of the outage did not reach and wipe clean his backup. It's the only place he kept the private, unpublished numbers of his immediate boss, Robert Fenton, and his boss, Sandra Nolan.

Upon reaching his street, he kicked up his hurried jog to a full out sprint when he saw the lights in his building were still on, keying in through the front door security and bypassing the rickety elevator for the stairwell, five flights which went by in a blink.

When he finally made it into the apartment and opened his secure electronics cabinet where he locked up all his current projects and his clone phone, he noticed he had several new texts and voicemail messages from the last ten minutes. Upon checking them, they were primarily from wall security personnel who had lost communication with the security office and each other.

After reading through the texts, he listened to the dozen audio recordings, all of which reiterated the same information until the guard in the northeast sector frantically reported air and ground activity just past the Third Avenue Bridge. It was then Silva called Fenton with no answer, followed by Nolan. It wasn't long after Silva was up to speed, and Fenton was being ferried to the rooftop garage of the Whitney Museum of American Art.

Fenton and Silva were now making their way back into security headquarters via blackened hallways and stairwells lit by handheld flashlights rather than the makeshift torches. Upon reaching the garage, Silva opens the locker room door and tosses a spare flashlight to the mechanics inside, instructing them to hold tight while he gets the power turned back on with Fenton. From there, they maneuver through the garage to the farthest end of the mammoth room where a single, windowless door is marked AUTHORIZED PERSONNEL ONLY – ACCESS LEVEL 1. The key card reader, which would usually be lit in red, is colorless. Fenton swipes his card anyway, but nothing happens.

"Wait," Fenton says aloud, though only talking to himself. "There's something about the reader, if the system shuts itself down...shoot, there's a manual entry. I need a screwdriver, Philips head, I think."

Silva grabs a handheld multi-head driver off a workstation and hands it to Fenton, who unwinds the four screws holding the key card reader cover in place. Silva keeps his light on the cover as Fenton removes the final screw, pulling off the glass panel with a tangle of wires connected to a microchip board attached to the back. He lets it hang down as he turns his attention to the numeric keypad now exposed in the wall opening.

"Do you know the code?" asks Silva curiously.

"I do," responds Fenton, entering in his twelve-digit identification number. Like tumblers in a bank safe, the series of magnetic locks disengage, allowing Fenton to pull it open. They both step inside, and their flashlight beams immediately catch the large metal box taking up most of the room. This room within a room has no windows and a single door, which they reach post-haste and open via the metal swinging lever to unlock. Inside are dozens of rows of network racks filled with thousands of servers and just off to the side, a C-shaped desk with four keyboards and a half-dozen wall-mounted monitors.

Between the four keyboards is a black box with a telephone headset and a push-button keyboard the same as in the wall outside the room. Fenton sits down at the desk and enters the same twelve-digit sequence into the keypad and waits.

One by one, the screens on the wall glow with activity. Laid out in two rows of three, the fifty-five-inch screens are each populated with predetermined data streams, real-time mapping of the island, security camera feeds, and more. Fenton uses a keyboard to toggle to the screen displaying the island ring of security, a digital map of the island showing the locations all of the tower guns currently as offline, each identified with a unique numerical designation starting with 001 at the northernmost tip of the island, then 002, 003 and so on.

From a menu of options, he chooses PERIMETER SECURITY - ALL and the numbers change in color from red to green, indicating they are again active.

"Hold on," Fenton mutters. "Something is off."

"If there is activity outside the northeast sector-" says Silva.

"-those guns should be going berserk right now," responds Fenton, finishing Silva's thought. "Let me bring up thermal and video." He clicks on 015, the tower gun almost directly above the Third Avenue Bridge. Another screen displays a split live feed video and thermal image, both displaying three hovering helicopters and the convoy of vehicles just across the bridge.

"Try the manual override," says Silva.

Fenton clicks through menu options and finds the manual override for 015 and selects MANUAL CONTROL.

It does nothing, he clicks it again.

"What in the hell is going on?" blurts Fenton. He tries a third time, but with no results, he backs out of the menu.

"Check the mode," says Silva, and Fenton clicks MODE, which shows ACTIVE and MANUAL both greyed out.

"That doesn't make sense," says Silva.

"Yeah, it does," Fenton realizes. "It's Lamb. He changed the settings so it would look like the guns are active, but he disengaged their targeting systems. All they can do it point their cameras."

"Oh shit, look." Silva points to the screen, and they watch as a Jeep, followed by a tractor-trailer, cross the Third Avenue Bridge towards the gate.

"Goddammit," Fenton slams his fist on the desk. "We did exactly what he wanted. Now he can open the gates, and they can start rolling in. How long will it take a semi to maneuver through the tunnels and reach us?

"If Lamb is guiding them through, he'll try to take them on a route with the least amount of turns," says Silva, thinking out loud. "That rig can't handle some of the angles and they'll have to keep the speed to ten or fifteen miles an hour, so twenty, maybe twenty-five minutes, tops."

Fenton calls Nolan on Silva's phone and relays the news.

"Get reinforcements, whoever you can," she tells them. "Get them to the sub and secure it. Do not let them board the sub. Take it out to sea if you must. But be ready to launch."

"Sandra, I can launch from fire control here, but I can't remote pilot the sub. If it comes to it, I'll detonate a torpedo and scuttle it."

She sighs. "Do what you have to," Fenton instructs Silva to recall every tower guard he can reach and send them to Pier 57.

"This is it," Nolan relays.

"They're not getting those nukes," responds Fenton.

"Wait a sec," says Silva. "There were four helicopters. That's what the guard reported in his message. So, why are there only three outside the wall?"

21

"Hold on!" yells Charlie as he pushes the Sea Stallion diving toward the unforgiving concrete of 6th Avenue and deploys a round of heat dispersing aerial chaffs to redirect the incoming sidewinder missile fired from the Apache helicopter trailing a half-mile behind them.

He banks the helicopter hard left down Canal Street as the chaffs redirect the missile to explode into the rooftop corner of a York Street apartment, sending concrete and steel crashing down to the street below as pedestrians scramble out of the way.

"We've got another mile, can we make it?" shouts Takeshi, strapped in behind Charlie. They make a hard-right down Church Street, temporarily losing visual of the pursuing attack copter.

"One more round of chaffs," barks Charlie. "Then we're sitting ducks. We can't outrun it. They're faster than us and closing in."

"It's Lamb," yells Bishop. "They're protecting him, trying to stop us from reaching him, right? We need to get on the ground fast and spread out."

Takeshi gives thought and agree.

"Charlie, you hear that?" Charlie gives Takeshi a thumbs up.

"Problem is," says Charlie, "there ain't exactly a good place to set down."

"We're not setting down," yells Takeshi. "Charlie, you get as close to the ground in front of that building as you can. Slow down, but don't stop. You hear me."

Charlie gives Takeshi another thumbs up.

"There are inflatable life rafts still on board," explains Takeshi, bracing himself as the copter makes another hard turn. "We open the back door and slide right out onto the street."

Bishop considers it.

"That's insane."

"I love it!" laughs Ollie. "White water rafting on the streets of Manhattan."

"We will be outside the front door in less than thirty seconds," yells Derek from the right front seat, mapping to the Brain on his tablet.

"Incoming!" barks Charlie as the chopper banks hard right north on Broad Street. A sidewinder explodes into an office building behind them, raining glass and debris onto the street.

"We're making a left on Pearl, that's the entrance," shouts Derek.

Takeshi unbuckles his harness and grabs the overhead straps restraining four emergency uninflated polyurethane-coated nylon rafts. He pulls the release, and they fall to the floor. Using the hanging storage straps, he works his way to the middle of the cargo bay where the rafts tumbled, grabbing at them as the helicopter throws him left and right.

He tosses Ollie, Tessa, and Bishop a raft and hurriedly explains how the cord releases the compressed gas from the attached canister, inflating the raft in just a split second.

They have guns in anticipation of a firefight, they had not expected to be kicked out of a moving helicopter in a life raft onto a street in downtown Manhattan.

"Ten seconds to Pearl!" yells Derek.

"Door. Inflate. Slide out. Got it?" Everyone nods to Takeshi. "Charlie, when we're gone, get back to the Mick."

A final thumbs up from Charlie. "Be safe!" he yells.

As the Sea Stallion makes the deliberate left turn hovering over Broad Street onto Pearl Street, it dives towards the asphalt. Charlie slows it to ten miles an hour, opening the rear cargo door so it drags a few feet above the two-lane road in the wrong direction of the one-way, though the thoroughfare had long since been converted from motorized to strictly foot traffic.

Pedestrians' frantically scatter from the asphalt to the sidewalks on either side. Takeshi grips the release cord at the open cargo door. It's then they see the Apache swing into view behind them.

"Get out of here, now!" yells Takeshi back to Charlie, who draws his 9mm pistol and fires off multiple rounds at the Apache as he inflates and jumps on the raft out the back of the chopper. Charlie pulls up hard and accelerates toward the sky. They each inflate and cling to their rafts as they bounce hard onto the street, the Sea Stallion cargo door closes as it ascends up and away from Pearl Street.

Takeshi, Ollie, Bishop, and Tessa tumble hard, bouncing off their inflatables before landing on the street, bruised but not broken. The Apache overshoots the spread of rafts, speeding in pursuit of the Sea Stallion, and is forced to make an awkward mid-street correction. They scurry towards the building, taking cover behind decorative brick planters and benches in anticipation of the Apache firing on them.

But it doesn't.

The helicopter hovers less than a hundred yards away, armaments trained on their position. Suddenly it slowly ascends straight up.

"What the hell is it doing," says Tessa. "It's got us dead here." They all look up.

"The roof," says Takeshi. "Lamb's going to try to escape off the roof. We gotta move. Now!" They sprint for the front glass door entryway of the Brain.

♟ ♟ ♟

Silva: in position, Fenton has link to Wy - 5:21 PM
Nolan: coordinates entered? - 5:22 PM
Silva: confirmed - 5:23 PM
Nolan: hold on my orders - 5:23 PM

♟ ♟ ♟

Using MOSAIC, Lamb has watched the helicopter chase between the buildings of lower Manhattan with the bemused detachment of an action movie viewer. It occurred to him since building security was no longer at his disposal, he would need to exit the premises via an option other than the front doors.

With an open channel to Reynolds' forces, he explained the situation to the Apache helicopter pilot, call sign Red Rider, who received permission via the ground commander, who Lamb has since learned was named Fisk, or formally, Commander Quinn Fisk of the reconstituted Fifth Armored Brigade out of Fort Bliss, Texas. Calling it reconstituted was an annoyance to Fisk, who had served at the actual Fort Bliss when Reynolds had purchased all the base assets, down to the uniforms currently worn by the men under Fisk's command. Now they are contracted mercenaries as the very concept of a volunteer citizen army was defunct. He even resurrected the various battalion nicknames: Vipers, Renegades, Rough Riders, and so forth, but it still rubbed him wrong after all these years.

It was neither here nor there. Today, as Reynolds had made it clear, Lamb was an asset worth protecting. At Lamb's insistence, or more accurately stated, panicked hyperventilating, Fisk had ceded Lamb's request to terminate pursuit of the transport helicopter to extract him from the Brain.

Lamb downloads a mobile satellite link program mirroring what he uses to connect with Reynolds to a tablet to take with him to maintain control of Brain operations while Reynolds men secure the nuclear missiles and then assist in the transition of power from Vinick to Reynolds. There would be loyalists, he ascertained, who would not take kindly to Reynolds takeover of Manhattan. But a clean, mostly bloodless transfer of power would have almost zero impact upon the general population.

Big picture planning aside, currently, four people are entering the building, and two of them had made it very clear they would kill him on sight. Lamb watches as the file transfer completes successfully on the tablet. He sticks a hands-free wireless headset into his ear to maintain communication with Apache pilot and Fisk on the ground.

"Red Rider, where are you?" asks Lamb as he shuts down his computer station before heading out the door with the tablet.

"Setting down on the rooftop, over."

"On my way," says Lamb as he exits his office, the door sealing shut automatically behind him. Rather than take the elevator, figuring security may trap him inside once they spot him on surveillance cameras, he opens the stairwell door and listens for footsteps. Hearing none, he steps inside and hurries up the metal staircase to the top landing, pushing open the door. A blast of chilled air hits him as the dimming of the winter sun behind the ever-present cloudy smog dims the horizon behind the Apache.

With the pilot seated in the rear position of the two-seater Apache, he opens the front glass enclosure as a sign for Lamb to approach. Not familiar with the height of the rotating blades above the helicopter, Lamb instinctively ducks to a near crouch and gradually makes his way across the fifty or so yards of gravel rooftop. Clutching the tablet under his arm, he takes a few steps, keeping one hand on his earpiece to protect it from the air blast coming at him from the spinning blades of the Apache.

"Oh, shit!" yells the Apache pilot in Lamb's ear.

Before Lamb can respond, multiple projectiles streak over ahead from behind and strike the engine located behind the cockpit. Consecutive explosions rock the Apache, engulfing the entire craft in flames and black smoke as the fuel lines ignite, erupting into a towering fireball that knocks Lamb onto his back in a painful thud.

Lamb twists his torso and looks behind him.

Standing just outside open elevator doors are Takeshi, Bishop, Tessa, and Ollie, the latter holding his M79 grenade launcher, smoke trailing from the tip of the barrel. Another thirty seconds and he would have been away in the Apache to safety. But those thirty seconds were unacceptable to Lamb when he moved into the Broad Street offices so many years ago.

The 1920s building had a sufficient yet antiquated elevator requiring a full minute to travel from the ground to the top floor, Lamb's level. In his various trips around the world, when there was a world to traverse, he envied the advances in elevator speed made by multiple Asian countries. He was particularly fond of the Taipei 101 building in Taiwan, which covered over a hundred floors in thirty seconds, traveling at a brisk thirty-seven miles an hour.

When Lamb made over the building and later its neighbor for his purposes, he installed similar high-speed passenger elevator systems specifically so he could go from the ground to his floor in just over twenty seconds. In his hurry to transfer his data and rush to the rooftop, he failed to consider the man wielding the spent grenade launcher behind him, with the help of building security no doubt, would use his renovation project against him.

Lamb brushes himself off as he rises to his feet, feigning outward indifferent confidence at odds with his internal trembling terror. He is sure he is about to die; he just hopes it will happen painlessly and without comment.

"Two people on this rooftop would love to disembowel you right here," says Ollie as they approach, standing face to face to with the man who conspired to kill, or help kill, all of them as the Apache burns brightly behind him in a pile of charred metal. "Myself, I'd just assume throw you off the roof and save myself the mess."

"Reynolds' men are already inside," Lamb offers. "They know

exactly how to get to the sub and offload the nukes. The only way you can stop them is me. You kill me, Reynolds still wins."

"We know," responds Bishop.

"So, we're going to have you make a call."

▲ ▲ ▲

After unlocking this office door, Lamb leads the group inside and restarts his computer station and VR unit. Ollie walks the unfurnished room, eyeing corners, vents, and finally, the computer and VR unit itself. Bishop stands closest to Lamb as if physically placing himself between Tessa and Takeshi in an effort from tearing him apart.

"This place needs an interior designer," remarks Ollie. "Goddamn depressing in here."

"Please don't touch anything," snaps Lamb.

Ollie throws his hands up in a mock apology.

"So, I'm calling Nolan, and then?"

"Then you're going to conference in Jasper Reynolds," says Bishop. "Nolan wants to speak with Reynolds directly. She's waiting for your call."

"Okay, I'll make the call."

"Put it on speaker," says Ollie, pointing to flush-mounted ceiling speakers. "If you wouldn't mind."

"Of course." Lamb puts on the VR goggles and haptic gloves, maneuvering through his contacts to find Nolan, who picks up immediately. The group watches on a screen as avatars of Nolan and Lamb appear

"Hello, Nathan. Are you ready to change the world today?" asks Nolan.

"Yeah, sure," shrugs Lamb with disdain. "Something like that. Hold on a sec, I need to uplink to a satellite to connect to Reynolds."

"Do me a favor, Nathan?" asks Sandra.

"What?"

"Keep your mouth shut and let me do the talking, got it?"

Lamb bristles at the comment, changing screens to recall and launch his satellite connection program. "Ok, here we go." A few seconds pass before the line is picked up.

"Mr. Lamb, I hope you are calling with good news."

"I'm sorry, Jasper. Nathan is a bit busy at the moment."

"Oh. Oh really? And to whom am I speaking?"

"Jasper, this is Sandra Nolan. I believe we've met, though, I'm sorry to say, I don't remember you all that well, or fondly. But you do know my boss, or should I say, former boss, Elton Vinick."

"Yes, Sandra. How are you? It has been a very long time. What's this about Elton, is he all right?"

"I'm afraid Elton has taken ill and been forced to step down from his position here on the island. As such, I am now in charge until the board votes on a new CEO."

"Oh dear, will you send him my best. I did so enjoy our time together. Great chess player that Elton, you know."

"Jasper, I'm afraid in our game, I'm going to have to say check."

"Excuse me? I wasn't aware we were playing a game."

"You have a small army at our gates, with some more moving inside our walls as we speak. They're attempting to steal the nuclear warheads from the submarine currently docked in the Hudson River. It is a bold move, I'll give you that. Crazy stupid, but bold."

"Just because you can see the move happening, doesn't mean you can stop it, Sandra. There will be a lot less bloodshed if you just hand them over. The soldiers are the best at what they do, and I have an army at my disposal in Boston. But one way or another, I'm getting those missiles."

"You're going to get one of those missiles, Jasper. I guarantee you. Robert, are you still on the line?

"I am," responds Fenton.

"Robert, please confirm you have the coordinates 29.7604 degrees north, 95.3698 degrees west."

"I can confirm," he says.

"Sandra," injects Reynolds. "What is this little performance you're putting on here?"

"I'm sorry, how rude of me. Also, on the line is Robert Fenton, our head of island security. He is currently seated at the remote launch console for the USS Wyoming, built by our mutual acquaintance Nathan Lamb many years ago. It gives us the ability to launch a nuclear missile from inside the island. Do you still want your missile, Jasper?"

"And those coordinates, I suppose they're meant to rattle me—a nuclear strike on millions of innocent people when you don't even know where I am. I control five cities, Sandra. I could be in any one of them."

"True," she admits. "It's a one-out-of-five shot. Twenty percent. But Houston is your hometown, isn't it? Any family still there."

"I see you've taken Elton's vindictive streak to a mass-murdering level."

"Considering you used to be a Solear board member,

responsible for global genocide, you're the last person to lecture on mass murder. Withdraw your men now, or we will launch."

"Have you ever made a decision like this before, Sandra? Have you ever held millions of lives in the balance? I don't think so. I don't think you're capable of this. I think I'm going to get what I want, and if you play your cards right, you can realign yourself with the new management team I'll be installing. So, what do you say, Sandra?"

Her conversation from earlier with Vinick flashes in her mind. "It wasn't until today I realized, no matter how hard Elton tried to shield me, my hands were just as dirty as his. Only, I didn't carry the guilt. I let him absorb that burden. No more. It's my burden now. Last chance, withdraw, or I launch."

"No," spits an agitated Reynolds.

"Robert, launch the missile."

Everyone is silent for a moment.

"Opening hatch one, missile launch in five, four, three, two, one. Missile away."

"Dear God..." mutters Lamb. Piggybacking the live security camera feed, he watches the plume of smoke in the Hudson as the Trident II ballistic nuclear missile rises slowly. The main booster ignites as the missile appears to temporarily hover weightlessly before a plume of fire and smoke boil the river below, passing the top of the island wall and speeding up into the sky.

"Flight time?" asks Nolan.

"Hold on, calculating." Fenton estimates a path of approximately twenty-three hundred miles at roughly twenty-nine thousand miles an hour. "About four minutes and forty-five seconds to impact, give or take."

"Jasper, they aren't bluffing," interrupts Lamb. "I just watched the launch happen live."

"You did it, you really did it," laughs Reynolds. "Elton would be so proud."

"You have about four minutes left," says Nolan.

"Actually," interjects Fenton. "he has two minutes. "I have redirect capabilities before reaching the apex. After that, there's nothing I can do to stop it."

"There's no abort?" asks Nolan.

"No."

"Well, there you go. Jasper, you now have about ninety seconds. Let me ask you, are you ready to die today?"

22

Second after second of agonizing silence passes. Takeshi, Ollie, Bishop, and Tessa trade worried glances. Bishop takes Tessa's hand, intertwines their fingers, and gives a gentle squeeze. Nolan closes her eyes - *what have I done?* Fenton raps his fingers nervously across the console desk, watching the time tick down.

"Okay," sighs Reynolds.

"Okay?" asks Nolan. "What does that mean, you'll withdraw?"

"We are, you can confirm for yourself."

Lamb scrambles to reactivate security cameras located throughout the subway system. He finds the lead convoy, a Jeep, pickup truck, and tractor-trailer stopped less than a half-mile from reaching the Pier 57 exit.

"They are awaiting new directions to return to the exit. I assume, Mr. Lamb, you can relay those to the commander like you did the original route." Lamb winces at hearing the information aloud. Another nail in his coffin, he supposes at this point.

"Now, about that missile," says Reynolds.

"Robert, can you-"

Fenton doesn't need to be told. "I'm on it. One moment."

Via the console keyboard, he enters a code to trigger the failsafe, immediately redirecting the missile two hundred and fifty miles into space. Lamb realizes although satellite imagery of the ground is impossible due to the atmospheric conditions, once the missile exited the atmosphere, it would be visible. He launches his satellite tracking program and searches for a viable camera over the United States, locating an active NSA reconnaissance satellite and taps into its real-time video feed.

At first, he thought he had missed it, or the missile had simply floated off undetected, but then a blinding light permeates the screen giving way to a blue-green aurora filled with snake-like tentacles reaching in all directions. The detonation continues to expand while it dissipates, particles of debris burning as they re-enter the atmosphere over Kentucky, Tennessee, and the Carolinas.

"Well, now that we've put this ugliness behind us, perhaps we should start discussing formal diplomatic relations between our cities," says Reynolds. "Trade, immigration, important topics nation-states need to discuss to coexist."

"Wow," exclaims Ollie. "The stones on this guy."

Everyone in Lamb's office chuckles, except Lamb, as slow panic sets in. He eyes Takeshi and Tessa, who have been sizing him up since the moment they set foot in the room. They stand between him and the door, only a few feet away. One quick move, he figures, and he could lock them in from the outside. But where would he run? Where on an island could he hide with no allies? He extinguishes the nonsensical thought.

"Jasper," says Nolan. "If and when we decide to establish diplomatic relations, we'll do it on our terms. For now, this call is over." Nolan terminates the signal on her end.

"Hello, Sandra?" asks Reynolds, not used to being dismissed so flippantly. Takeshi leans over close to Lamb's face, practically breathing down his neck.

"Terminate the call now." Lamb shuts off the satellite program.

"I need to relay the return directions to Reynolds' people," explains Lamb. "So, can you back off, just a bit?" Ollie puts his hand on Takeshi's shoulder, who breaks his gaze and takes a step back.

"We'll deal with him," says Ollie. "He's not going anywhere. Why don't you get Charlie on the walkie so we can get a ride back to the Mick?"

"Yeah, good idea," says Bishop.

He stares at Tessa while trying to defuse the tense situation, he can see her laser-focused on Lamb. He pulls her a few feet away from the group situated around Lamb's computer and VR setup. He hugs her tight, feeling her body temporarily become loose, and whispers into her ear. "You don't have to do it, you know."

She pulls back and looks him in the eyes. They had both killed before. For survival. In defense. Neither had been an executioner.

"Takeshi is a soldier. He's been on the wall, like me," he says. "Whatever happened, if you cross that line, it can be hard to come back." Before she can respond, Takeshi announces Charlie is returning with the Sea Stallion, and they are heading to the rooftop.

"What's the security on this set-up?" asks Ollie. "You got a password? Is it password1234?"

"Biometric, actually."

"Really? What, like a retinal scan?" Lamb would be mildly impressed someone like Ollie would know what biometric meant, but now isn't the time.

"It's the haptic gloves. They have a built-in fingerprint reader. When I put my hand in, the system automatically reads my fingerprints and unlocks."

"Fascinating. Very cool stuff."

Takeshi looks at Ollie impatiently.

"Are you two done talking tech? Let's get to the roof." Lamb powers down the computer system, and the group exits the office, making their way down the hall to the stairwell and back up to the rooftop. As the doors open, they can hear the familiar sound of the Sea Stallion rotors on approach. They step out into the darkening chill and watch the smoldering embers of the still-burning Apache as Charlie brings the helicopter over them and carefully descends.

Because of the Apache wreckage, he's forced closer to the edge of the roof than he'd prefer, with barely enough room to fit the wide stance of the rear landing gear on the rooftop. Takeshi, Tessa, and Bishop make their way to the lowering rear cargo door first.

"You're not going to blow this one too, I hope," snarks Lamb, walking next to Ollie. Ollie slaps his hand hard on Lamb's back, gripping the base of his neck with this thumb and forefinger. A power move of dominance, causing Lamb to wince.

"It's important to keep your sense of humor," laughs Ollie.

Takeshi, Tessa, and Bishop walk up the cargo bay door first as

Ollie pushes Lamb towards them, then abruptly changes course and shoves Lamb over the short wall at the edge of the roof. Ollie grabs Lamb's left arm with his own, leaving Lamb to dangle thirty-three stories above the street below.

"What the hell are you doing?!" yells Takeshi from the rear of the helicopter.

"You heard him," replies Ollie. "All we need is his hand."

With the professional agility of a trained killer, Ollie unsheathes a long bayonet knife from his right leg holster, swings it up to Lamb's left wrist, and slices cleanly through the skin, bone, tendon, and muscle. Holding Lamb's severed left hand, he looks over the edge to see the body slam into the metal awning over the entrance.

He turns and walks into the back of the helicopter; a trail of blood follows him. He locates a metal medical kit off the wall and unlatches it, finding a plastic Ziploc bag full of various sizes of band-aids, empties it, and drops the bloody appendage inside. Takeshi grabs Ollie's shoulder and spins him around.

"That was my kill. Our kill. You had no right-" Ollie turns fully to him and puts his hand on Takeshi's shoulder.

"You don't want him on your conscience. Trust me. Once you start executing people, right or wrong. You can never go back. You're not an executioner. Neither of you are."

Ollie pats Takeshi's shoulder and walks to the cockpit, strapping into a seat behind Charlie. For all her rage at Lamb, Tessa silently agrees, giving Ollie a confirming nod. She walks up to Takeshi and, without a word, embraces him. Takeshi closes his eyes before they fill with tears.

"I'm hungry," announces Ollie. "Whaddya say, Charlie. Let's get this bird in the air and get some takeout."

▲ ▲ ▲

Charlie lands the Sea Stallion on the Mick rooftop; everyone makes their way back to Vinick's floor where they find Nolan in a hushed conversation with Wolcott and the recently arrived Lloyd Rust. Vinick watches from his med chair, coughing and looking frail.

"Where's Lamb?" asks Nolan.

Ollie approaches and nonchalantly hands her the Ziploc bag, which she tosses onto the kitchen table before realizing what it is.

"We got what we needed," he replies. "You can send some janitors to scoop up the rest of him later." Rust looks sick and covers his mouth before looking away. Bishop steps up.

"What's the status of Reynolds' forces?" he asks.

"Fenton just let me know the last of them just exited the Third Street Bridge. The gate is closed, and all security is back online. We're still assessing the damage done by your little stunt-"

"Did she just call our EMP blast a stunt?" Ollie asks sarcastically. "I thought it was pretty badass myself."

Bishop nods in Vinick's direction. "And what's going to happen with him?"

"We're still trying to decide," says Nolan. "This is Lloyd Rust, CFO, and our most senior board member." Rust tries to compose himself.

"Elton had floated a contingency, I'm sure at the time just out of spite towards Lamb," explains Rust. "We have the option to create wards based on certain geographic boundaries and give citizens the ability to elect representatives. Those representatives would then be tasked with selecting a CEO. The board would stay on, but more as an informal advisory commission. The details are not yet set in stone. But-"

"But," interjects Nolan. "It would change the city, hopefully for the better, going forward."

"And Vinick?" asks Bishop.

"We're still deciding. For now, he will be confined to his floor," says Nolan. "But he will lose his status. I'll assign my staff to look after him, but no more special treatment like the other executives are afforded."

"So, he wipes out half the planet and just gets to walk away from it and live in a penthouse?" spits Takeshi. "Nice, real goddamn nice."

"What do you want, a trial? An execution?" she fires back. "He'll die alone up here, with no control over his kingdom. For a man like Vinick, powerlessness is death."

"Whatever," snipes Takeshi. He spots Ollie rummaging through kitchen cabinets. "Let's go check on Sanders and get back to Fenton, find out what's what."

"I assume my credits will be in the mail, Ms. Nolan," says Ollie. She half-smiles, "sure." Takeshi and Ollie exit via the stairwell, Tessa steps into the fray. "What about us?"

"I promised you both debt-free citizenship if you returned with Doctor Wolcott, and you did. I will honor my promise. I'll look at employment openings myself and find you something." Sandra looks over to Vinick, glaring at her from his med chair. She steps to him and leans in.

"Tell me why," her voice trembling. "Why did you turn my parents away, why did you do that to them? To me?" He can barely look her in the eye, shifting his gaze around the room.

"When was the last time you spoke to them before they left?

Do you even remember?" he fires back. "You were nothing like them, they would have obscured your moral outlook. We didn't need morality back then, we needed pragmatism and vision. I did you a favor. I saved you from a path of upper-middle-class liberal bullshit. Your parents were nothing but a burden to your development, and they would have burdened you here. Did I act selfishly? You're damn right I did. I needed you all to myself, I was not about to share you with those people."

"Those people?" she says, her rage building. "Those people were my parents, and you sentenced them to die out there. I might not be able to kill you with my bare hands, but the rest of your life is going to be alone and miserable."

"I knew you had ice in your veins, but is this the new Sandra Nolan," Vinick asks. "One who is willing to lob nuclear missiles across the country, commit her own genocide?"

She's about to step away but stops.

"Oh, Elton. I'm not a killer like you." She holds up her phone him, displaying the last text stream:

Nolan: hold on my orders - 5:23 PM
Nolan: target away from population, gulf of mexico - 5:26 PM
Nolan: but give me lat + long for houston - 5:26 PM
Silva: got it - 5:27 PM

♟ ♟ ♟

"Doctor Wolcott?" asks Bishop. "What are your plans? Are you staying, or are you going back to Bangor?"

"There's no reason for me to be here," he responds. "Charlie and the folks from Bangor are going to fly back up the coast when it's light in the morning. Ms. Nolan is going to put us all up in her place for the night."

Bishop looks at Tessa, then Wolcott. "Do me a favor, doc. Don't leave without saying goodbye."

"Oh, okay," responds Wolcott, caught off guard by the request. They share a handshake; Tessa hugs him. They exhale for what feels like the first time in days, maybe years.

Bishop opens the door to his apartment, located at the Towers on East Thirteenth, previously some sort of medical building. His unit is a lower-end option, a former hospital recovery room, converted to an apartment furnished with a cot and dresser, minus one of its three drawers.

He and Tessa step inside, drop their various bags onto the floor and collapse together onto the bed. She scans the sparse surroundings.

"And I thought I lived in a shithole," says Tessa. He ignores the playful taunt.

"What I'm about to say is going to sound crazy," he starts. "But I want to take you back to Bangor, I want you to see it with your own eyes. I know this is everything we were building toward, everything that we just went through, but I just want you to see what I've seen."

"Why? We've been so many places that seemed stable."

"I know, but Bangor is different. The last year on the island,

I've seen what happens to people. We'll just work and be trapped inside these walls. No purpose other than to keep this shitty little apartment, maybe get a promotion someday. I thought I wanted the security, but now I'm not so sure."

"I want to see it."

"See what?"

"The city. Show me the city. Then we'll make the decision. Together."

He kisses her forehead, they hold each tighter, then relax as they both fall asleep from exhaustion.

Around midnight, Bishop awakens and slides off the bed, stripping off his clothes to check his wound, then stepping into the shower to wash off the multiple days of blood, sweat, and dirt covering his body. After a few minutes, Tessa joins him. They don't say it aloud, but their frailness disconcerts them both. A pair of once physical specimens reduced to emaciated survivors.

She borrows one of his few clean t-shirts, and they bundle up to deal with the now below freezing overnight temperatures. He gives her a spare surgical mask and explains the air quality. In short bursts, it's passable, but they'll be trekking a fair distance. Free from regulations, the city air quality becomes suffocating when exposed for long periods.

Back outside, on the slick sidewalk, they scurry uptown, and Bishop checks his current credit at an automated teller machine. Nolan had kept her word, his automatic debt payment was absent, only his balance showed. They had enough to splurge on something more appetizing than synthetic fast food burgers and water. Though he enjoyed the kitschy atmosphere of the lone remaining name-brand fast food joint left in existence, it was merely for show. The menus reflect the limited and mostly unremarkable offerings that paled in comparison to an actual, pre-asteroid hamburger, fries, and milkshake. Things he dismissed before as trivial, like so many others, were now the most cherished.

Like Manhattan before the asteroid, the city streets were always alive with activity. Only now, instead of bar-hoppers and partygoers at one in the morning, there are shift changes at factories and twenty-four-hour merchants selling their wares. The city that never sleeps is sleep-deprived, a non-stop workday, seven days a week. Millions of people to be fed, clothed, and housed, a monumental interconnected undertaking that never rests. Most city dwellers with citizenship debt are like Bishop and Silva, spending the off hours from their official employment on a secondary position, racking up a minimum of seventy to eighty hours of workload a week. Like Bishop and Silva, some are city-sanctioned, others are improvised.

Hand in hand, Bishop leads them on a half-hour stroll through the bustling throng. They finally arrive at a formerly sports-themed watering hole frequented by much of the island security personnel in their off-hours, the closest approximation he could find resembling he and Tessa's favorite bar, The Dank.

In the early months on the island, he had stopped in a few times to make small talk with fellow security personnel, trading stories for shocks and laughs. Once he landed the second gig riding shotgun in the garage hauler with Pete, he didn't have the time to make pleasantries.

As they enter the subterranean establishment, he takes notice nothing has changed. It was dark, dirty, smoky, and somber, just as he liked it, an approximation of the bar in which he met Tessa a lifetime ago. A non-stop loop of pre-recorded football, basketball, hockey, and baseball games from the previous forty or so years playing on the wall-mounted television.

Most inside have just wrapped an eight-hour shift at midnight and are huddled four or five around tables sharing cannabis vaporizers over plates of greasy bar food, a break between second jobs or back home for brief bouts of shuteye. Bishop spots an open leather and wood encased booth and guides them through the establishment, sliding in and around the curved half-circle, Tessa at his side.

A waitress appears and hands them a menu detailing their current selection of edibles, both semi-nutritional and illicit, as well as locally distilled spirits. Thanks to the scarcity of grain, beer has become a luxury item brewed in small batches by an elite, the inverse of its former place among the working class.

"This place isn't bad," says Tessa, eyes darting around, taking it all in.

"Yeah, the pizza ain't bad here from what I remember. Real sauce and crust, too. Cheese isn't real, it's soy or something. Tastes close enough."

"If you like," says the waitress, a tired-looking woman who fakes enthusiasm well, "we can do it by the slice. The better deal is the whole pie, but if it's just the two of you."

They each order a slice with preferred vegetable toppings and one of the lower cost synthol drinks. The waitress hands Bishop a tablet for payment, which Tessa looks over.

"Two hundred credits?" she asks. "Is that a lot?"

"That would be how much I spent on food for a week, normally. But we're celebrating."

"But that's only two pieces of pizza and two drinks."

"I know and look at this place."

"How did you live like-"

"Hey, I had a roof and a job and could scrape by. You were on the outside, that was worse."

"Yeah, at least you never got drugged and kidnapped," she quips.

"Even in a city as tightly controlled as this, there is still a black market. It's just…"

"Just what?"

"It's bad. Everything is legal here. Drugs, prostitution, you name it. But underneath, there is some dark, dark stuff. When I work the garbage pick-up with Pete, we'd find bodies chopped up and dissected for the organs. The rich pay for them. I mean, there are legal means to get them, but sometimes there's a shortage, so there are other ways."

"We saw stuff just as bad out there."

"We did, you're right. But that's when I thought we only had two options. So, I ignored it."

The food arrives, big triangular slices of New York-style pizza and Old-Fashioned glasses filled with clear mind-eraser liquids. They devour the food and drinks orgasmically.

"Thing is," he continues. "If we leave, we give up our spots. They'll find a replacement for me in a heartbeat."

"You know I trust you. I just want to stop running."

He takes her hands in his and kisses them.

"One more drink."

♠ ♠ ♠

The sun rises behind the cloudy gray morning sky as Bishop and Tessa wind their way through shoulder-to-shoulder pedestrians back to the Mick. Instead of surreptitious entrance methods like the previous day, this time they are approved by Nolan to pass the front desk and security check and ride the elevator to her floor.

In the kitchen, they find Charlie, Wolcott, and Derek enjoying a spread of fruits and pastries with cups of coffee and tea.

"I could get used to this spread," bellows Charlie, inhaling a jelly danish. "You better get some of this before I eat it all."

Bishop and Tessa each fill a coffee cup and grab some assorted fruits. He smells the coffee and takes a sip. Though it's hot, he doesn't care. He hasn't tasted coffee this pure in years. Tessa bites into an oversized strawberry and closes her eyes, savoring it.

"This is how the other half lives," she says, smiling.

"Yeah, only it's not quite half."

They hear a pair of footsteps approach as Nolan and Zach flank a corner, straight up to Bishop and Tessa.

"I never got a chance to say it yesterday, but thank you. What you did, what you both did, was extraordinary," Nolan extends a hand to both. "Tessa, Kell told us what you did for him, getting him free from Lamb's men, leading him back to safety. I think you would make a great member of our security forces here on the island."

Tessa smiles, "He would have done the same for me. He's a tough kid. Where is he now?"

"His mother is resting on the executive medical floor below; you're welcome to visit them after if you like." Bishop and Tessa exchange a knowing glance.

"Tessa and I talked last night; we're going to head back to Bangor on the chopper today. I messaged Commander Fenton this morning. He's sending over a satellite phone and some equipment. Since we have access to Lamb's communications array, we can set-up Bangor with a direct line."

"Good thinking. With Reynolds' men still in control of Boston, we need all the allies we can get," says Nolan.

"After we've established communication, we'll turn everything over to Bloom and his folks. Then we'll figure it out from there. I wanna show Tess Bangor, figure out where we want to settle down."

"You're sure about this?" interjects Wolcott.

Bishop grips Tessa's hand and squeezes, "Yeah, we're sure."

"Sounds like we need to get a flight plan together," says Charlie.

"Also, we need to make a quick stop in Waterville, Maine, just off the highway, is that okay?"

"Waterville? What's in Waterville?" asks Charlie. Tessa follows as well, "Yeah, what's in Waterville?"

"A friend."

Tessa's bemused by the thought.

"A friend? When did you have time to make a friend?"

"Just trust me. We've got more allies out there than we know."

"Derek, get on your computer and plot our route home with a stop in Waterville. I want wheels up in twenty minutes."

Charlie turns to Nolan. "And ma'am, if you wouldn't mind, please tell Mr. Fenton and his folks to turn off the tower guns in the northeast sector for a bit so we don't get our assess shot off."

"I will," she says. Bishop perks up, "Can I get in on that call?"

"Sure." A minute later, Nolan dials up Fenton via video chat. In Fenton's office, seated at his desk, he accepts the call, but instead of Nolan, he sees Bishop.

"Well. Hello, soldier. Did the sat phone packages arrive?"

"Just arrived and being loaded as we speak, sir."

"Good to hear. Anything else?"

"Heading out in about ten minutes and would greatly appreciate it if the tower guns did not prematurely end our return trip, sir."

"Noted."

"Have you spoke to Arch today, sir?"

"I have. He was in my office first thing looking to get back into rotation. I advised him we still had some loose ends to clean up from yesterday."

"Does he mean Ward, Lamb's security lead?" asks Tessa off-screen.

"Since Ollie took it upon himself to deal with Lamb, I gave Arch the task of sorting out Ward Whaley."

"Understood, sir," says Bishop.

"Best of luck to you both. Stay safe. I look forward to getting this set-up, and to a detailed report upon your return."

"Yessir, thank you for the opportunity, sir."

▲ ▲ ▲

Nolan watches as everyone files up into the rear cargo door of the Sea Stallion on the Mick rooftop. The rotors slowly turn, churning up to speed. Bishop looks back and gives a wave, which Nolan returns as the cargo door slowly closes. Finally, the helicopter ascends into the sky, tilts forward, and moves northeast over the city. She watches it grow smaller, passing over the island wall, climbing higher as it shrinks in the distance until it is a soundless speck in the gloomy wash of emptiness.

EPILOGUE

A tired Vinick awakens in his bed. The first morning no attendant has rustled him with medications. This is his new reality.

After a stop in the bathroom to urinate, he visits the kitchen and pulls one of his dozen or so premade green health shakes from the refrigerator before settling into his med chair. His security camera feed screens are now auspiciously blank, where once Xeno and his men would be positioned throughout the floor, there is nothing. Displays one, two, and three could be still photographs.

Screen four shows the chessboard. However, the text on the screen has updated, "Awaiting Your Move."

Vinick takes a small remote keyboard off the table to his left and utilizes the keypad to enter his next move, pressing enter. The text changes back to "Awaiting Player Two." Immediately, a new message flashes, "Incoming Chat Request - Y/N?"

Vinick presses the "Y" button, and on-screen via video chat appears Player Two - Jasper Reynolds.

"I was wondering if you'd be playing today," says Reynolds. "Based on that move, I'd say your head is still in the game."

Vinick smiles. "Don't you worry, my old friend. It is, it is."

♚ ♚

ACKNOWLEDGEMENTS

Thank You...

To my wife Katie and daughter Nina, for letting me steal time to chase ideas, ask questions on mind-numbing minutiae, and supporting me every step of the way.

To my mother Coni Minneci and Aunt Judy Holstrom, for reading along chapter-by-chapter as I was writing the first draft and providing me feedback and encouragement every step of the way.

To Cortney Dziak, Susan Laser Range, Doug Beebe, Jodie Cantwell Robinson, T'Lisa Macon, Michael Ferraro, Jodi Lugibihl Quint, Amanda Gradisek, Andrea Hoo Chempinski and Christie Robb for reading at various points throughout the development of the book.

To Kat Howard (kathowardbooks.com) for the detailed and expert feedback.

To DX Ferris for being a voice of reason and a knowledgeable sounding board.

To Jason Tharp for the coffee and encouragement.

To Jacob Slichter, who provided me my "500 words a day" mantra, keeping me on track.

To Mike "Beeple" Winkelmann (beeple-crap.com) for graciously letting me use his artwork for the book.

To Andy Weir, whose methodology of writing The Martian inspired completing The Black Sky.

To the countless musicians and artists that helped me escape to another world when writing, especially to Shawn Smith and Gordon Downie, who passed while I was writing – *you are wrapped in my memory like chains.*

ALSO BY TIMOTHY D. MINNECI

Power Ballad (2013)
Small Stories (2017)
Are You Making A Sound? (2018)
35 Days In The Air (2019)

THE INSTRUMENTAL ELECTRONIC SOUNDTRACK ALBUM INSPIRED BY AND CREATED FOR THE BLACK SKY

STREAMING AND DOWNLOADS AVAILABLE ON ALL SERVICES

COMPACT DISCS AVAILABLE VIA AMAZON.COM

SOLEAR
The Future Of Tomorrow, Today

Visit **solearindustries.com** to learn about:

Aerospace
Bio En9ineering
Commercial Aircraft
Dri7ling
Energy
Media
Mining
&
Real E5tate Investing

Or find us on **LinkedIn at solear-industries**

And on **Twitter @solearinc**

CPSIA information can be obtained
at www.ICGtesting.com
Printed in the USA
LVHW111009050920
665161LV00001B/220

9 781734 521306